To Joyce
With love

The author is the owner of the
hairdresser 'Salon' at the Plough, Boddington.
She lives locally in Wallyster.

A Suitable Ending

An excellent read! Read in 2004
and 2024.

A Suitable Ending

Sally-Ann Wilding

*Blackie & Co
Publishers Ltd*

A BLACKIE & CO PUBLISHERS PAPERBACK

© Copyright 2003
Sally-Ann Wilding

The right of Sally-Ann Wilding to be identified as the author of this work has been asserted by her in accordance with the Copyright, Designs and Patents Act 1988

All Rights Reserved
No reproduction, copy or transmission of this publication may be made without written permission. No paragraph of this publication may be reproduced, copied or transmitted save with the written permission or in accordance with the provisions of the Copyright Act 1956 (as amended). Any person who does any unauthorised act in relation to this publication may be liable to criminal prosecution and civil claims for damage.

First published in 2003

A CIP catalogue record for this title is available from the British Library

ISBN 1 84470 034 8

**Blackie & Co Publishers Ltd
107-111 Fleet Street
LONDON EC4A 2AB**

Dedication

For my sister, June –
the one person who probably
won't want to read this . . . again!

PROLOGUE

My earliest memory is of Christie. During her short life she was to become my only true friend - in death, my torment.

It's important now that I discover the truth. Was I responsible... or was my guilt a product of my mother's insanity?

For so long, believing myself to be culpable, I accepted the blame for what happened. But now, so many years later, I know this to be irrational. I have to go back to discover the truth – back to that dark, evil place where I last saw Christie alive.

CHAPTER ONE

Sunday 23rd September, 1990

Partially blinded by the bright September sun, he stared, unseeing, at the countryside beyond the hawthorn boundary of his garden. A shadow rippled across the plain on the north side of Gibson's farm. There was barely a sound, bar the occasional drone of distant machinery that grew ever nearer. Soon the landscape would change, by virtue of Gibson's combine. It was harvest time again. If he listened carefully he could hear the stutter of an engine – see the occasional puff of black smoke as the tractor started up. Mark Jordan's eyes scanned the horizon, searching - but for something he knew he wouldn't find.

For six years it had eluded him, and today was no different. He knew the answer couldn't be found in the waist-high barley that soughed and swayed before him, any more than it could be found in the crumpled sheets of paper that lay at his feet. He stared reproachfully at the blank pages, and wondered if the day would ever come when this would no longer rule his life. How long could it take to write one chapter?

Some tiny disturbance from the house caught his attention and forced his protesting mind back to reality. He threw his pencil down in a gesture of self-disgust. He should never have started this again, not when they had guests arriving at any moment - and there was one in particular who certainly wouldn't appreciate his efforts.

"Oh, to hell with it!" He snapped the notebook shut with unnecessary firmness and sank back in his chair, feeling slightly disorientated. Trying to ignore a familiar dull ache behind his eyes, he forced himself to concentrate on the importance of the day ahead.

The long-awaited birthday weekend had arrived. Tim was four years old and the event was to be marked in the usual way. The kids had had their fun yesterday. He'd dutifully dressed as a clown, something he enjoyed immensely but never would admit to, and suffered the indignity of tripping and stumbling about in an effort to make them laugh. He'd helped Susan serve jelly and ice cream – most of which, he'd ended up wearing. All in all, though, the day had gone well. Today, however, it was time to entertain the grown-ups. Mark sighed, and wished it were yesterday again.

There were times when he'd cursed the fact that their only child had seen fit to be born during the month of September. In fact, if he had his way, there would be no September at all. Silly really; until six years ago it had always been his favourite time of year. He cast a critical eye around the garden and wondered why he could find no joy in it. The lawn was immaculate, the flowerbeds at their most colourful and, thankfully, the weather was holding. Susan had prepared enough to feed an army, and he should be set to enjoy it all – but it was all too familiar.

It had been just as glorious then, he remembered. A perfect autumn until... he pressed his hands to his temples as if to rid himself of the memory. He couldn't let this take hold again – not now.

He was unaware that Susan was watching him. Perhaps, had he seen the expression in her eyes – or recognised the familiar signs of anxiety in her behaviour - he might have made more effort. But that day he was too deeply entrenched in the past to notice.

Susan Jordan crossed the lawn silently. She was fully aware of her husband's obsession with what had happened all those years ago, but had never quite understood it. Sometimes, in rare moments of bitterness, she would accuse him of being selfish. After all, it was she who was most affected – it was she who suffered the nightmares. She cleared her throat as if to warn him of her arrival.

"I'm surprised you can keep your eyes open," she said, "seeing as you were pacing the floor for half the night."

Mark, startled by the intrusion on his thoughts, jerked forward in his seat. "What...?" He looked around quickly to see if she was alone.

"It's all right, relax, they're not here yet." She sat beside him on the bench. "I could see you were miles away..." she held up her hands, "and no, don't bother to try and explain. I can guess where you were."

"Am I that transparent?"

"Not always. But when it comes to this..." she patted the notebook that lay face-down across his knees, "I'm afraid you are." She concentrated her gaze on the toes of her shoes. "It's that last chapter again, isn't it?"

He tried not to look at her. Her direct approach was out of character and left him floundering for an answer; some witty remark that would divert the conversation onto safer ground. At last, forcing a wry smile, he said, "I sometimes wonder if I'll ever finish it."

"Well, you'd better put it away for now, they'll be here any minute."

Still avoiding her eyes, he began briskly gathering papers together. Silently he cursed the day. But for Tim's birthday these twenty-four hours would come and go without note. He straightened, red-faced and slightly breathless with frustration, and tried to force the papers into some kind of order. "You know, there are times when I'm tempted to burn the entire manuscript and stick to what I do best. Quite frankly I doubt whether anyone would believe all this really happened - except perhaps..." He paused for a moment and allowed his gaze to wander. Quite suddenly he raised his arm and waved towards the far end of the garden.

An elderly woman had emerged from the trees near the boundary. A child, running closely behind, caught her hand, then skipped and pranced around her, giggling with delight. He carried something in his free hand – something that glistened and sparkled brightly in the sunlight. As they drew nearer Mark could see their expressions, hear the child's excited laughter. The woman raised a weathered face and looked directly at him. Mirrored in her faded grey eyes he could see a trace of the same anxiety he felt. She knew what he was thinking. She always did.

More voices from the side of the house heralded the arrival of their guests. They came in high spirits, laughing, heavily laden with gaily-wrapped parcels. Mark wished it could be just the four of them, he could have done without a crowd this afternoon. Somehow he forced his features into a welcoming smile. "Come in, it's so nice to see you," he lied, then eyeing the parcels, added, "I suppose these are all for Tim?"

"Well, they're certainly not for you," one retorted, "unless you've taken to playing with crayons."

"Hardly." Mark took one of the parcels and shook it gently. He could tell from its size and weight that it contained something far more elaborate and expensive. "Crayons, my eye!" he said. "I hope you haven't gone too mad. You spoil him, you know."

"And why not?" Slightly flushed with exertion, the elderly woman sank stiffly, and with a certain amount of relief, onto the bench. She whispered something in the child's ear then smiled as the little boy ran to greet the newcomers.

"Look," he cried, holding up a jar. "We've been collecting caterpillars."

A solitary cloud, skimming across the sky, dimmed the bright September sun. And a curious, uneasy silence fell on the group.

Mark stepped back, apprehensively scanning their faces. It was nothing more than a jar of caterpillars, but the effect was immediate. It shocked him to discover they all remembered, but his main concern was Susan. The smile had frozen on her lips, and he could tell from the expression in her eyes that her thoughts, like his own, were now firmly centred on that fatal autumn of six years ago.

CHAPTER TWO

Sunday 23rd September, 1984

For the first time in many months there was a spring in Susan's step. The heavy weight of anxiety, that had darkened her days for so long, seemed to dissolve and disappear on the breeze as she revelled in the beauty of the countryside. She could see and feel everything with such intensity now. The sweet smell of newly cut grass, the warmth of the sun, the stillness... Of course, it had all been there before – she just hadn't noticed it.

She could see now that her friends had been right all along – she needed to get away. Here, in the heart of the Derbyshire countryside, in her pretty rented holiday cottage, there were no ghosts, no imaginary footsteps on creaking floorboards, and no eerie noises as the wind whistled about the eaves. She wasn't that far from home - but far enough, it seemed. The shadows that haunted her might be a million miles away. Maybe life wasn't so bad after all; and maybe, after a week or two in this quiet place, she would be able to put the past few years into perspective and forget the events that had brought her here.

Following a heart attack her mother had become a permanent invalid, forcing Susan to give up all thoughts of a career in order to look after her. At first it hadn't seemed so bad, but as time went on her mother grew weaker and more demanding. Susan had had to do everything for her – as one would for a child. She had coped reasonably well with the physical strain of it, but emotionally it had left her feeling insecure and vulnerable. Never knowing when the end might come, she'd grown to dread entering her mother's room for fear of what she might find. Even in the comparative peace of

6

her own room she could never totally relax. She would lie in bed listening, ears straining for the slightest sound.

The end, when it came, was very calm. Susan had found the frail form sitting up in bed, propped against the pillows, just as she had left her. She looked as she always did except for her eyes, which stared sightlessly at their own reflection in the mirror opposite the bed. In the dark weeks that followed, Susan had often wondered, rather morbidly, and certainly irrationally, whether her mother had actually watched her own death.

She breathed deeply and smiled as she watched Lexer, her beloved German Shepherd, snatch up his new toy and bound mischievously into the woods. "Right, my lad," she called. "You asked for it - I'm coming to get you." She gave a whoop of delight and ran after him into the woods laughing aloud - but not for long. Within seconds the unaccustomed sense of freedom, a latitude denied to her for most of her adult years, was gone.

Striving for control, she moved nearer to the bundle of crumpled rags that lay, half buried, under a pile of rotting leaves. Something about it, the way it lay, alarmed and fascinated her at the same time. She wanted to walk away, pretend she hadn't seen it, after all, it was nothing to do with her. But when the unmistakable stench of death reached her nostrils, she knew it was **everything** to do with her. She moved nearer still silently praying she was wrong. She had to be wrong – maybe it was the light playing tricks – her imagination – please God, let it be just that!

Pale blue material, once a pretty dress, clung damply to the crumpled form. It lay on its side in a foetal position but for one arm which, seemingly dislocated from the shoulder, projected awkwardly at right angles to the body. A fine gold chain, fastened loosely around a pathetically thin wrist, glittered in obscene contrast against bruised, blackened skin. A matted veil of straight, almost black hair obscured the dead woman's face. Susan's eyes widened in horror as she peered through the damp strands and saw something move.

A year ago she might have kept her head and dealt with what she had found more efficiently. Her customary clear logic would not have deserted and allowed mindless panic to take control. But death and logic were strangers - and life, at times, unfair.

Swallowing hard as the bitter taste of bile rose in her throat, she drew away from the rotting corpse, sickened, yet unable to tear her gaze from it. Retreating still further she tried to think what to do - where to go, but as her eyes darted frantically from side to side, a pulse began hammering in her head. She was lost. All about her the woods seemed to be closing in, she couldn't remember which way she had come. Fighting desperately to stay calm she drew deep gulps of air until the hammering in her head subsided, to be replaced by a faint, but blissfully familiar, whining sound.

Lexer pawed at the ground close to the body. "Leave it!" Susan's voice seemed to echo in the silence of the woods.

Startled at the sharpness of the command, the dog stood quite still, eyeing her warily, then after only a cursory glance at the object before him, went to Susan's side. With trembling hands she attached the lead to the dog's collar while muttering aloud. "Come on boy, we've got to get help..." But who? She knew nobody; she'd only arrived in the village an hour ago.

It didn't occur to Susan until much later, that if she had only allowed the dog to lead her, the following tortuous minutes might have been avoided. Without thought she had begun running blindly in what she assumed was the direction of the village. Tripping and stumbling she grazed her knee badly – branches caught at her hair, tore her clothes, lacerated her face, but on she ran until, finally, an exposed root brought her crashing to the ground. Struggling to her feet, she looked around. This wasn't right - there was no way through, no path and - no dog!

Realisation that she was alone brought further panic. She ran again, blindly, verging on hysteria until again the dog saved her reason.

Lexer, also realising he was alone, set up a continuous bark for attention until Susan found him, miraculously, in the clearing where she had first come chasing after him. Within seconds she was on the footpath racing down the steep hill to the village.

To call it a village was something of an overstatement. The hamlet of Carlton amounted to less than a dozen buildings situated either side of a narrow lane. However, unremarkable as it appeared, to Susan, it was like waking from a nightmare.

In the deserted lane, breathless and dishevelled, she looked around desperately for signs of life. Somewhere a door slammed. At last, someone was coming.

CHAPTER THREE

Friday 21ˢᵗ September, 1984

At the junction of the motorway he hesitated. It had taken him two days – two very bleak, agonising days - to make the decision. He was going to quit!

In an act of almost desperate determination, Mark Jordan pressed his foot hard on the accelerator and manoeuvred the jeep into the fast lane. For the first time in ten years he found himself questioning his chosen profession. Ten years, and almost as many published books, and suddenly he only had to look at his computer to break into a cold sweat. He'd even considered, briefly, trying another genre; maybe he'd exhausted the possibilities of crime fiction. After all, he reasoned, there are only so many ways to commit a murder - or solve it.

As the distance from London grew greater Mark became calmer, but no less dejected. He knew he'd got to get his act together. If he couldn't write, what else could he do? Until now it had all been so enjoyable, almost easy, but his last work had deprived him of sleep and, when finished, left him exhausted and confused. Thus, in a rare state of depression, he'd taken it to his publisher. He cringed inwardly. His behaviour that day had been less than perfect.

"There!" Mark, grim-faced and defiant, tossed the manuscript on the already littered desk.

Richard Lumley stared at it, his expression that of one who had been this route before.

"Well, go on then," Mark growled. "At least have a look at the bloody thing. You've done nothing but bang on about it for months."

Inclined to argue the injustice of the remark, Richard chose instead the line of indifference. He carefully turned the manuscript around to face him. "OK, I've looked. Now, do you want to tell me what brought all this on?"

Mark responded with a bad-tempered grunt, which was hardly an apology, but the nearest he could manage. At last he muttered, "I've had enough, Richard." He pushed the manuscript to the edge of the desk, as if its very presence in the room was distasteful to him. "And this is the last you'll get from me – so you'd better make the most of it." He paced about the room waiting for a reply. When none came, he flung himself into a chair. "Well, what have you got to say about that?"

Richard returned the rebellious stare with an irritatingly level gaze. "If you're expecting me to throw up my hands in horror and beg you to reconsider, forget it." He watched Mark rise from his seat and move towards the door. He'd met some prima donnas in his time but somehow he knew this was different. A smile softened his features as he studied his friend's expression. "Look, I can see you're upset about something, Mark. What is it, the girlfriend? ... what's-her-name?"

Mark toed the carpet sulkily. "Jacqueline."

"Right, Jacqueline. What's happened – have you had a falling out?"

"Nothing as exciting as that."

Richard waited, then seeing it was going to be a struggle, came straight to the point. "I take it she's gone off in search of greener pastures, then?"

"Right." Mark looked as if he didn't care much one way or the other. "I expect that's what it was. And I expect it was largely my fault." He began pacing the room. "You know what I'm like when I'm into a book. I go off into deep thought for days on end, forget to phone and - well you know what I mean. You can't expect any woman to put up with that for long, they start feeling neglected. Anyway, that's only part of it..." He came to a halt at the window, wondering how he'd ever got into this. Jacqueline had absolutely nothing to do with his present state of mind, and he wanted to tell Richard so. He wanted to explain how he was feeling – how his inability to write was affecting him - but he couldn't. Now that he'd had his moan he was bitterly regretting his behaviour, and wanted to leave with as much dignity as possible.

Richard remained impassive. Still thinking Mark's mood was due to his unsatisfactory love life, he offered the usual condolences. "Never mind, chum. You just haven't met the right one yet." He patted the manuscript. "Anyway, you've finished this, so you can take a break now. You'll soon meet someone else, you know."

Deciding it easier to continue the deception, Mark laughed mirthlessly. "What's the point? If I do, and then start another book, I'll still have the same problem, won't I?"

Richard gave up. "OK, so your love life's a bit of a disaster at the moment, but the books are great. You're probably just tired. Why don't you take a holiday, go on one of those walking trips of yours? Personally, I can think of less taxing ways of relaxing, but it seems to work for you. That last trip of yours - Derbyshire, wasn't it? Did you the world of good, as I recall?"

"Yes - yes it did, I suppose."

"Well there you are then! Go home, pack a bag and head for the hills." Grinning broadly, he added. "And stay away from women and work for a while."

Mark smiled as he guided the jeep north on the M1. Richard was right. Loath as he was to admit it, Richard was always right. Maybe a little hill-walking would blow the cobwebs of crime fiction away.

It was mid-day when he pulled off the motorway and followed the A6 into Matlock. Situated at the southern edge of the Peak National Park, the town provided a variety of hotels and guesthouses and appeared to be a good central point from which the tourist could explore, but it wasn't what he was looking for. Eventually, purely to stretch his legs, he made his way into the Hall Leys Gardens, which offered an excellent view of the gloomy, haunted-looking building known as Riber Castle. Surrounded by hordes of noisy holidaymakers, he stood frowning at the gaunt, embattled facade, which brooded over the town - but the atmosphere of the place was lost on him. If anything, it was making him feel worse. Acutely aware of his solitary existence, he made his way back to the car. What he needed was somewhere quiet yet uplifting – if such a place existed.

He passed through several sleepy villages before arriving in Carlton. It was ideal for his purpose, he thought. The sort of place where nothing much ever happens.

Mark was to reflect on this thought more than once in the weeks to come. There was no premonition or sense of foreboding, nothing to indicate that the peace he sought would last but a few short days.

The light was just beginning to fade when he pulled up outside the Royal Oak. In the lane, he stretched the stiffness from his limbs and, ignoring the chill in the air, breathed deeply, enjoying the subtle fragrance of a late-flowering honeysuckle that scrambled, untamed, over a nearby porch. Yes, this would do nicely.

The pub, typical of many others he'd visited in Derbyshire, proved, small, cosy, and in early evening, practically empty. As a newcomer from London, he got full attention and in no time at all had established his intentions. By nine thirty that night he'd met the publican and his wife, booked his room for the week and, with the assistance of several drinks, poured his troubles over the bar into the tolerant ears of George Tanner.

The publican patiently allowed him to talk himself out, then, with an understanding smile, took Mark's empty glass. "I think you're just about all-in, lad. I'll get the wife to show you to your room." He lifted the bar to allow Mark through. "Just one thing though - you say you're a writer. It is just books, isn't it? I mean, you haven't come from a newspaper or anything?"

"Good heavens, no - why?"

"It's just that some of the villagers are a bit iffy about reporters, but if it's not your line - well that's all right then, isn't it?"

Mark shrugged. "If you say so. What have they got against reporters?"

George Tanner shook his head. "Can't say for sure. It was something that happened here years ago." He lowered his voice. "Something about a young village lass - terrible tragedy, by all accounts. The wife says she was murdered but you know how gossip blows things up out of all proportion. I know the mere mention of reporters is enough to stir 'em up, though."

Joan Tanner emerged from the kitchen, effectively suspending further enquiry. "Ready to go up then, Mr Jordan?" She inclined her head to the stairs, "Come on, I'll show you your room."

With a nod to George, Mark followed her through into a narrow passage and embarked on what turned out to be a whirlwind tour of the building.

She bustled ahead, pointing out rooms as she went. Mark heard her mention the lounge, the kitchen, then after two short flights of stairs they were on the landing. She paused here to show him the bathroom. "You'll only be sharing with one other guest, so there shouldn't be a problem." Moving along the landing, she added, "So you're a writer, Mr Jordan. What sort of writer - war, westerns...?"

"Crime."

"Oh." She stopped in her tracks and looked at him through narrowed eyes. "Crime, eh?"

"Purely fiction, I assure you, and, before you say anything, George has already warned me about the locals." Mark contrived his most engaging smile. "What happened here - he mentioned a tragedy?"

"He probably told you not to ask about it, as well," she returned dryly. "Anyway, I don't know the details of it. It all happened before we came back to live here, and is probably best left alone." She indicated to a room on the left. "Here we are, what do you think?"

"It's delightful," he murmured, walking straight in. He'd been effectively put in his place, and knew better than to persist. Directing his attention to the room, he admired her taste. "Nicely done," he said. "Very nice indeed."

Two large windows gave the room an air of space. The first, he discovered, offered nothing more interesting than a view of the house next door. However, the second overlooked the rear garden and in daylight, he knew, would offer an uninterrupted view of the countryside beyond.

A reddening sun was fast disappearing over the horizon, but there was still enough light for him to establish the terrain. Beyond the boundary wall the land swept upwards, quite steeply, away from the house. A small building at the top caught his attention. "Is that a church up there?" he asked.

Joan Tanner busied herself unnecessarily, plumping pillows and straightening the bed covers. "It was," she said without looking up.

Something in her tone made him curious. "Was?"

"It's just a ruin now – hasn't been used for years. It should have been pulled down a long time ago."

15

Mark tried to judge the distance between the church and the village. "It's quite a climb, I should think. Have you been up there to see it?"

"Only once."

"And was it worth the effort?"

"What do you mean – worth the effort?"

Mark was struggling. Every question he put seemed to be regarded with suspicion. "I mean, is it worth visiting? What did you find when you went there?"

She joined him at the window and followed his gaze to the top of the hill. "Nothing," she said at last, "nothing except...." She turned away quickly.

"Except what?"

At the door she paused, then looked directly at him. "There's nothing there, Mr Jordan. It's just a place I visited once - and I don't want to visit again. At least, not on my own."

"Why?"

"It's hard to explain - I just felt uneasy. Old churches can be eerie places, full of creaks and groans." She shrugged. "Anyway, it was probably just my imagination, but I kept getting the feeling I wasn't alone." She gave a wry smile. "You know Mr Jordan, you mustn't take too much notice of us country-folk. We're a superstitious lot. It's just an old church - nothing more."

Long after she'd gone, Mark stood at the window staring into the darkness. Country-folk or not, Joan Tanner didn't strike him as the type to take flights of fancy - but something had spooked her, and for the first time in weeks there was a glint in his eye.

CHAPTER FOUR

Saturday, 22nd September, 1984

Mark watched a shaft of bright morning sunlight dance on the mirror opposite his bed and wondered idly what he might do with his first day in Carlton. In many ways it was a relief to know he didn't have to do anything if he didn't want to. There was no phone to answer and no computer to stare at in empty-headed confusion. Conversely, he also knew that total inactivity would soon begin to pall. He eased himself back into the warmth of soft downy pillows. Maybe he'd climb that hill - then again...

A gentle tap on the door interrupted his thoughts, and then George's beaming face appeared. "The wife said to bring this up," he said, placing a tray on the bedside table. "Its fresh coffee, she says you're to drink it while it's hot"

Mark grinned. In many ways George reminded him a lot of his father. He was always passing on instructions from his mother: Eat your greens, take your feet off the furniture. "Thanks," he said while struggling to sit up. "I didn't know you did room service."

"We don't. This is something quite different from the norm." George chuckled. "The wife seems to have taken quite a shine to you. What were you two chatting about last night?"

"Nothing much. I asked her about the church on the hill, that's all."

"Oh." George dismissed this as unimportant. "Well lad, you're looking a lot brighter than you were. Did you sleep well?"

"Like a log. What's the time?"

"It's just after nine. Joan said to let you sleep on, she thought you looked worn out. Anyway, there's no hurry, you've got the bathroom to yourself, Mr Wade left about an hour and a half ago."

"Mr Wade? Oh, your other guest. I haven't met him yet."

"Aye, and you'll be hard pressed to, he's never here. Doesn't have any meals, just goes off in his car every morning and comes in after closing each night. Funny sort of chap." He shrugged his shoulders and turned to leave. "Still, he's no trouble, which counts for something, I suppose. About twenty minutes then - for breakfast, I mean?"

"Oh, yes - thank you, George."

An hour later, Mark watched Joan bustle around the kitchen clearing the breakfast things.

"You're starting to make me nervous," she said at last.

"Sorry, was I staring?"

"Sort of. Is something the matter?"

"Nothing, that's the trouble. Suddenly I have all this time to do exactly as I please, and I can't think how to use it. The original plan was a good brisk walk in the hills, but after that breakfast, I think I'll just settle for a gentle stroll around the village."

"Well that shouldn't take long. Apart from a couple of small-holdings and the cottages opposite, there's nothing to see but fields."

"Perfect," Mark said without conviction. "What sort of small-holdings?"

"There are only three. There's the dairy, the pig farm, then a bit further on you'll find the nursery."

"Nursery?"

"Plant specialists, you know, roses and things."

"Oh I see. Well, that will do for a start. Maybe after lunch I'll do something more energetic."

As Joan had predicted, it didn't him take long to walk the lane. At the southern end he stopped at the junction to study the length of it, and wondered if he'd been a little over-optimistic thinking he could spend an entire week here.

By mid-morning, bathed in the warm glow of autumn sunlight, the village was picturesque enough, but deadly quiet. Glumly, Mark suspected he might have to look further afield for something to interest him. Suddenly, having nothing to do wasn't quite as appealing as he'd expected.

Looking around dismally, he found himself faced with a choice of three routes, all looking very much the same. One, he knew, would take him up to the ruined church, but he was in no mood for a climb. He mentally tossed a coin between the lane, roughly sign-posted 'To Harold Village' and the unmarked lane leading heaven knew where. Opting for the latter, he set off with brisk determination, but once past the dairy and pig farm, he'd very soon left all signs of life behind him.

Content to be alone for a while, he walked for twenty minutes without sight or sound of another human being, and was on the verge of turning back when in the distance he noticed a dark plume of smoke rising above the trees. He walked on until, through a break in the hedgerow, he saw smoke billowing from a solitary farmhouse. Imagining all kinds of horrors, he began to run along the lane. People might be trapped or injured - where was the nearest phone? At last, in front of the building, coughing from the fumes, eyes smarting, he didn't see a little dog as it raced through the gate into his path.

"Christ!" he muttered under his breath as he stumbled against the fence. He watched the small, white terrier scuttle across the lane then, finding no sign of anyone chasing after him, called out, "Hello, is anybody there?" There wasn't a sound except the crackle of burning wood. By this time he'd established, with a certain amount of relief, that the building itself wasn't on fire. The smoke was coming from somewhere behind it. "Hello!" he called louder.

This time he was rewarded with a faint but urgent reply. "Here... I'm here at the back, can you help me?"

He ran across the front garden and around the side of the house. Only ten metres or so away from the building, a bonfire burned dangerously out of control. Dense smoke stung his eyes and caught in his throat, but he pushed on looking for the owner of the frail voice that had cried out to him.

She lay on the ground, an elderly woman, struggling unsuccessfully to pull herself away from the flames.

Within seconds he'd covered the distance between them, scooped her up and carried her to the back of the house where, uncertain what to do next, he asked. "Are you hurt?"

"Of course I'm hurt!" she snapped. "Why else would I have been sitting there? And you can just put me down, young man."

It was hardly the response he'd expected, but he put it down to shock. Ignoring both her ingratitude and her instructions, he tried again, "Where are you hurt?"

Her lips formed a thin line of indignation. "My ankle - twisted it - but I'm perfectly capable of walking, thank you."

"So I noticed," he replied dryly. "Now, how do we get inside?"

She sighed heavily. "Just lean against the door, it's on the latch."

Disregarding her protests, and in spite of their uncertain progress across the quarry-tiled floor of the old lady's kitchen, Mark gained an impression of old-world charm from the parchment-coloured walls and black oak beams. He looked around for somewhere to put her. The room glowed warmly with the reflection of sunlight on copper and brass, but the most striking feature was a huge circular table, beautifully carved in solid yew, surrounded by four matching chairs. Onto one of these he lowered the old lady.

"Right, let's have a look at this ankle," he said.

"Are you a doctor, young man?"

"No - but..."

"In that case, you're no better qualified than I am to

understand my condition."

"Good grief! Are you always this difficult? Can't you see I'm trying to help?"

Quite unexpectedly, she smiled. "Well, it's not often I get put in my place, I can tell you."

"I don't doubt it," he muttered.

She went on smiling as she continued, "I'm Maude Brandon, who are you?"

Mark introduced himself and explained briefly how he came to be there. "I was on the verge of turning back when I saw the smoke from your bonfire."

In sudden alarm she tried, quite unsuccessfully, to stand. "Oh my goodness - the bonfire - and where's Robbie?"

"Robbie?" The old lady's sudden pallor concerned him. "Please, sit down, at least until we've established what damage you've done to your ankle. Now, who's Robbie?"

"My dog – he ran..." As if on cue the little white terrier padded into the kitchen and jumped onto her lap. "Oh there you are, you naughty boy!"

Mark watched her as she admonished the offending creature. The thought of what might have happened to her if he hadn't noticed the smoke unnerved him a little. He marvelled at her calm and wondered if he should get her to the nearest hospital for a check-up. Delayed shock could set in and, although her appearance gave very little away, she was obviously no youngster.

"Well, at least he's all right, and your bonfire is dying down a bit now." Mark frowned at her rapidly swelling ankle. "Now what about you? Would you like me to call a doctor?"

"I most certainly would not, it's only a sprain." The old lady glowered at him. "In any case, I don't trust them. I'm certain to end up with a bottle of pills that will cure one thing only to give me another. No, I can manage well enough without the aid of a doctor."

Mark wondered just how old she was. Greying hair,

scraped tightly back into a knot, did nothing to soften her lined face, but there was a toughness about her that defied age. "OK, you win, no doctor," he said, "but I can't just go off and leave you to get on with it. How will you manage - is there a neighbour or someone I can ...?"

"There's no one."

"Well, I don't like the look of you. I wouldn't be surprised if you're suffering from shock, or something. I know – hot sweet tea - that's what you need. At least let me do that for you?"

A look of extreme exasperation settled on her stubborn features. "I'm perfectly capable...." she paused when she saw the determination in his eyes, "oh, all right, if you must. You'll find the tea things in the cupboard by the sink." She added grudgingly, "You'd better make yourself a cup, I suppose."

Sensing a breakthrough at last, Mark got on with it in silence. He knew that one wrong word would set her off again. Nobody spoke until the tea was made and he was seated with her at the table.

Eventually the old lady spoke. "You seem very capable, Mr Jordan. I suspect you're used to doing things for yourself."

"Yes, and no." He grinned. "Yes, I'm used to looking after myself, but I can't claim to be capable – not in the kitchen anyway. Making tea is something I've got down to a fine art. As for the rest of my culinary skills – well, just don't ask me to cook you a meal. Believe me, you'll be sorry."

Maude Brandon grunted. "At least you're honest."

He looked into her searching grey eyes. "Not much point in being otherwise, is there?"

"I suppose not." She stirred her tea unnecessarily. "What brings you here, Mr Jordan? I mean, why Carlton?"

"No special reason. I set off with no particular place in mind, and this is where I ended up."

Maude Brandon shrugged. "Well, I don't suppose you'll be around very long. There's not enough going on for most city folk, and you can see all Carlton has to offer in a couple of hours."

"I agree, it's quiet, but I'm sure I'll find enough to interest me for a day or two. There's the old church for a start."

"What do you mean - which old church?"

Mark almost flinched at the sudden hostility in her eyes. "I mean the ruin, the one at the top of the hill – how many are there?"

She ignored his question. "Why do you want to go there?"

"No special reason, I thought it would be a pleasant walk, and - well, I quite like looking around old buildings."

Maude Brandon straightened her shoulders and spoke in more level tones. "If you'll take my advice, you'll give it a miss. There's nothing to see there - nothing at all, certainly nothing worth trekking all that way for." She turned her attention to her swollen foot. "Now, if you've finished your tea, and if I'm to deal with this ankle, I would be most grateful if you could leave and allow me to get on with it."

Mark rose uncertainly. He was dismissed and there was no arguing with it. "Yes of course, but I still don't like leaving you on your own like this."

"Nonsense, I shall be perfectly all right. Enjoy the rest of your stay in Carlton Mr.. er..?"

"Jordan." He offered lamely then, turning to leave, added. "Look, I'm staying at the Royal Oak, please call if...."

But Maude Brandon wasn't listening.

Mark returned to the village in rather a sombre mood. The old lady bothered him more than he cared to think about. He knew her irascibility was little more than a brave show of independence, and that she was alone and needed help. Maybe he would have a word with Joan when he got back; there must be someone in the village who would offer to lend her a hand – always supposing she'd let them. And what was all that stuff about the church? Clearly she didn't want him going anywhere near it - very odd, and she was the second person to react strangely when it was mentioned. He walked on, knowing that before long he would have to investigate. By the time he reached the pub he'd already decided to return to the farmhouse the next day to see if he could find out more - and to see if she was all right, though he doubted she'd thank him for it.

"I'm a bit worried about her," He told Joan later that afternoon. "I was just beginning to sense a thaw when she dismissed me like a naughty schoolboy. She even pretended to forget my name."

"Yes, that sounds just like Maude. She's always been a bit too independent for her own good. Don't worry, I'll have a word with Eve in the shop across road. She delivers Maude's groceries – yes that's the best way round it, I think."

Mark felt easier now that he knew someone was on the case. "It sounds as if you know her quite well."

Joan nodded. "I do, in a way. She was the local schoolmistress, until she retired. I used to live in Harold when I was a child and went to the school where Maude Brandon taught history. She was a bit of a tartar, even then. Most of us kids were terrified of her, but she was a good teacher." Joan gave Mark an amused look. "Go back and see her, if you must, but don't be surprised if you get your knuckles rapped."

CHAPTER FIVE

Sunday, 23rd September, 1984

The following morning Maude Brandon showed a remarkable lack of surprise at finding Mark on her doorstep. "Thought you'd be back," she snorted. "Well, now you're here, I suppose you'd better come in."

Mark trailed after her – he didn't dare do otherwise. He thought of the conversation he'd had with Joan, and could imagine just how easily the old lady had controlled a classroom of young tearaways. Here he stood in her kitchen, twenty-nine years old going on eight, and tried desperately to think of something to say.

"Sit down," she commanded. "I'll put the kettle on."

"How's the ankle?" he ventured cautiously.

"Fine." She turned to stare at him. "Why have you come?"

"I just thought..."

"Worried about me, were you? No need."

"Clearly." He felt oddly deflated. This was a mistake. Apart from anything else, he could see any chance of further information about the church was out of the question. "Look, if you'd rather I left, just say so."

She surprised him then with a sudden smile. "I'm doing it again, aren't I? I'm afraid I'm being very rude. In truth, I should be thanking you for your help yesterday. Please, stay for coffee. The kettle's almost boiled."

Mark cautiously took a seat at the table. She really was a most difficult woman to deal with. No wonder she's a spinster, he thought. How could anyone live with it? Up one minute, down the next - puts a chap on edge. At last, reluctant to say anything that might put her back up, he muttered, "I was admiring your table when I was here yesterday. It's very unusual."

"My father made it," she said. "He made all the furniture in this house. He was a carpenter, you see."

"Clever man," Mark replied, hoping she would enlarge on the subject, but she didn't. Sensing conversation on any subject was going to be hard work, he watched in silence while she pottered around the kitchen.

When she joined him at the table, she chuckled with unexpected warmth. "As my father would have said, you look about as nervous as a long tailed cat in a room full of rocking chairs, Mr Jordan. You don't need to be anxious, you know. I'm afraid I never was much good at the social graces - comes of spending all one's working life with children, and the rest of it alone."

"My landlady, Joan Tanner, told me you were a schoolmistress."

"Yes, that's right."

"History, wasn't it?"

"For the most part. Sometimes I took English Lit. but history was my main subject. Are you interested in history, Mr Jordan?"

"Historic buildings interest me."

A wary look came into her eyes, reminding him he was still on shaky ground. "So you said yesterday," she replied in a colourless voice.

Here we go, he thought. The barriers are in place again. Mark bit his lip and braced himself. The old lady was becoming a bit of a challenge – one he couldn't resist. "I know you think it's a waste of time, but I thought I might wander up to the old church this afternoon."

She remained silent.

"After all, it can't hurt, can it? And I could do with the exercise." It was as if he hadn't spoken. He watched her carefully. There was no reaction – not a spark. Eventually, impatience got the better of him. "Miss Brandon, why *did* people stop using the place? I thought the church was the nucleus of village life." He waited for a rebuke, and was surprised when she spoke without anger.

"It was. It was the one thing that united the people of this village. We were all involved in its upkeep, one way or another. Sam Fletcher and Archie Crane used to do the repairs and keep the garden up to scratch. Mary Tyler used to clean once or twice a week, and Blanche Armitage and I took it in turns to do the flowers. Between us we kept it looking nice and, I think without exception, everyone in Carlton attended." She reached across the table for his cup. "Another?"

"Thanks...but."

She carried on as if he hadn't spoken. "Of course in those days things were different. People cared about each other – cared about the village. But ever since..." she paused, as if realising she was going too far. "What I mean is," she spoke hurriedly, "times have changed. Folk keep themselves to themselves. Maybe it's better that way. Anyway, the locals go to St. Peter's church in Harold nowadays. I used to go myself until getting to and from by bicycle became a bit too much for me."

"But why travel all that way when all they had to do was walk up the hill?"

"They had their reasons."

Mark chewed on his lip. They'd reached the tricky bit and he knew he either had to abandon the subject altogether, or jump in with both feet and risk the consequences. "It must have been something pretty dreadful. What happened?"

Her eyes narrowed. "What is it about the place that fascinates you so much, Mr Jordan? Why do you want to know all this?"

Mark relaxed a little. At least she hadn't blown him out of the water altogether. "Curiosity I suppose, and the way people react when they speak of the church."

"What people? Who have you been talking to?"

"Only Joan Tanner- and you." He was beginning to feel foolish.

The old lady snorted. "You must have a very active imagination, Mr Jordan. Two people, apparently reluctant to talk about an old ruined building and you've got yourself a mystery. You're not a policeman by any chance, are you?"

Mark grinned and shook his head.

She looked as if she didn't believe him. "What did young Joan tell you about it? She must have said something to fire your imagination this way."

"Actually, she didn't tell me very much at all. She said she felt uneasy about the place but didn't know why." He waited for a response but nothing came. "She felt she was being watched – as if she wasn't alone."

The old lady's gaze shifted from his face to the window. "Did she now," she murmured softly.

Mark watched her expression as she stared out at the garden. Her eyes, once steely and hard, softened visibly. Instinctively, he knew if he pressed her now she would clam up altogether.

Several minutes passed before she looked at him again. Then, without prompting, she said. "Everything changed after the murder, you see."

"Murder – in the church?"

She nodded. "After that the congregation grew smaller and smaller, until in the end nobody went any more. Attitudes changed, people began to cut themselves off – they took to locking their doors at night. No one felt really safe any more."

"When did it happen?"

"About fifteen years ago. It was a child from the village. Her father found her, poor man - and I found him."

Although the last was uttered in barely a whisper, Mark heard a distinct tremor in her voice. He looked away, hoping she wasn't going to cry. It was the last thing he'd expected, or wanted.

The old lady brushed a stray wisp of grey hair from her temple. "They never caught the murderer, you see. At first everyone thought it must be a tourist, but when the police came up with nothing, they started looking closer to home." Slumping a little in her chair, she rested her arms on the table. "Things got very unpleasant for everybody. But that was all a long time ago, best forgotten." Her hands trembled a little as she loaded the coffee things on a tray and carried them to the sink.

Mark gave her a moment to collect herself, then said. "George mentioned a tragedy, but I didn't link it with the church."

"I doubt he could tell you the details of it," she replied. "As far as I can remember, he didn't live here when all that was going on. And I doubt he'd get anyone in the village to enlighten him."

"Did you know the child?" Mark asked gently.

"Yes, I knew her, she was one of my pupils." Abandoning the dishes she returned to her seat. "Christie Abbott." she whispered. "She was a bright child, only seven years old. The family still live in the village, you're bound to see them if you stay here long enough. The mother, Kathleen, has coped pretty well in the circumstances. Mind you, she had to, she had two other youngsters to worry about, and her husband, Jim." She shook her head sadly. "Poor Jim, the shock of finding Christie like that affected him very badly - and still does."

Mark knew she was no longer seeing him. Her mind was elsewhere, back in that church on the hill.

"I'd gone to the church that day to change the flowers. It wasn't really my week, but Blanche was still recovering from a bad cold." She smiled briefly. "I remember it was early spring, a lovely day, the first real sun of the year. My garden was full of daffodils and I'd decided to take a basket of them up there. You know, I must have walked up that hill a hundred times, or more, and thought nothing of it. But that day, everything seemed different – I felt different – as if I was expecting something to happen. Even now, I can recall every second of it. As I drew nearer to the church I noticed Samuel had cut the grass and, wonder of wonders, he'd repaired the gate. I'd been grumbling at him for ages about it, you see. I turned as I closed the gate behind me..." She paused as if remembering something then, with a slight shake of her head, continued. "Yes, I closed the gate and stood for some time looking down to the village, thinking how perfect it all looked." She gave Mark a quizzical look. "Isn't it strange how one can remember the tiniest detail after such a long time?"

He knew she didn't expect an answer so he waited quietly, anxious not to intrude on her thoughts. He studied her face carefully. What little colour she had in her cheeks had vanished. The smile still lingered on her lips, but the pain in her eyes concerned him. He began to question his motives – what right had he to stir all this up again? Was any story really worth causing this much anguish?

"It was a calm, still day," she continued. "No birds sang. Nothing moved. I remember thinking how lucky I was to live in such a beautiful spot." Her smile vanished. "I also remember how alone I felt, until I heard a faint sound from inside. I was glad for some company and went into the church expecting to find Reverend Matthews, but... "

Unshed tears brightened her eyes and caused Mark to leave his seat. "Look, don't go on – not if it's going to upset you." He hovered by her side uncertain what to do.

"No, I'm all right, really. It's just that I haven't spoken of it like this, not since it happened anyway. Those of us in the village went through quite an ordeal in the weeks following, what with the police, and then those dreadful newspaper people. Since then we've been careful to avoid the subject. The odd thing is, I'm remembering things now that I didn't give much thought to at the time. When the police questioned me, all I could tell them was how I'd found Jim Abbott kneeling in front of the altar table cradling his daughter's body in his arms. He just knelt there, rocking to and fro, crooning, 'there, there...it'll be all right,' over and over again."

Dismayed, he watched as the tears spilled onto her cheeks "I'm so sorry." He spoke gently. "Shall I get you something – some water?" He stared wildly round the kitchen, dithering, completely at a loss.

Brushing a hand across her eyes, she said. "No - I should have talked about this before, doesn't do to keep things bottled up. I'll make some more coffee. It'll give me something to do. Why don't you go into the sitting room, it's more comfortable in there." She smiled weakly. "Don't look so worried. I'll be all right in a minute."

All available wall space in the sitting room displayed the skill of old Mr Brandon. The room was like a small library; bookshelves everywhere, all decorated with the same beautiful carving as the kitchen furniture. There were no ornaments, just hundreds of books carefully placed in groups according to their subject; each separated by a framed photograph. Mark wandered around aimlessly. Things weren't going at all well. He'd finally got what he wanted, but at what cost? Questioning people in depth was all part of the job, but going around upsetting old ladies wasn't. He looked at his watch – whatever was keeping her? Knowing she was probably sobbing at the kitchen table made him feel worse. He took down one of the photographs and stared at it without really seeing it

"You can put that back where you found it." Her voice, which had recovered some of its normal stridency, preceded her into the room. "That's the class of 1966, and of no interest to you whatsoever." She placed a tray on a low table and, before he could do as she asked, took the photograph from him. "The likeness of every child I ever taught can be seen on these shelves somewhere. Some of them still write to me." She replaced the photograph among the books and carefully selected another. "Here, this was Christie Abbott."

Mark studied the child's laughing face for a long time. He wanted to ask more questions but feared the consequences. "Pretty girl," he managed at last.

"Yes, she was. All the Abbott children were good-looking, as I recall. They got it from their mother. She was the village beauty, you might say. There was great competition among the village lads for her, and she broke a few hearts before she finally settled on Jim."

"Has it been a happy marriage?" Mark lowered himself onto a window seat.

"I think so, although we were all surprised at her choice. Jim was such a gentle boy, inclined to be nervous, even as a youngster. Kathleen was quite different, lively and outgoing; she liked the good life. Of the two, she was the stronger. Maybe that was the attraction. Kathleen always liked to be in control, you see."

"What about the other two children, do they still live in the village?"

"Jamie's in the RAF; he's the eldest. He comes home on leave of course, but not very often. Rebecca's still at home, though. Let me see - she must be seventeen or eighteen now. She's been working in Harold for the last year, training to be a hairdresser. I expect she'll be up and away like her brother once she's got some qualifications. All the youngsters from the village have gone now - well, most of them. The only ones who stay are those who want to work on the land." She released a wistful sigh. "Still, as I said, some of them still write to me. I like to hear how they're all doing."

Mark could see they were gradually wandering from the point and, although reluctant to upset her again, attempted to steer the conversation back to the matter of the murder. "If it isn't too painful..."

"Please, Mr Jordan – or may I call you Mark?"

"Please do."

"Well, Mark, please don't worry about what happened before, a good cry never hurt anyone, you know. Now, what are you trying to ask?"

"What happened next - I mean, after you found Jim Abbott in the church?"

Maude Brandon's brow creased. "Why do you want to know all this? There must be some reason why it interests you so much."

"Let's just say I have an enquiring mind." He smiled ruefully. "Standard equipment for a writer."

"Ah, now I see. What sort of writer?"

For reasons best known to himself, Mark always felt faintly embarrassed when asked about his work. "Crime stories mostly," he mumbled.

"Well, that explains everything, doesn't it? Are you successful?"

"To a certain extent." He gazed out of the window, trying to avoid direct eye contact. "But I'm going through a difficult patch at the moment."

"Mm, I believe they call it writer's block, don't they?"

"Something like that," he muttered, wishing they could change the subject.

Maude Brandon looked at the photograph again. "Well, I don't imagine you'll get much inspiration from this tragedy. The police were left baffled and, as far as I know, the case remains open. All kinds of rumours went around at the time. Somebody even accused Reverend Matthews. Believe me, that child's death brought misery to more than one family in the village." She looked at him steadily. "But I haven't answered your question, have I?"

He'd become so intent on what she was saying, he'd quite forgotten what he'd asked. Thankfully, he was saved from embarrassment when she continued. "You want to know what happened after I found them in the church. Well, that part is still a bit hazy. I remember putting my hand on Jim's shoulder and saying something - I can't remember what - probably something totally inadequate, but whatever it was it didn't matter - he didn't even know I was there. He just went on crooning and stroking the child's hair from her face. Next thing, I was running out of the church and down the hill to the village. I must have been shouting because people started coming up the hill towards me. I'm afraid it's all a bit muddled after that. As soon as the others arrived I just sat at the side of the footpath watching folk go up and down. There seemed to be people everywhere, all the folk from the village, then the police came - followed by an ambulance. How they ever got up that hill I'll never know. They had to drive across the fields because the path is so narrow. Suddenly it seemed they were all gone. I felt somehow set apart from it all. I don't even know how long I sat there. It was Blanche Armitage who persuaded me to go down with her. She lives in the corner cottage, the big one with the thatched roof, and that's where I was when the police came making their enquiries." She stared into space, her mind still turning over the events of fifteen years ago.

"What was it that you remembered?" Mark ventured softly.

"Remembered?"

"Yes, you said earlier that you were remembering things now, that you didn't pay any attention to at the time."

"Oh yes - well, it's probably nothing, but when I saw them - Jim and Christie, I wanted to help but the look on Jim's face frightened me, and there was so much blood, I'm ashamed to say, I just turned and ran without thinking. Since then I've tried very hard not to think too much about it, but when I was talking earlier I was seeing it as if for the first time, that's when I remembered..."

"Yes?" he prompted.

"It was just a feeling really, as I ran out of the church I was conscious of someone else being there, and then the gate, that's the oddest thing."

"The gate?"

"When I arrived I closed the gate before looking down at the village, but when I ran out - the gate was wide open."

"You're sure of that?"

"Oh yes, quite sure. Odd I should remember it after all this time, still, I don't suppose it's anything important."

"No." He spoke absently, seeming to agree. In truth, he wasn't so sure.

They sat in silence for some minutes, each for different reasons. Mark's brain was stirring into action. Already he was weaving a story around the events that the old lady had related.

Maude Brandon studied him shrewdly. He thought she had been reading his mind when she said. "You're going to write about it, aren't you?"

"I only write fiction, Miss Brandon," he smiled. "But I will admit you've given me an idea." There was something else he wanted to know. "You said something about the girl's death affecting more than one family - what did you mean?"

"Oh, nothing specific. Christie's death affected us all, and it seemed to be the start of a chain of disasters, but that's another story. Perhaps another time?"

"Yes, of course." She was looking very tired and he knew it was his fault. "I'm sorry I've taken up so much of your time."

"Not at all," she assured him. "Talking has done me good. I don't see many people these days. Maybe you'll come again?"

"Yes, I'd like that."

She laughed with genuine mirth. "I can see you're surprised. I suppose the villagers have been telling you what an old dragon I am?"

He felt uncomfortable. "Well, not exactly. Joan said you were very independent."

She laughed again. "I don't mind, you know. I used to be quite proud of my reputation, but if nothing else, age has taught me independence brings little joy. It's usually accompanied by loneliness." As they walked to the door, she touched his arm. "What are you going to do with the rest of the day?"

"I'm not sure yet. I may look around at some property. If I'm going to stay in the area for a while if might be a good idea to rent a cottage. Who knows? I might even buy one. It would be nice to have a retreat from the city - I don't know, I'm still thinking about it."

She stood at the door watching him walk away. He was almost out of the gate when she called, "Mark, would you like to come to lunch tomorrow - we could talk again?" She spoke as if she expected him to refuse, and could barely disguise her pleasure when he didn't.

CHAPTER SIX

Long before leaving the farmhouse, Mark had decided he would visit the church as soon as possible. He had no clear idea what he was looking for, or what he could hope to find after fifteen years. Nevertheless, he commenced the steep climb in a curious state of anticipation.

About half way up he stopped to catch his breath. Too many hours sitting at his desk had wrought havoc with his body. Beads of perspiration glistened on his forehead, his thigh muscles tightened and cramped uncomfortably, and a dull ache in his lower back warned that he was going to pay dearly for his curiosity next morning.

He sat on the grass verge looking down at the village, which presented the sort of scene used to decorate holiday brochures and chocolate boxes. Maude was right, it looked perfect - almost too perfect, he thought. Scanning the area, he recognised the smallholdings to the left of the path. To the right, the large thatched cottage he now knew belonged to Blanche Armitage. Next, the pub where Joan would be pottering in her garden – then three small cottages marking the end of the lane. It would be nice to think it would stay this way; that no well-meaning developer would want to build on it.

He noted with surprise that, in only two short days, Carlton had become as familiar to him as his London home. It was going to be difficult to leave. Maybe he wouldn't, he mused. Maybe his throwaway remark to Maude Brandon about buying or renting a cottage wasn't too far from the truth, after all.

With more difficulty than he cared to admit to, he struggled to his feet to get a broader view. He could just see the rooftops of the cottages on the far side of the lane and wondered about the people who lived in them – and what secrets they might have to tell. Beyond the chimneys, miles of unspoilt countryside swept upwards, in shades of green and yellow, like an intricately woven quilt. It was hard to believe that somewhere within this idyllic but limited landscape a murderer might dwell, undetected. With a wry smile, Mark resumed his climb. This was all purely the stuff of fiction – and what he did best.

Having been a Londoner all his life, Mark's idea of a church ran to vaulted ceilings, pews and stained-glass windows, so he was somewhat disappointed to find a building which could only be described as a chapel at best. A drystone wall, which had once enclosed the garden, lay crumbled to an untidy heap of rubble. The gate Maude had spoken of had long since gone, and the path he trod was barely distinguishable between the weeds. One of the big chapel doors lay across the path, the other hung awry from a rusty hinge.

Inside there was nothing. Not a sign that people had once worshipped there. Even the glass, whether stained or otherwise, was gone from the windows. At the far end he spotted a wooden staging. This must have served as the altar, he thought, and walked towards it. He stared at the bare boards, split and rotting now, and knew this must be where the distraught Jim Abbot had cradled his daughter's dead body. Suddenly all kinds of questions manifested themselves: Why here, in the church – at the altar? Was Christie killed here or brought here after her death?

Without really knowing why, he took a couple of steps back. He had no desire to mount the creaky steps to examine the altar further. He concentrated instead on the doors, one on either side of the staging. They were identical, miraculously intact – and closed.

Opting for the one on the left, he opened it slowly and with a certain amount of trepidation, but again he was disappointed. The square window-less room was empty, lit only by a gaping doorway in the back wall. A second door, on the right, led to a small kitchen, and in turn completed the circuit back to the altar where he stood for a few seconds, listening to the silence.

Unlike Joan or Maude Brandon, he had no feeling of another presence, no sense of the drama that had taken place so long ago. Yet something bothered him.

Deep in thought, he retraced his steps to the path outside. He started the return journey, thankful it was all downhill, barely noticing the woods on his left until the sound of twigs snapping underfoot brought him to a halt. He remained still, listening, then moved on, reflecting how easy it would be to imagine some unknown being watching from the bushes. This was probably what had unnerved Joan. A light breeze brought the sound of rustling leaves, then more twigs snapping. Mark smiled at the thought of small woodland creatures scurrying about, completely unaware of the effect they could have on an active imagination.

Continuing the descent his thoughts returned to the church. He still felt there was something amiss - but what?

He'd almost reached the lane when it came to him. He stared back up at the ruin. A building, empty as long as this one had been, without windows or doors, on a hill exposed to the elements, should be littered with all kinds of rubbish. That's what was wrong - the chapel was completely void of debris. Someone had given the place a thorough cleaning - and recently, too.

In his room, Mark cursed and swore as he rummaged through his things. Ideas were coming thick and fast and he didn't have a pencil to his name.

Downstairs, Joan searched the kitchen drawers and eventually came up with a ballpoint pen. "Here, you can have this. As for paper, all I've got is an old writing pad - will that do?"

Mark grimaced involuntarily.

"Well, you'd better try the shop across the lane, then. If you hurry you'll catch Eve before she shuts. Go out the front way – it's quicker."

A brilliant sunset momentarily blinded him as he came down the front steps. Then, as his eyes rallied to the light, he noticed a girl with a large dog at the end of the lane. Something about her, the way she looked - even the dog seemed agitated. Assuming she was lost, Mark moved towards her. At the same time she turned to stare directly at him. Immediately he noticed how dishevelled she was, her shirt was torn and splattered with mud, and there was blood on her face. "Dear God!" he muttered. She looks as if she's been beaten up.

She came towards him, half-running, clutching tightly on the dog's lead. "Please...can you help?"

Within minutes the quiet country lane was bustling with noise and activity. To Joan's irritation, people massed around the girl, trying to see what was happening, while she did her best to minister first aid to her cuts and grazes. "What's happened?" Someone asked. "Don't ask me," came the reply. "It's this lass – reckons she's found summat up in the woods." The dog, thoroughly alarmed, barked incessantly. Mark took hold of the lead and tried to coax him to one side, but the animal would have none of it.

George, having phoned the police, stood at the top of the steps watching the proceedings with a certain amount of concern. He could see things were getting out of control. In the general melee, no one noticed him slip quietly away to the cottage next door to the pub. Here he found the one person in the village who could deal with the situation.

Bob Witchell possessed an air of authority that few would argue with, Mark thought. He watched as the villagers, as if in response to some unspoken command, stood aside to let the big man through.

Without a word, and with no hesitation, the man ignored everyone except the dog. Mark held his breath as the great German Shepherd first snarled at the man's extended hand, then as curiosity took over, sniffed and eventually licked the offered fingers.

Bob Witchell slowly smoothed his roughened hand over the dog's head and along his back, then applied a firm but gently pressure to his rump. "Good lad," he murmured, as the dog obediently sat down. "I think that's quite enough barking for one day, my beauty." The dog gazed trustingly into the big man's eyes. He, for one, had found someone who could take control.

Once the dog was settled, the man placed himself beside the girl on the bench. "Right, let's have a bit of calm, shall we?" His eyes scanned the stunned crowd. "I suggest you all go back to your homes. There's nothing to see here." Then, as the village folk began to drift away, he turned his attention to the girl, gently questioning her until he had the whole story.

"Right!" Bob Witchell rose from the bench. "The police will be here soon and things will be a lot easier if this chap isn't around." He stroked the dog's ears. "With your permission, lass, I'll take him into my place. He'll be just fine in there with Shona."

Susan looked as if she'd never understand anything ever again. "With Shona - who's...?"

"Shona's my dog – ex-police, just like me."

"You're a policeman?"

"Retired."

After that things moved very quickly. Susan was taken back up the hill to point out the area. "It was my dog that found her," she said with tear filled eyes. "I don't have to go into the woods again, do I?"

"No, Miss, don't worry, " Sergeant Williams gently touched her elbow, "we'll find it. Just wait here a moment, will you?" Leaving her alone, he walked back to the path where another car had just pulled up. A tall, well-dressed man emerged from the vehicle, together with three uniformed policemen.

"What have we got, Williams?" The well-dressed man glanced at Susan. "Is that the girl who found it?"

"Yes sir, but I don't think she can tell us much. She only arrived here this afternoon – s'posed to be on holiday."

"Well, she's off to a good start, I must say. Probably came here for peace and quiet – and ends up with a dead body."

Williams nodded. "Sod's law – or what? Shall I get one of the lads to take her back to the pub? If you ask me, she's just about had enough, anyway."

"OK, but tell her I'll need to talk to her later. Get the details, address and so on. Oh, and find out who owns that field. Whoever it is, isn't going to be too happy. We had to drive right across it. There's no way we could get up that path."

Inside her rented cottage that evening, Susan wandered around in a state of preoccupation. From the moment the policeman had dropped her off at the Royal Oak until the time she reached the cottage she'd found it impossible to fasten her mind on anything but that mutilated bundle in the woods.

She had a vague memory of thanking those who had helped her, then someone brought Lexer in. The next moment Joan was giving her a card with a telephone number written on it, and helping her into Mark's jeep. What a day it had been - and now it was over she felt completely drained, wanting nothing but sleep.

An hour later, her things neatly stowed away and Lexer sleeping peacefully, she soaked in the comfort of a steaming bath. Even then, try as she might, she couldn't rid herself of the coldness that had stayed with her since the discovery of the body. She so wished she'd been a bit calmer. All that crashing around in the undergrowth probably hadn't helped the police much. Whatever had made her behave like it? She never used to panic.

Long before she'd drifted into a restless sleep she knew exactly why, but it didn't serve to make her feel any better. She had, in fact, identified all too clearly with the victim. She was, in many respects, as Susan saw herself – alone, abandoned and unwanted. The only difference being that Susan was still alive.

CHAPTER SEVEN

For once the Royal Oak was full to capacity. Wishing he'd gone to the back door, Mark manoeuvred his way through the over-spill of people loitering on the forecourt. Inside it was worse. He had to push and elbow his way, amidst much protesting, to reach the bar.

George, red-faced and flustered, grinned above the heads of those vying for attention. "Got her home safely then, did you?"

Mark nodded. "Where did all these people come from - are they all from the village?"

George snorted. "Never seen most of 'em before. News travels fast around here, they've all come hoping to see something grisly."

"Well if nothing else, it's good for business."

"I suppose so. It's a bit sick though, if you ask me."

Mark smiled wryly. "Human nature – here, do you want a hand?"

George pushed a glass of Scotch across the bar. "No lad, Joan will be out in a minute. Anyway, it's a good chance for you to meet a few of the locals." He inclined his head towards the far end of the bar, where Bob Witchell stood head and shoulders above the crowd. "There's one you've already met."

"Oh good, just the one I wanted to see." Mark eased his way along the bar until he reached the big man. "I'm glad you were around this afternoon." He had to shout to make himself heard.

"Pleased to be of assistance. How was that young lass when you left her?"

I think she'll be all right after a good night's sleep. I offered to stay for a while but I think she wanted some time alone." His eyes scanned the crowd. "I think this lot would have just about finished her off – it looks like the whole village has turned out."

"Aye, there's a few of 'em here, but that lot over there are from Harold."

"George was just saying he'd never seen most of them before."

"Probably won't again, either. Once they find there's nowt to see, they'll push off."

"I expect you've seen a lot of this sort of thing?"

The big man nodded. "Whenever there's trouble, you'll find a crowd like this. You're on holiday, I hear."

Mark nodded. Conversation was becoming impossible, but he was determined to manoeuvre the ex-policeman away from the mundane and onto the more interesting topic of the murder. "Nasty business, though. What do you make of it all?"

Bob shook his head. "Right now it's anyone's guess. I might find out a bit more when I see my nephew. He's on the force, one of those that came from Harold this afternoon."

The writer studied the big man's face closely. A bushy grey moustache that tilted slightly at the corners gave him the appearance of perpetually smiling, but Mark sensed there was more to the ex-policeman than his benevolent appearance suggested. Those penetrating grey eyes would miss nothing. He would be a hard man to deceive.

"You were at Harold police station, too, weren't you?"

Bob finished his pint. "I was. There's some say I still am." He chuckled. "Jack, that's my nephew, says he doesn't know why I retired. Reckons I spend more time there now than when I was on the payroll."

Mark glanced over his shoulder. "Look, there's a table just coming free. Why don't you go and grab it? I'll get some more drinks."

In fact, the crowd was beginning to disperse quite rapidly, leaving no more than four or five people sitting around. Bob sat back in his chair with satisfaction. "Good, we're almost back to normal. By the time we've finished this you'll see just how many of 'em are local. I reckon, without even looking around, I can tell you just who's left and where they're sitting."

"It's that predictable, is it?"

"I'm afraid so. Bit boring, I suppose."

"Not really, but it is surprising. I'd have thought they'd all be in here - curious to know what's happened."

The big man shrugged. "Old Amos might come in later, he lives next door to me, but the others only come in on high-days and holidays."

"Or murders?"

"Huh, they don't have to come in here, lad. If anyone wants to know anything, all they have to do is go in the shop. Eve Simpson knows everything and everybody, and she's only too pleased to share it – if you see what I mean."

"Actually, now you mention it, I don't remember seeing her in the crowd this afternoon. I'd expect her to be in the thick of it – wonder where she was?"

"Where she always is, lad, behind that counter of hers. I can't remember the last time I saw her outside that place, but mark my words, she'll be better-informed than any of us." Bob grinned. "I've often wondered how she does it. It's one of the great mysteries of the village, you might say. Anyway, most of the other village folk are here; there aren't many of us left, you know. Apart from Eve and her son, the only ones missing are Mary Tyler and the Abbotts, and the last thing they need is another murder." He gave a Mark a knowing look. "But you'll know all about that, of course. I hear you've already met Maude Brandon. I suppose it's my turn to be questioned now, is it?"

"I'm beginning to think everyone in this village is telepathic." Mark looked sheepish. "Do you mind me asking questions?"

"Not at all, but I doubt I can tell you much."

"Were you on the Christie Abbott case?"

"Well that's straight and to the point, if nothing else. Yes, I was on the case, but that doesn't mean I have special knowledge. We were no better informed six months after the murder than we were an hour after it happened. In the end everyone decided it had to be a tourist who did it. We get a lot of hill-walkers passing through, maybe staying long enough for a drink, then off again. We followed it up as far as we could but there was no real way of checking, you see."

"I'm surprised the family are still living here after an experience like that. Why do you think they stayed?"

"Aye, everyone thought they'd move on, but truthfully, I don't think Kath could have coped with it on top of everything else. If it wasn't bad enough losing her little girl like that, she had Jim to cope with. She needed her friends around her – people like Mary Tyler."

"Mary Tyler?"

"Aye, you'll no doubt meet her eventually. She and Kath used to be great chums - went to school together. The funny thing is they don't have much to do with each other now. Not since it all happened, anyway."

"Why's that?"

"Dunno. It started after Mary's husband died. And that's another mystery you'll probably want to get your teeth into. I hope you're not the squeamish type?"

"Hardly. If you'd ever read any of my stuff, you'd know that."

"Ah, but this is real lad, not the stuff of penny-dreadfuls."

Mark resisted the desire to argue the implied aspersion and tried to steer the conversation back to the matter in hand. "Good point. So what happened to Mary Tyler's husband, then?"

"One day Mary found him in the shed where he'd been cleaning his rifle. Of course the man drank too much and, well anyway, the shot had gone clean through his eye, blew his brains out - very nasty."

"Indeed, but where's the mystery? Do you think he did it on purpose?"

"I don't know. Nobody does." Bob took a pipe from his pocket. "Do you mind this...?" Mark shook his head. Filling the pipe from a battered leather pouch, Bob continued. "There was summat the matter with those two, that's for sure - Mary and Len I mean." He rummaged in his pockets for his matches then took a few minutes making sure the tobacco was alight. "They married not long after Jim and Kath. The four of them spent a lot of time together in those days, until Kath had Jamie. Two or three years later she had Christie and that's when the trouble started. I think Mary was a bit envious. She and Len hadn't got any kids, you see. Anyway, about that time they adopted a little girl, Helen her name is. That seemed to settle things down a bit, especially as the two children were such good friends. They were inseparable, never saw one without the other."

"Except the day Christie died."

Bob nodded. "That day Mary had taken young Helen to the dentist in Harold, so Christie went off to play on her own. I've often wondered whether that was fortunate or not."

"Fortunate - for whom?"

"Think about it. If the two had been together, would that have stopped the killer - or would we have had two dead children on our hands?"

"Hmm, I see what you mean." Mark wondered why he hadn't thought of that himself. "What made Jim Abbott go up to the church in the first place?"

"It was the obvious place to look for her. All the kids used to play up there, either in the church or the woods - never again though."

"So what happened to Mary's daughter, Helen?"

"Helen left Carlton a long time ago. After Christie's death she became a bit of a loner. To be honest, there was dark side to that kid that I could never fathom. She used to walk around hanging her head, staring at the ground so she didn't have to talk to folk – far too withdrawn than is healthy, I'd say."

"Where did she go?"

"London, I think. She's been back to see her mum once or twice, but I haven't seen her around the village for ages now."

Watching the big man smother a yawn, Mark sensed he was starting to find the conversation a bit tedious. He decided to change the subject. "What do you think of this lot today then?"

Rubbing his chin thoughtfully, but looking marginally more interested, Bob replied. "Until we know who it was up there, it's hard to know what to think. It can't be anyone local, in a place like this, if anyone was missing we'd hear about it pretty quick."

"When do you think you'll be seeing your nephew?" Mark tried to sound casual.

Bob chuckled. "Tomorrow probably, but I doubt he'll tell me anything you could write about. It is a detective story you're doing, isn't it?"

"Well, sort of ..." Mark felt foolish.

"Don't worry lad." He stood up and put a friendly hand on the younger man's shoulder. "If I hear anything interesting, I'll let you know. Come on, it's my turn. What'll you have?"

That night Mark slept fitfully, his mind racing with the events of the day, together with his conversation with Maude Brandon, and now with Bob Witchell. His thoughts drifted back and forth between the past murder to the present but, try as he might, he could not connect the two. Pity - it would make a good story...

CHAPTER EIGHT

Slumped on the edge of the bed cradling his aching head in his hands, Mark reflected, with a modicum of remorse, there was a price to be paid for everything - still, it had been worth it.

Talking and drinking into the early hours with Bob Witchell had proved both entertaining and rewarding. He'd learned a lot more about the people of Carlton, the murder of Christie Abbott and its effect on the lives of those closest to the family. But he needed more information, and for that he'd have to talk to some of them. For the moment at least, he had enough to get started – well almost. He had everything he needed except decent writing equipment.

Stumbling across the landing he had his first encounter with the mysterious and elusive Mr Wade. The man had come out of his room so fast he almost knocked Mark off his feet.

"I'm so sorry, I didn't see you, are you all right?"

A pulse throbbed relentlessly behind Mark's eyes as he tried to focus on the voice. "Yes, I'm fine, " he mumbled. "My fault - you must be Mr Wade."

"Right." The voice bellowed.

Mark winced and leant against the doorframe for support.

The voice continued to bombard his eardrums. "Look I'm sorry, I've got to dash - you sure you're all right? Blissfully, the noise receded as Mr Wade disappeared down the stairs. "Maybe I'll catch you later, eh?"

"Maybe." Mark muttered, and breathed a sigh of relief. "Well, there's nothing mysterious about you, chum - except why you have to talk so bloody loud!"

"I wish you'd eat something." Joan refilled Mark's cup.
"I couldn't Joan, really."
"That'll teach you to go drinking with the locals, my

lad. And if you're thinking of going back to bed, forget it. I want to get those sheets changed today."

"It's all yours. Much as I'd like to just slump somewhere, I really must get on. I'm going to have another crack at getting to the shop. I almost made it yesterday when all hell broke loose."

"Are you going to see her?"

"Who?"

"Young Susan."

"What for?"

"I think someone should see if she's all right, Mark. After all, the girl is here alone, and she's had a dreadful shock."

"Oh all right, I might try later, but it'll have to be after lunch."

Peering over her gold-rimmed half spectacles, Eve Simpson watched as Mark carefully selected a large notebook and several pencils. "Going to get started on it today then, are you?" she said.

"What?"

"Your book. I suppose you're going to write about the murder?"

He stared in amazement. Not another clairvoyant?

Quite obviously pleased with herself, she laughed knowingly. "You'll soon learn you can't sneeze around here without half the village hearing about it. But don't you worry now, I'm not going to ask too many questions." 'Just as well,' Mark thought. "Bad business that yesterday," she went on. "I s'pect the police will be round this morning wanting to talk to us all. Don't s'pose you can tell them much though, after all, you weren't up there, were you?"

"No, I wasn't." Mark found himself lying. "Well, not in the woods, anyway."

"You are going to write about it, aren't you – the murder, I mean?"

Mark shook his head. "Hardly. Not at this stage anyway. After all, it hasn't been confirmed as a murder yet. For all we know, she may have died of natural causes."

"Oh." She sounded disappointed. "I didn't think of that. What are you going to write about then?"

Mark shuffled about uncomfortably. "Right now I'm more intrigued with a much older crime, in fact you might be able to help me." He tried to ignore the warning signals as she folded her arms and stared at him through narrowed eyes. "Were you already living here when the Abbott child was murdered?"

There was a long silence before she answered, her voice now crackling with suspicion. "So, you want to know about Christie – I might have known."

'Here we go again,' he thought, and tried to reassure her. "I'm not from the newspapers, Mrs Simpson. And, if I do write about it, it will be in a purely fictional way."

"If that's so, why don't you make something up? Folk won't want all that dragging up again, believe me."

"I'm sure you're right. The last thing I want is to upset anyone, but not all fiction is make-believe. It has to be based on something – and in this case..."

"In this case, you're asking the wrong person," she interrupted. "Yes, I knew Christie, but that's all I know." She placed his shopping in a paper bag. "Take my word for it, Mr Jordan – leave well alone. That'll be three pounds fifty, please."

"Thanks." He placed the exact amount in her hand and headed for the door.

"Mr Jordan," she called. Mark turned to find her smiling, a little guiltily, he thought. "I'm sorry if I was blunt – bit of a sore point, you see. If there's anything else I can help you with, come and see me."

Returning her smile, he nodded his thanks and left. This was going to be trickier than he'd thought. From now on he was going to have to be very careful how he handled things – pity he hadn't packed his kid gloves!

In the sheltered courtyard garden at the back of the pub, Mark sat, content for a while to do nothing but allow the stillness of the village to soothe his aching head. He was very close to sleep when, all too soon, another sound reached his ears, the strangled cry of someone in pain. He turned sharply to find a woman staring at him as if he were the devil himself. She stood by the kitchen door, painfully thin, clutching a broom as if her very life depended upon it.

Mark half-rose from his seat. "Are you ill?"

She flinched as if she'd been struck and drew back against the wall, gurgling sounds coming from her throat.

"It's all right, really. I won't hurt you."

Dark eyes stared at him in terror, while she edged her way along the wall away from him.

He was becoming alarmed. She looked as though she was having some kind of seizure. "Look, please don't be afraid - I'll get someone to help."

Joan's voice came from inside. "Mary, I've done upstairs..." she stepped into the courtyard. "Oh there you are." Immediately assessing the situation, she gently put her arm around the woman's shoulders and led her into the kitchen. "Come on, I thought you might make a start on the potatoes for me."

She returned a few minutes later to reassure Mark. "Don't be upset about that, Mary's nervous of strangers."

"Nervous?" he spluttered. "I thought she was going to conk out right there and then. She looked petrified. "

"I know, it's a bit unnerving isn't it? She's been like that since her husband died."

"I assume that was Mary Tyler. Bob told me about her last night, but I wasn't expecting that. She looks very ill."

Joan nodded. "Yes, she worries me. I suggested a doctor once but she got so upset, almost hysterical, I've been frightened to mention it since." She sat next to him on the bench. "She's like a coiled spring. I don't think it would take much to push her over the edge."

"Has she ever talked to anyone about how she feels?"

"She doesn't talk to anyone about anything. Perhaps that's the trouble. Everyone says she can't talk but sometimes, when she's working in the house, I can hear her talking to herself, or what's worse - her husband."

"Sounds a bit scary to me."

"It was at first, but I've got used to her." She smiled. "Don't look so worried, she's probably happy enough in her own way - and so are you by the look of it. What's all this?" She pointed to the crumpled sheets of paper on the ground. "I thought you were here to rest?"

"That was the general idea, but events seem to have overtaken me. You know, Joan, it's very strange. I've been here a little over two days and I know more about this village and its inhabitants than I know about my own home town."

"George says the same thing. I kept on for years about coming back here to live when he left the army. He wasn't keen at all, kept saying, 'What do you want to bury yourself out in the sticks for?' Now, he wouldn't go back to the city for a fortune."

"I know what he means."

She studied his expression with amusement, then patted him on the shoulder and said. "Maybe you'll soon start looking for a cottage, then?"

Smiling to herself, she disappeared into the kitchen, leaving Mark staring after her in amazement. Now, how did she know about that?

CHAPTER NINE

Susan's first full day in Carlton was devoted to slow recovery. After a long night of fitful sleep, the first moments of full consciousness were painful and unpleasant. Struggling to sit up, she reflected dully that, judging by her symptoms, she was either coming down with flu or suffering the effects of shock. In different circumstances she might have stayed in bed, content to let the day go by, but there could be no such luxury here. She glared at the sleeping dog beside her bed with a mixture of affection and resignation. She had originally acquired the German Shepherd puppy for company and, for the most part, he had lived up to, and at times surpassed, all expectations. But that, as Susan was soon to discover, was not the end of it. No longer could she pander to her own whims, fit or otherwise. Fulfilling her obligations to the faithful creature, she stumbled down to the kitchen to let him out.

Bleary-eyed, she surveyed the little patio garden. A hard knot began to form in her stomach as her vision progressed beyond the courtyard to the rear wall. Before locking up for the night she'd carefully checked that the back gate was securely latched... and there it was - wide open. She ran to close it quickly before the dog could run off, but Lexer was busy crunching on something he'd found by the wall. With hands that were cold and damp with something akin to fear, she fumbled with the gate's rusty latch, then quickly turned her attention to the dog.

"Leave it!" She grabbed the great head and forced his jaws open. Reluctantly, he allowed her to scrape the remains of what looked like a biscuit from his mouth. "You bad dog." she grumbled. "You know you mustn't eat things that you find." She checked the garden for further delicacies then, finding none, returned to the kitchen to slump at the table. She really didn't feel well at all.

An hour later, after a determined effort, she was dressed and attempting to explore the cottage that was to be her home for the next two weeks. Carrying a mug of coffee, she wandered listlessly from room to room, barely taking in the details, until she arrived in the main bedroom. At the window, she took a moment to study the meadow beyond the lane, where her attention was drawn to a solitary figure hurrying away into the bushes. Perhaps it was her muddled state of mind, or maybe she was still jumpy from the events of yesterday, whichever - something about the figure struck her as unusual. His demeanour seemed almost furtive - and why wear a heavy jacket with the hood pulled up? The meadow was bathed in sunshine and she knew, from her brief experience in the garden, that the air was quite warm. She watched until the figure had disappeared from sight then, deciding her imagination was getting the better of her, continued her exploration until, unable to settle anywhere, she returned to the kitchen.

Raking her fingers through her hair for the umpteenth time, a habit she had whenever she felt at odds with herself, she picked up the kettle and promptly put it down again. This wouldn't do at all; coffee, on its own, would set her nerves jangling. What she needed was food. Shocked to find it was already two o'clock, she grabbed her purse and Lexer's lead.

Simply to be out walking was therapeutic, as clean country air and the warmth of the sun began to work their magic. By the time they reached the junction she felt better. Quickening her step, she purposely ignored the footpath on her right. She didn't want to think about the woods and what she had found there yesterday, and was determined to concentrate on other things, but inevitably she found herself wondering if there had been any further developments. Who was she? Was she a local girl? How did she die? She was still deep in thought when she entered the shop.

"Yes m'dear, what can I do for you?"

Susan stared at Eve Simpson blankly. "What? Oh – um – I need some groceries."

Eve Simpson looked amused. "Well now, any idea what exactly?"

With a weak, apologetic smile, Susan said. "I'm not sure. Goodness this is ridiculous, I can't seem to remember what I came in for!"

"You're more used to supermarkets, I'll bet. I can always tell. Folk can wander around in those places hoping to see what they want. In here they have to ask for it." Eve Simpson smiled kindly. "Let's see if I can help. What about some bacon?"

"Oh yes, that would be nice."

"How many rashers?"

Susan bit her lip. "How many?" She was beginning to feel very foolish.

"Shall we say four, for now?"

"Yes, make it four." She tried to sound decisive. "I'm sorry to be so stupid. I don't know what's the matter with me – can't seem to fasten my mind on anything."

"Well, I'm not surprised, m'dear. It's probably a reaction to yesterday – must have been a nasty shock. I mean, finding her – then getting yourself lost..."

"Yes, that's probably what it is." Susan didn't even question how this woman knew so much. She only knew she didn't want to go into it yet. "Right, now I must concentrate."

Eve smiled kindly. "You just leave it to me. Now, you'll need eggs, cheese, butter..." Eve Simpson chattered away cheerfully while they got the groceries together.

Susan hardly noticed how skilfully she was being pumped until the shopkeeper mentioned the woods again. She had happily explained where she came from, where she was staying and for how long, but the woods – oh no, she couldn't cope with that yet. They had just got onto debating who was to be questioned by the police, when she heard the door behind her open and close again. Susan breathed a sigh of relief. Hopefully, another customer would draw the shopkeeper's attention away from the subject of the body and she could leave quickly without seeming rude.

"Thanks for your help, Mrs Simpson." She hurriedly stuffed the last of her groceries into a bag. "I expect I'll be in again soon, and a bit better organised, I hope." She turned towards the door and stared into the tortured face of Mary Tyler.

Dark, frightened eyes bore into her as the woman held her arms outstretched. Mary Tyler backed away, the palms of her hands paddling the air as if she were trying to push the image of Susan away from her. Susan took a step forward as the woman's dry, cracked lips open and closed without sound. "What is it?" Susan whispered.

An agonised groan came from deep within the woman's throat, and she pulled her hands back as if to shield her eyes.

Thoroughly alarmed, Susan looked to Eve Simpson anxiously. "I think she must be ill."

"It's all right m'dear, leave this to me." Eve came around the counter carrying a cardboard box full of groceries. "Here you are, Mary, I've got your order ready, dear." She pushed the box into the woman's outstretched arms and led her to the door. "Don't worry about the money, pay me next time."

Susan hadn't moved. "What on earth was all that about - did I do something?"

Eve shook her head. "No, it's nothing to do with anything you did."

"But what frightened her?" She suddenly thought of Lexer. "I hope it wasn't my dog. I left him tied up outside."

"You mustn't worry. It's nothing to do with you or your dog. The poor soul's been scared to death for years."

"What of for heaven's sake – and what's wrong with her voice, can't she speak?"

"Oh, she can talk all right, at least she used to. All that just now was probably because she doesn't know you. Once she's seen you about in the village a few times she'll be fine. She's just a bit simple, that's all."

"Oh, I see," Susan said, as if that explained everything, when in truth it confused her even more. Simple wasn't the word she'd have used to describe Mary Tyler, but she was in no fit state to labour the point. She reached for the door handle. "Well, I'd better get going. Thanks again, Mrs Simpson."

Feeling better after a late lunch, Susan took her book and settled in a sunny corner of the garden. After half an hour the book lay, still unopened, in her lap. Her mind was too full of recent events to concentrate on anything else. Every time she closed her eyes she saw them, like snapshots in her mind. First, the haunted face of Mary Tyler, then the decomposed features of the body in the woods. Faster and faster they alternated - until they became one. Eventually, she fell into a troubled sleep.

Some small disturbance brought her to consciousness. With a start, she sat up to find Lexer crouched low, staring menacingly at the back wall while emitting a low growl. She looked warily around the garden but nothing had changed. Certain she'd heard something, possibly footsteps, she gestured to the dog to lie down. Then she climbed carefully onto a low rockery wall. The light was fading but she could see well enough that the field beyond was deserted. Shivering slightly she climbed down, persuading herself that Lexer had probably caught the scent of a fox, and she, no doubt, had been dreaming.

CHAPTER TEN

At midday Mark knocked on Maude Brandon's door, hoping he looked in better shape than he felt. Instinctively he knew she would be neither impressed nor sympathetic if she knew his enfeebled state was down to drink. However, an invitation to lunch was precisely that - and lunch he would have to endure.

To Mark's surprise, the meal was not the ordeal he'd thought it would be. From what he could see, the old lady had taken considerable trouble over the event. A fresh green salad with home-made quiche was just light enough for him to cope with. He even managed a helping of dessert, a concoction of fresh fruit liberally juiced with a heady, aromatic liquid he couldn't quite identify. He strongly suspected it was alcohol-based and immediately reassessed his opinion of his hostess. Maybe she wasn't quite so strait-laced after all.

That afternoon, sitting in the garden in companionable silence, Mark watched the old lady from the corner of his eye. He was glad he'd come. Her delight at seeing him, and her pleasure at the flowers Joan had sent, made it worthwhile. He wondered how long she'd lived alone like this, with only her dog for company.

"That was a lovely lunch," he said at last.

"What? Oh, lunch - I'm glad you enjoyed it. I was still thinking about that young girl."

"What girl?"

"The girl who found the body. I wonder how she's feeling today?"

Mark smiled. During lunch he'd told her everything he knew about yesterday's performance, and all she was worried about was the girl. At the time he'd wondered why, but as the meal went on, and his head began to clear, he realised that she, above all, would identify with Susan Forest. After all, she'd been in the same unenviable situation herself. "I thought

I might call on her on the way back, just to see if she's all right," he said.

"Good idea. Where's she staying?"

"Rosemoor Cottage on the Harold Road."

"I know it, in fact there's a short cut from here. Tell you what, I'll walk down the lane with you. I could do with the exercise, and there's something I want to show you."

"What?"

"You'll see," she said, her eyes twinkling. "Now, I'll just take these dishes in."

While helping her put the lunch things away he told her of his talk with Bob Witchell. "He told me quite a lot about the village, the people - and the drama that's gone on over the years."

The old lady sighed. "Yes indeed, we've had our fair share with one thing and another."

"Actually, I met someone yesterday." Mark went on to describe his meeting with Mary Tyler. "She's so thin, Miss Brandon – almost emaciated – and the look of fear in her eyes... bit of a shaker, I can tell you. Joan says she's always looked like that and not to worry – but I was rather hoping, could you tell me a bit more about her?"

"Is this more research for your book, or just curiosity?"

"Bit of both, I suppose."

"I thought it was about time you started asking questions. Come on, let's sit in the garden a little longer and I'll tell you what I can." Outside, she wasted no time getting into the subject. "Of course everyone says it's because of the way her husband died."

"What is?"

"The fact that she can't speak, of course," she looked impatient. "I'm not so sure though. Finding Len dead in the shed like that was certainly enough to put her into severe shock – but there was something very wrong in that family before that happened. Mary's had problems for a long, long time – and I think part of the blame has to lie with the girl."

"Which girl?"

"You know young man, for a writer, you can be remarkably slow at times. You asked about the Tyler family - now who do you think I mean?"

"Oh, you mean their daughter, Helen?"

"Yes. I suppose you know they adopted her?" Mark nodded. "The child was three when they got her. At first, she seemed the answer to their prayers, but she was such a difficult child. She wanted everything she saw and, because Len and Mary doted on her so much, she invariably got it." She looked at him. "This is only my opinion, you understand?"

"Did you teach her?"

"Yes, she was in the same class as Christie. Now that was an unlikely partnership if ever I saw one. They were like chalk and cheese, those two. Christie was a delightful child, always laughing and full of mischief. Helen, on the other hand, was just the opposite, inclined to be sullen, suspicious of everybody and everything, yet she and Christie were as if joined at the hip. One wouldn't go anywhere without the other. After Christie's death Helen became much worse."

"Worse - in what way?"

"Lies! Every time that child opened her mouth, she lied. As she grew up she seemed to improve a bit, or that's what we all thought until she was arrested for shoplifting. It was a first offence - at least, the first anyone knew about - so she got off with a caution. She was about sixteen by then I think, anyway, shortly after that she left the village."

"A bit young to go off on her own, don't you think?"

"I do, and I said so at the time, but then it wasn't my place to interfere."

"Didn't her mother try to stop her?"

Maude shook her head. "I very much doubt it. I got the impression her mother was glad to see the back of her. It might seem an odd thing to say, but Mary always seemed to be rather frightened of her daughter."

"Have you seen Helen since she left the village?"

"Not to speak to. She's been back a few times to visit her mother, but I'm inclined to think it was more to squeeze some money out of her than for love. In truth, she'd have done better staying away. After each visit Mary seemed worse than ever." Maude stood up. "Come on, let's not get too maudlin. Maybe we should go for our walk before it gets too dark. I'll go and get my coat if you'll round up Robbie. He'll be down the bottom of the garden somewhere."

Saddened a little by the old lady's story, Mark strode to the end of the garden whistling loudly, attempting to lift his spirits and summon the dog at the same time. Leaving the cultivated area behind he soon found himself in a woody spot that had been left entirely to nature. Overgrown trees and lanky shrubs crowded together, providing the perfect place for a little dog to play unseen. A narrow path, well worn by constant walking, led him to the boundary wall. It was here that he gained some insight into the lonely life of Maude Brandon. Against the foot of the wall stood a row of tiny gravestones. He paused to read an inscription, "SCAMP" 1951-1962".

Not, by nature, a sentimental man, Mark studied the row of neatly clipped grass mounds and was surprised by a sudden moistness in his eyes. His love of animals and a growing fondness for the old lady made the discovery more affecting than he would have thought possible. He turned hurriedly away. Better not return looking like a bawling eight-year-old, he thought. She'd probably box his ears. By the time he reached the house he'd regained his composure. "I couldn't find him, he must have..."

"It's all right he's here - came back a moment ago. Come on, or it will soon be too dark to see anything."

Mark had intended trekking back to the village to get

onto the Harold Road, but Maude had other plans. In spite of her ankle injury she strode off, away from the village, along a part of the lane that Mark hadn't yet explored.

Half a mile later, with no sign of life at all, he ventured. "Are you sure this is the right way?"

"Perfectly sure. Look, can you see that cottage ahead?"

"Cottage? I can't see a cottage."

"Well it's there, believe me. And just a bit further on you'll see the main road." She took his arm and pulled him along the lane. "Here, you see." She stopped at a gate buried deep in the hedgerow.

Mark followed her gaze. "I say, this is rather lovely."

"It is pretty, isn't it?" They stood at a lych-gate, looking through a neglected garden to the cottage beyond.

"Who lives here?" he asked.

"Nobody now. It used to be Archie Crane's place. He died last year and left everything to his son Lionel." She pushed the gate. "Come on, let's have a closer look."

Mark followed, carefully inspecting the structure. "Seems to be well cared for, considering it's been empty for so long. Bit of a waste really, you'd think he'd let it out or sell it, wouldn't you?"

Maude walked on. "I suppose that would be the best idea."

Mark trailed after her. "Nice large rooms," he mused peering through a window at the back. "Do you ever see this chap, Lionel?"

"Not often, but I think I've got a telephone number somewhere. Here look, we'd better make tracks, time's getting on."

"Hmm, I suppose so." He followed her out thoughtfully.

At the gate, she gave him directions to Rosemoor Cottage. "I won't go any further with you, if you don't mind. I'd like to get back before it's completely dark."

As she turned away, he said. "I thought you wanted to show me something?"

She shook her head in exasperation. "I just have!"

In the pub later that evening, Joan eyed Bob suspiciously. "I hope this isn't going to turn into another session," she said.

He replied, "I only asked for a couple of pints!"

"Yes, well if you'd seen the state of Mark this morning..."

Bob Witchell looked amused. "Bit rough was he?" He glanced across the bar into a narrow hallway where Mark was talking on the telephone. "He seems all right now."

Joan snorted. "Yes well, this morning he looked as if he'd been embalmed - and I don't suppose you were much better. What's this all about anyway, you're not usually in here this early?"

"Just making the most of the company, Joan. We don't get too many fresh young faces around here, especially one that's prepared to spend time with us oldies."

"That's true." Joan agreed. "And this one is certainly making an impact. He had lunch with Maude Brandon today, and that's her on the phone."

"Lunch eh?" Bob chuckled. "I bet he wasn't asking questions about ancient history - look out, he's coming back."

Mark joined them looking very pleased with himself. "Maude Brandon has arranged for me to meet Lionel at the cottage tomorrow." He grinned at Joan. "Would you like to come with me? I wouldn't mind another opinion."

"I'd love to, but what about Susan?"

Bob looked confused. "Is someone going to tell me what's going on?"

Mark told him about the cottage. "It's the one in Cherry Lane."

Bob nodded. "I know it, Crane Cottage. It's a nice place but are you really thinking of buying it?"

"Yes. Why, don't you think it's a good idea?"

"It's not that. I just assumed you'd be heading back to the great metropolis soon. Since you arrived this village has been a hive of activity, but it isn't like that all the time you know, you might find it a bit dull under normal circumstances."

Mark smiled wryly. "Bob, if you want to know what it's like to live somewhere dull, you go and stay in my one bedroom flat in Bayswater for a couple of weeks. Mind you, I doubt you'd last that long."

"I believe you, but then I was born and bred in the country. What made you decide on all this anyway?"

"I don't really know. It was something I said in conversation with Maude. I didn't really mean it at the time, but once I'd said it I found myself warming to the idea. Then, when I saw Crane Cottage this afternoon, I was certain."

"So what's young Susan got to do with it?"

"Nothing. At least, nothing to do with the cottage. After leaving Maude I called in to see if she was all right."

"And was she?"

"She's still a bit jumpy, which isn't surprising. Anyway, I said I'd call in again tomorrow. I'd better go and phone, maybe she'd like to see the cottage, too."

Bob picked up the drinks. "Aye, well I'll take these over to the table, lad. And, you'd best be warned, we'd better make 'em last - seems we're to be put on ration tonight."

Mark slid onto a seat opposite the ex policeman. "I'm hoping you've got some news," he said.

Bob shrugged. "Not as much as I'd like. I went into Harold this morning to see my nephew, but I didn't get much out of him - except they've got one hell of job on their hands.

They don't know who she is, or why she was up in those woods, in fact, the only thing they can be certain of is that she didn't die from natural causes."

"So it's murder," Mark said unnecessarily.

"Aye it's that all right, couldn't be anything else by all accounts. After what Jack told me, I'm glad it wasn't me who found her I can tell you."

"Bit of a mess, eh? I suppose you can't tell me anything - against the rules and all that."

Bob chuckled. "I'd like to think that was the case, but Jack only tells me things that are already common knowledge." He studied Mark carefully. "I hope you're not squeamish lad, because it's not a pretty tale."

"I think I can handle it."

"Aye, well according to forensics, the body had been in the woods for anything up to three weeks. At this stage they can't be more precise - apparently it's all to do with larvae."

"Larvae - you mean maggots?"

"Aye, it's the only way to get an estimated time of death. It all depends on how advanced the larvae are, and what species. It's a problem bedevilled with difficulties, and it all takes time."

"So what happens next?"

"They wait for the official pathologist's report. Jack says they're pretty certain the cause of death was strangulation, it's the other injuries that are puzzling."

"What other injuries?"

"Apparently all her facial bones were stove in. Now why would somebody want to beat her to a pulp after she was dead?"

"Rage?"

"Maybe, or it could have been to prevent identification. It's going to be a tough one all right. She had nothing with her, no bag, her pockets empty."

"What about fingerprints?"

"They won't be much use unless she's got a record."

"Her clothes..." Mark volunteered. "What about things like manufacturers' labels?"

"Sounds like you've been watching too much television, lad. Tell me, is all this interest purely for your book?" He gave Mark a penetrating look. "Or is there another reason?"

Mark grimaced. "It's for the book. At least, it started that way."

"And now?"

"Now I don't know. It all just seems too... coincidental, for want of a better word."

Clearly puzzled, Bob said. "You're going to enlighten me, I hope?"

"As long as you promise not to scoff."

With a look of pure innocence, Bob replied. "Now would I do that? Oh go on then, I promise."

"When I arrived here a couple of days ago, a chance remark got me digging into a fifteen-year-old murder, then within twenty-four hours it's all starting again."

"You're saying the two are connected?"

"I don't know what I'm saying. I rather hope it's the sinister side of my imagination going into overdrive, because if it isn't, and I'm right about this, then I've stirred something up. I'm the catalyst."

CHAPTER ELEVEN

"I'm afraid I got rid of all my uncle's old furniture," Lionel Crane apologised. "Still, it was pretty ancient. I doubt it would have been much use to you. Have you got some furniture you can bring in?"

"Not enough to fill this place, I haven't." Mark roamed around the large sitting room. "Everything I've got would probably fit into this one room alone."

"Bigger than you thought, is it?"

Mark nodded. "It is, but don't worry, it won't put me off."

Lionel relaxed. "Look, you probably want to look round on your own for a bit. I'll go up and check that water tank – feel free to wander."

Mark watched him leave. He'd meant it when he said nothing would put him off. He'd made that decision as soon as he'd crossed the threshold. True, it was a lot bigger than he'd expected – and it could stand a bit of attention, but he knew he wouldn't find better. The place was a bargain.

The sound of a dog barking reminded him of the others waiting in the next room, and he wondered what chaos they had wrought. He and Joan had arrived at Maude's farmhouse in the middle of a cloudburst, which was why the three of them, together with Robbie, had driven the short distance to Crane Cottage. They had barely got inside when Susan, with a drenched German Shepherd in tow, came running up the path. Mark smiled to himself; it had been worse than a night at the circus.

Maude's little white terrier had thrown himself at the confused Shepherd, first running under then around him until, exasperated, Lexer had jumped onto a wooden packing case barking furiously. The terrier, in turn, had yapped and whined until the noise had become deafening. Susan had grabbed Lexer; Mark had scooped up Robbie, but all to no avail, until

Maude Brandon's voice had risen above it. "Quiet!" Even Lexer, who rarely took any notice of anyone, was immediately silenced. All eyes had centred on the old lady. The dogs cautious, the others in amused admiration. "Years of practice," Maude had said airily. "It's nice to know I haven't lost the knack."

Her words had sounded casual enough, but Mark hadn't failed to notice Maude's expression when she first saw Susan. A mixture of polite curiosity and something else – something akin to fear.

Assuming she was merely waiting for an introduction, he'd taken Susan's arm. "You haven't met Miss Brandon, have you?"

"No, I haven't." Susan had also been startled by the look on the old lady's face. Something about it was faintly reminiscent of the look Mary Tyler had given her.

Eyes narrowing, Maude had said. "Is this your first visit to Carlton?" then before Susan could reply, "we've met before, haven't we?"

"I don't think so. I've never been to Carlton before. In fact, this is my first visit to Derbyshire." Susan had looked puzzled, but feeling the pressure of Mark's hand on her arm, had smiled and turned away.

"Susan, this is Lionel Crane." She'd looked up at a heavily set man in his early fifties.

Shaking her hand warmly, he'd spoken apologetically. "I've been hearing about you too, I expect you're sick of people wanting to talk about it – the murder, I mean?"

She was saved from having to think of a suitable answer by the intervention of Maude Brandon. "I suggest we ladies make ourselves comfortable here in the study, while the men get down to business."

71

Joan put her head round the door. "Oh there you are, Mark. What are you up to in here on your own - and where's Lionel?"

"He's checking the water tank. He'll be down in a minute."

"Right. Well when you've finished, we've decided were all going back to the pub for lunch."

"Oh good. Does that include Maude?"

"It certainly does. Why?"

"No reason – I just wondered, that's all."

Joan came right into the room. "So you noticed it too – the way Maude reacted to Susan?" Mark nodded. "What do you think it was all about?"

"I've no idea. How are they getting on in there?" He nodded towards the study.

"All right. Apparently Susan had a bit of a rough day yesterday and Maude's been reassuring her. Telling her that it's all due to shock. She even said Susan should visit her at the farmhouse if ever she felt like some company." She patted Mark's arm. "I don't know what you've been saying to the old girl, but she's not the tyrant I remember from my childhood, that's for sure."

Mark grinned. "It's got nothing to do with me, honestly. Come on let's go and tell Lionel what the arrangements are."

There was a relaxed atmosphere in the sitting room at the Royal Oak that afternoon. Maude sat motionless in a fireside armchair and quietly observed her new companions. First she studied Mark. Somehow, she sensed that the arrival of this young man was going to be important to the village. That Carlton, for many, would never be quite the same. She didn't know how he would change the course of their lives – she only knew, with absolute certainty, that he would. She cringed inwardly when she remembered how she'd behaved that first day, and marvelled that he'd bothered with her at all. But for his persistence she might never have realised that having so little contact with others had drawn her into an unhealthy introversion.

Her eyes roamed next to George who, having eaten rather more than usual, was blissfully dozing. A nice man, she decided. Ideally suited to Joan. Maude studied her old pupil, who was idly leafing through recipe cards. Yes, she thought with satisfaction, Joan has found her niche in life. The only blot Maude could see on their horizon was the lack of children, but Joan wasn't the type to let that ruin her life.

When her gaze settled on Susan, the old lady's eyes dulled with concern. She had noticed it straight away, and wondered if anyone else in the village had. Watching the girl toss back a mane of blonde curls as she laughed at something Mark had said; she felt a brief twinge of fear. It's the eyes, she thought. Those large, blue, sparkling eyes were going to be her downfall.

"Well, Miss Brandon," Mark broke the silence. "You've been very quiet this afternoon. Have we exhausted you?"

"Not quite." She smiled at him with something close to affection, and put down her teacup with great deliberation. "There is something I'd like to say, though. I know I've always been a stickler for propriety, but I really feel it's about time people starting calling me Maude, don't you?"

Once again she had everyone's attention, and feeling someone should say something, Susan spoke up. "I once had an aunt called Maude."

"Well, Aunt Maude it is then." Mark sat back in his chair, pleased to see the old lady relax a little.

At this point Susan stretched and said. "Well this is all very nice, but I think it's about time I took Lexer home and fed him."

"I'll take you back." Mark volunteered.

"It's all right, it's not far, we can walk."

"It's pouring with rain, and I'll be taking Aunt Maude home soon anyway. Are you coming back this evening for a drink?"

"Yes, I'd like to. Can I bring Lexer?"

"Of course you can, lass," George suddenly surfaced. "Or failing that, you can leave him with Shona next door."

"That's settled, then." Mark started searching for his car keys. "It'll give you a chance to meet some of the locals."

"I've already met a couple." Susan told them of her visit to the shop and her meeting with Mary Tyler. "She tried so hard to speak to me, but nothing came out."

"Well, I wonder what brought that on?" Joan looked at her husband. "She hasn't spoken a word to anyone since we've been here, has she, love?"

"Nothing coherent anyway. We've had to communicate by pointing and signing, jolly difficult at times."

"Well, she had a jolly good try when she saw me." Susan pulled a face. "In fact, she really got quite distressed about it."

"I think I can explain that." Maude looked directly at Susan with a curious expression in her eyes. "I'm sorry, my dear, you must have noticed me watching you, and probably thought me quite rude - it's just so strange, you see."

"What is?" Joan was fascinated.

"The likeness." She touched Susan's arm. "It's quite uncanny, but you are the image of Christie Abbott."

All but Susan sat in stunned silence.

"Christie Abbott - who's she?"

Maude sighed wearily. "It's a very long story, my dear. Mark will tell you about it later, I expect."

Once he'd seen Maude and Robbie safely into the farmhouse, Mark drove Susan to Rosemoor and spent the next hour relating the tale of Christie Abbott.

"What a dreadful story," she said when he'd finished.

Belatedly, Mark noticed her pallor. "Here. Are you all right?"

Susan's attention had been drawn to a watercolour hanging close to the fireplace. She hadn't noticed it before, but it was clearly a crudely painted study of the village as it might have looked thirty years ago. Apart from the absence of cars and one or two cottages that now occupied the southern end of the lane, it looked pretty much the same as it did now. She allowed her eyes to follow the path she'd taken that first day. There was no hedgerow bordering the path when the picture was painted, and the building on the left at the top of the hill looked more like a barn than a church. A blob of dark green paint to the right of the path lacked detail, but Susan knew what it was meant to depict. She didn't need reminding what it was like in those woods. She could almost feel the rotting leaves underfoot, smell the damp earth... the decay. It had felt cold in the shade of those gnarled old trees... the further she allowed her memory to take her, the colder it became... Susan shivered slightly....

"Susan!" She felt a sudden warmth as Mark gently touched her arm. "What's wrong? Are you ill?"

She turned, and was surprised to see concern in his eyes. "I'm sorry, I was miles away. What did you say?"

Relieved to see some colour returning to her cheeks, Mark smiled. "Nothing of any importance. You just seemed a little distracted. I wondered if it was something I ..." He stopped as realisation dawned on him. "God, you must think me an insensitive so-and-so. After your recent experience, Christie's story is the last thing you needed to hear."

"It's OK. I'm just being silly." There was little humour in her smile as she added. "Two days and two deaths... makes you wonder what tomorrow will bring." She rose from her seat and went to the window. "It's sad about that little girl, but it has nothing whatever to do with what's happening now."

She tried to make her next question sound casual, but the answer was important to her. "Did they ever find out who killed her?"

"Apparently not." He looked at her closely. "I hadn't noticed it myself, but Maude's right, you do look like her, or rather how she might have looked if she'd lived. I saw a picture of her at the farmhouse - it's the eyes and the colouring, just as she said. You don't think you could be connected with the Abbotts, do you?"

"Not a chance. My resemblance to that child is purely coincidental." Susan realised she was sounding defensive and softened her tone. "My father was an only child, and he died when I was ten. As you know, my mother died recently. She did have a sister, that's the Aunt Maude I mentioned, but she died years ago, unmarried and childless." She became pensive. "Actually I have no relatives at all now."

"Join the club – neither have I." Mark suddenly grinned, and immediately lightened the atmosphere. "But, fear not, there's hope for us both. Today we gained an aunt. Come on, you go and get yourself ready while I take this dog for a walk. Joan warned me to get you back in time for dinner, so we'd better get a move on."

CHAPTER TWELVE

Driving back to the village for the second time that night, Mark tried to convince himself that for once in his life he was being sensible. Richard had advised him to stay away from writing and women. Well, he'd failed miserably with the first, but success was certainly in sight for the second.

As he drove into the village he looked up at the light in the Tanners' bedroom, and reflected glumly that there was another apology due. Joan had only been trying to help. Like most women, she'd jumped at the chance for a spot of matchmaking, but her timing was completely off. He'd have to try and explain tomorrow.

Mark would have felt even more uncomfortable if he'd known how much trouble Joan had taken with the meal, and how George had found her busily setting the scene in the dining room.

"What the devil are you up to? You've been fiddling around with those flowers for ages."

"I'm just trying to make the table look nice." Joan stood back to admire her handiwork. "There - what do you think?"

"Very nice, but what's it all for?"

"Mark and Susan, of course." She moved the flowers microscopically nearer the centre of the table. "I think candles might be a touch too much, don't you?"

"Depends," George replied dryly.

"On what?"

"On whether or not we have a power cut."

"I don't know why I bothered to ask. You've got no romance in your soul, George Tanner."

Wandering back to the bar, he muttered. "I just hope that young fellow knows what he's in for."

"And what's that supposed to mean?" She followed him out.

"I seem to remember your mother doing something very similar when you took me home for the first time - and look where it's got me."

Parked at the rear of the Royal Oak, Mark spent several minutes churning over the events of the evening and wondered just where and when precisely the mood had changed.

The first part had actually gone rather well but, on reflection, he could see this was largely because most of the time had been spent talking about his writing.

"Have you ever read one of my books?" he'd asked.

"More than one. In fact, if you must know, I've probably read them all".

"I'm flattered."

"Yes, I thought you would be."

Mark had then gone on to talk about his latest idea. "I'm furiously making notes at the moment, but it just won't come together. Of course I don't have all the facts yet."

"Sounds as if you're writing real-life this time. That's a bit of a departure for you, isn't it? Still, I suppose even writers need a change of routine from time to time."

He'd thought about that for a while, in fact he'd thought about nothing else for the rest of the evening - and that, he realised, was the turning point. He hadn't intended upsetting her, he was just being his usual preoccupied self. Throughout the meal, and even in the bar later, he was preoccupied in the extreme. People came and went, bought him drinks – he even returned the favour, but all this was done on automatic. From start to finish, his mind had been somewhere in the shadowy chapters of his unwritten book, forming situations, holding two-way conversations - in short, he'd ignored her. It wasn't until he pulled up outside Rosemoor and noticed her expression that the penny finally dropped. Before he could attempt an apology, she had jumped out of the car, called the dog, and stormed into the cottage, slamming the door behind her.

To his credit, he did spend a few minutes debating the advisability of following her, but again the book got first consideration. He was impatient to get back and get it all down on paper - but first he had to see Bob.

"What's up, has something happened?" Pulling a tartan dressing gown around his large frame, Bob glanced up and down the lane. "Is Susan with you?"

"No. Look I'm sorry to knock so late, but I've been wanting to speak to you all evening."

"Well, why on earth didn't you?" Bob gestured for him to come in. "I'm just making some cocoa, will you have some?"

"Thanks. I couldn't say anything in front of Susan earlier, I didn't want to alarm her."

Bob poured milk into a saucepan. "Alarm her - in what way?"

Mark paced around the kitchen. "You'll probably say I'm nuts, but I'm pretty sure someone's watching the cottage."

"Now what makes you think that? And do stop pacing, lad. You're starting to make me nervous."

"Sorry." Mark pulled out a chair and settled at the table. "At first I thought I was imagining it. This afternoon, when I took her back to Rosemoor, I thought I saw a movement in the bushes opposite, but didn't think much of it. Later on, while Susan was changing, I took Lexer out, and that's why I'm here, really. As soon as we came out of the gate he started growling and trying to pull me across the lane. I thought about letting him off the lead but I was worried he might dash off and I wouldn't be able to catch him. He gave me a hell of a time, he'd got the scent of something and was pulling me all over the place. In the end I dragged him away and walked him up the Harold Road as far as Cherry Lane and back."

Bob gave him his cocoa. "It's possible he caught the scent of a rabbit or something."

"That's what I thought – until we got back. As we drew near to the cottage he started growling and straining on the lead again. This time I decided to risk it, and let him have a run. But, as we crossed the lane he became quite frantic, and I distinctly heard rapid footsteps, like someone running away. It was nearly dark by then so I couldn't see much, but it was no rabbit, that's for sure."

"Maybe something bigger - a deer?"

"No, the footsteps sounded heavy, like boots on wet grass." He sipped his cocoa. "I'm sure I wasn't imagining it."

Bob rubbed his chin, then looked at his watch. "I wonder if Jack's on duty?" He stood up. "I think I'll try the station."

"You think we should report it then?"

"I do. A dead body in the woods, now strange noises in the bushes? I definitely think we should report it, besides..." he stroked Shona's head. "I would never underestimate the instincts of one of these." He finished his cocoa. "Right lad, you get off to your bed. I'll ring Jack. You know, I might just take this beauty for a stroll up there tomorrow. She hasn't worked for a year or so, but I don't think she'll have forgotten her training, will you girl?" The dog gazed at him adoringly. Mark got the distinct impression she understood every word.

In his room, Mark scribbled away until the early hours, finding, as usual, that as the words filled the pages, the picture became clearer. It was four in the morning when he finally put down his pencil. He knew which direction to follow now, but there were still a couple of bits of the jigsaw to find. He fell asleep unaware that the next, and probably most important, piece was about to present itself.

CHAPTER THIRTEEN

Gulping air into his burning lungs and his muscles straining, he ran fast as the steep incline would allow. On he went – every step a separate agony – but he dared not stop; he had to get to the top – where it was safe. He knew instinctively that if he could just get inside, everything would be all right - inside he could escape.

It was dark and very quiet, but the feeling of terror had left him. The chapel was a warm and friendly place - and he wasn't alone now. Someone was there, waiting, he could feel it - hear it - a slow rhythmic breathing coming from... he turned, and the merry-go-round began. Slowly at first, round and round, then faster and faster, the crumbling walls whirled about him. The wind swirled around his head throwing up dust, he could taste it, feel it stinging his eyes. But something was wrong, there could be no dust... the chapel was clean.

"Mark! Are you all right, lad?"

Only half conscious, Mark could hear concern in the deep voice. With considerable effort he managed to mumble. "Fine, I'm fine." His tongue seemed to be stuck to the roof of his mouth.

"Well, open your eyes then."

"I can't - it's the dust, you see."

Mark felt warm, firm hands grip his shoulders. "Come on lad, wake up - it's me, George."

At last he forced his eyelids open. "What's the matter?"

"I should be asking you that. What was it, a nightmare?"

"Mm, something like that," he struggled to sit up. "What's the time?"

"Half past ten. Joan's been nagging me to come up for the last half hour, she's worried you might be ill."

"No, I'm all right, I just got carried away with my notes last night, didn't get to bed until about four. I'll be down soon."

"There's no hurry. Now I know you're all right you can stay there all day if you like. In fact, I'm sorry I woke you now."

"I'm glad you did, George. Dreams like that I can do without."

George chuckled. "You'll have to explain it to me sometime – maybe when you've got the dust out of your eyes."

"What?"

"Nothing lad, just something you said." George left, still chuckling.

Mark found Joan in the kitchen, looking contrite. "I'm sorry for sending George up like that," she said. "If I'd known you were up working so late I'd have let you sleep on."

"Thank goodness you didn't, I'd have felt lousy all day. Can I do some toast?"

"Help yourself." She watched him with ill-concealed curiosity. "It must have been something interesting to keep you up so late?"

Pottering around the kitchen, he answered absently. "It happens like that sometimes. I get an idea, brood on it for a couple of days, then suddenly it all comes together and I have to write it down."

"Must have been a good idea, - there's some marmalade if you want it, in the cupboard on the left."

"It was, thanks." He filled his mouth with toast.

"I can see you're not going to tell me what it's about."

"Not yet. Soon... we'll see."

Joan sighed. "Are all writers like this?"

"Don't know, maybe. I know I'm difficult when I'm into a story." He wiped some butter from his chin. " And I think I've upset Susan without meaning to."

"How?"

"You may well ask." He tried to think of a way to explain. "Have you ever read a book that interests you so much that you shut off from the people around you - don't even hear them?"

"Yes, now and then."

"Well I'm like that when I'm thinking about my writing. The trouble is, when you're reading, people can see what you're doing and understand why you're being remote. When I'm thinking – well, it's not immediately obvious, is it?"

Joan suppressed a smile. "I suppose not. Still, I'm sure Susan will understand if you explain it to her."

"Maybe."

"Why not go up and see her this morning?"

"No, I can't, I've still got some notes to write and I've run out of paper. I really wish I'd brought my lap-top with me." He flexed the fingers of his right hand. "Now I know what they mean by writer's cramp."

"Couldn't you pop in to see Susan before you buy your paper?"

"No, I'll see her later. When I've finished this I'm off to the shop. I really want to get on before I forget things. I just hope Eve Simpson is a little more receptive this time."

Joan stood before him with her hands on her hips. "Don't tell me you've upset her as well?"

"I think I did, at least I touched a nerve. I asked her about Christie."

"Oh dear. I probably should have warned you." Joan joined him at the table. "It's a touchy subject for some."

"What, even after fifteen years?"

Joan nodded. "For some of the older villagers, yes."

"Why?"

"It's a complicated story, and it's only my impression of it. Now look, Mark, I want you to remember that when you're writing your notes. What I'm going to tell you isn't fact – OK?"

"I understand – I'm a fiction-writer, remember?"

"Well, as long you don't quote me, then. Firstly I know nothing about what really happened back then. I wasn't even in the country. George was in the army in those days - doing a stint in Germany. My family still lived in Harold then, and everything I know is through letters from home."

Mark got up and filled the kettle. "I'll make some coffee – you carry on."

"Naturally, when the murder happened, letters were coming over thick and fast. My brother was the one that kept us informed." Joan sighed heavily. "I wish I'd kept those letters now. You could have got all this first-hand, so to speak. Anyway, his first news was largely about the horror of it all, and how everybody was so upset. My brother went to the funeral and found it most distressing. The whole village turned out, filling the churchyard to capacity."

"Where is she buried?"

"At St. Peter's in Harold. Greg, that's my brother, said that although there were so many people, the silence during the burial was unnerving – at least, until near the end. He said Jim Abbot threw himself onto the coffin, wailing and screaming his daughter's name. In the end he had to be physically restrained from tearing the lid off – and was eventually taken away in an ambulance."

"Poor man." Mark placed two mugs of coffee on the table and sat down. "But what's this got to do with Eve?"

"I'm coming to it – be patient." Joan sipped her coffee. "Actually, it has nothing to do with Eve or anyone else in the village. The point I'm trying to make is that during that time, immediately after the murder, the entire village was united. It was several weeks later when the trouble started. I don't know whether is was because the police hadn't come up with a suspect, or whether it was a collective need to draw a line under the whole thing, but certain members of the community took it upon themselves to solve the crime once and for all."

"Sounds like a bit of a witch hunt."

"Precisely. You've heard the saying 'turning brother against brother'; well that's more or less what happened. Everyone started blaming everyone else. Neighbours who'd known each other for years started feuding. Friends of long standing, fell out. Some even moved out of the area altogether."

"Was there really any serious suspicion against anyone?"

"No, I don't think so. Greg said, it reached the point where almost anyone would have done. The village folk didn't care whether they had the right bloke or not, just as long as they could bring the whole thing to an end."

"So how did it end up?"

"As I said, people moved away. In the end, those that were left came to realise what they'd done. No one knows who pulled things together, but at some point it was decided to abandon the search and try to rebuild the community. To do that, they had to agree never to speak of it again. So you see, Mark – you have transgressed," she grinned wickedly. "You've broken an unwritten law, if you like."

"Haven't I just! Trust me to go jumping in with my great size nines. Trouble is, how do I know who I can talk to and who I can't?"

"How many informants do you need? You've already got Maude and Bob on the case. Isn't that enough?"

"I suppose it'll have to be, won't it? Anyway, I've got enough for the moment, and you've helped a lot, thanks."

"My pleasure," she said. "Now, what about Susan – and that apology?"

"Susan? Oh, right. I'll deal with that later. Right now I need to get that paper."

Watching him bolt the remains of his coffee, then race around the kitchen trying to clear up, she observed, with some humour, that charming though he might be, patience was not his strong point. Then, if only to save her china, she took the tea towel from him. "All right," she said, "you get off. I'll do this."

With a rueful smile, he gave her a quick peck on the cheek, muttered, "Bless you!" and was gone.

Hurrying, trying to remember all the ideas that had come to him in the early hours, he flung open Eve's door too quickly. He caught a brief glimpse of blonde curls before staring dismayed at the groceries rolling around floor. "Oh I'm so sorry Su...." He stared, open mouthed, into amused blue eyes - but the face of a stranger.

She might have been Susan, twenty or thirty years ago, but not now. Her blonde hair, streaked with silver at the temples, lacked the lustre of youth, as did her coarse, toughened skin. The eyes were the same if one ignored the tiny lines at the corners - and yet perhaps not. There was something different, a guarded look. After what seemed a long time, he apologised again. "I'm sorry, how clumsy of me."

"It's all right, nothing's broken." She spoke with a soft country accent.

Eve Simpson joined them. "Kath, this is Mark Jordan. He's going to buy Archie Crane's old place."

Mark was long past astonishment with this woman. She's done it again, he thought, and seriously began to question her methods. Either she really was clairvoyant, or she had a tap on every phone in the village.

"So you're going to live here, Mr Jordan?" The soft burr fascinated him.

Mark nodded. "It certainly looks like it, if all goes well."

"I'm Kathleen Abbott." She held out her hand.

"Oh, so you're..." he stopped, recovering quickly, but not before she'd seen the look of surprise on his face. "Look, let me help you with this lot." Trying to ignore the silent warning flashing in Eve Simpson's eyes, he picked up the bag of groceries.

"There's no need, really."

Mark knew he couldn't let her go. He wanted to talk to her - needed her input.

"I insist, besides this is far too heavy for you to carry."

"I can manage, really. I only live a few doors away."

"In that case it won't take me long, will it?" He started for the door. "Which way?"

"Mr Jordan!" Eve's voice carried the length of the shop. "I presume you came in here to buy something."

He hesitated for only a moment. She was silently threatening him, and he knew it. "It's not important, Mrs Simpson. Another time." He registered the full force of her anger in one brief glance, as her expression arranged itself into a mask of resentment. He smiled curiously before turning to his attention to Kathleen Abbott. "Now, which way?"

"Left," she said, following him out.

Mark maintained an inconsequential chatter until they reached the cottage at the end of the lane. After insisting he carry the bags into the house, she allowed him to follow her through into a small kitchen. "There you are." He placed the bags on a table. "And no breakages."

"You're very kind." She hesitated, then seemed to come to a decision. "Would you like some coffee?"

This was more than he'd hoped for. "Thanks, if it isn't too much trouble."

"It's no trouble. I'm going to make some for Jim, anyway. He's my husband, but you know that already, don't you?"

"Well I... er."

She smiled warmly. "It's all right, don't be embarrassed. I know how news gets around. You've probably heard about all of us in one way or another." She looked directly at him. "But I'm the one that interests you most, I think." Without waiting for a response, Kathleen started unpacking the groceries. "I can just imagine what the locals have been telling you. They still refer to us as 'that poor family.' I'll bet you've been warned off, as well. They mean well, but it's been fifteen years now. You can't mourn forever, can you?"

"I suppose not." Mark couldn't decide whether she was simply putting up a brave front or whether she really was as tough as she sounded.

"If I'd had my way," she continued, "we'd have moved away, but... I expect you've heard about Jim?"

"Only that he suffers with his nerves."

"That's one way of putting it, I suppose."

Mark was puzzled. She sounded almost impatient. In fact he was finding the entire situation confusing. He hadn't asked a question yet – he hadn't needed to.

Then the door behind him opened and, expecting to see Jim Abbott, Mark smiled in anticipation. He'd estimated Christie's father to be in his early forties, but the terrified creature standing in the doorway looked much older. Mark took a step forward, his hand extended, but the haunted face shrank away from him. Sunken eyes darted around the room as if expecting to see something lurking in the corners.

"Ah, there you are Jim, I'm just making some coffee. This is Mr Jordan, he's... Jim!" The man had gone.

Kathleen Abbott, kettle in hand, stared at the empty doorway. Suddenly her shoulders drooped wearily. "I'm sorry about that," she said quietly. "That was very rude."

"Please, don't apologise. Look, perhaps I should go?"

"No." She was suddenly angry. "This always happens. People take one look at him and leave. Please stay." She quickly grabbed three mugs from the draining board and placed them on the table as if, by doing this, she could prevent him from leaving. "There," she said, "the kettle won't take a minute – please, sit down."

Mark did as she asked. "Has he been like this since..."

he stopped, wishing he hadn't started.

"Since Christie was murdered?" she finished for him. "Yes, although he used to be much worse. The first year he practically lived in the bedroom... too frightened to come out, you see. It's been a long haul for both of us, but he's better now."

"But he looks so ill."

"Yes, I know. I suppose he is ill, mentally."

"But he must be getting some treatment, surely?"

"He's got pills – tranquillisers, for all the good they do. The doctor tried to get him to see a psychiatrist once, but he wouldn't hear of it."

"Does he ever go out? I mean, what does he do all day?"

"He does just what he's doing now, sits up there in his shed, hiding from the world." She sighed. "He makes wooden toys and ornaments to sell at the market."

"So he goes out sometimes then?"

"Only if I go with him. He'd never go alone - too frightened. It means he'd have to talk to folk, you see."

Mark watched her while she arranged biscuits on a plate and thought how attractive she must have been twenty years ago. She still was, in a way. Her eyes, vivid blue, held his for a moment. Eyes like Christie - and Susan. He could see what people were talking about, and why Maude had been so affected; it would be easy to think the two were related.

"Anyway, I'm sure you don't want to hear all this Mr Jordan - or maybe you do." She looked directly at him. "Eve tells me you're writing a book. Is it about what's happened here this week, or is it about us?"

The question was so bluntly put, Mark found himself floundering. "Well... both, in a way."

She smiled. "Don't worry, I don't mind. In fact, in many ways, it will be a relief to talk to somebody. Ever since it happened folk have been careful to avoid it. After the initial shock they all behaved towards us as if it had never happened. I suppose that was largely due to Jim as well." She looked directly at him. "Would you excuse me for a moment? I should take Jim's coffee up to him. He won't come in now, not until you've gone."

Left alone, Mark looked around the kitchen. On the surface it was clean and tidy, but he couldn't help noticing distinct signs of neglect. Yellowing paintwork, peeling and worn by constant cleaning. Cracked linoleum and threadbare curtains. There were the usual appliances: an old gas stove that should have been in a museum, as should the twin-tub washing machine that was partially hidden beneath an old wooden draining board. Mark suspected that this was pretty much how it had looked when the child was alive. Had this family, as well as losing their beloved Christie, also lost the will to live? He wondered. He tried to imagine what it had been like for them, and failed.

Kathleen returned preventing further thought. "Is he all right?" Mark asked.

"He's fine. When he's on his own, he's at his best. It's facing people and having to talk that's the hardest for him. He can't find the words, you see, so he shuts himself off from folk. He has no conception of what goes on outside this house."

"Then he won't have heard about...."

"About the woman in the woods? No, thank goodness." She stared into her coffee cup. "It's strange though, don't you think, that they found her there?"

"Strange?"

"That she was killed in almost the same place." Her voice had subsided to a whisper.

"Look, this isn't going to upset you, is it?" Mark was starting to feel uneasy.

She shook her head. "Not now. We'd always told Christie not to play in the church - only outside or in the woods." She sighed. "Now, I wonder if it would have made any difference. That woman wasn't in the church, was she? Do you know how she died?"

"I don't know," Mark lied. "I shouldn't think there's any connection, though."

"Really? I'm not so sure."

"It's fifteen years, Kathleen. Hardly what you'd call a serial killing."

"I suppose not." She looked thoughtful. "Fifteen years and I'm still trying to find reasons. Silly isn't it? Sometimes I think if only we knew why Christie was murdered, maybe Jim would find it easier to accept. He was so close to her - too close. When she died, he shut us all out, me, Becky, even Jamie. We could never speak of it or even mention her name. Maybe if I'd told him the truth..." She stopped suddenly. "It's too late now anyway."

Mark waited for her to continue but she remained silent. Eventually he asked gently. "What is it he doesn't know?"

She looked at him, a little frightened now. "Nothing," she said quickly. "Please forget I said that."

Dismayed, he saw her eyes brighten with unshed tears. "Please don't be upset." He reached across the table for her hand. "Look, we've only just met and you have no reason to trust me, but I promise you nothing you tell me will go any further if you don't want it to."

Kathleen brushed a hand across her eyes. "Do you always have this effect on people, Mr Jordan? Does everybody you meet lay bare their secrets for you?"

He smiled but remained silent.

"I'd have thought you would have guessed, anyway," she continued. "You see, if I'd told him the truth he might not have loved her so much, and then maybe he'd..."

Mark was barely listening. Her voice had faded into the background as he thought back to the conversations he'd already had with Maude and Bob. The friendship between

Kathleen and Mary Tyler that had ended so abruptly, the death of Len Tyler – maybe it had been suicide after all. At last Mark had the missing piece. "Christie wasn't Jim's child." Without meaning to, he uttered the words aloud. He looked at Kathleen but her eyes were firmly fixed on her empty coffee mug. "She was Len Tyler's daughter, wasn't she?"

The silence hung between them for what seemed an eternity until, at last, Kathleen spoke. "I can see you think you have all the answers now."

"I doubt that. There must be much more to the last fifteen years than can be summed up in a simple statement. I can't imagine how life has been for you. Did you never think of telling Jim?"

"Many times, but it seems I've spent my entire life making wrong decisions. At the time, I told myself it was because I didn't want to hurt people. Apart from Jim, Mary would have to know, our parents - it was easier this way."

"Did you tell Len Tyler?"

"Yes, and that was another mistake. It started Len drinking even more than he usually did, trying to drown his guilt. You see, Christie wasn't the result of an affair, it was one of those isolated things, never to be repeated. Jim and I were going through a rough patch, and Len and Mary were blaming each other for their childless marriage. The perfect breeding ground for trouble, you might say."

"Am I right in thinking you weren't a willing player in this union?"

"You put that very sensitively, but yes, you're right."

"So he raped you?"

Kathleen bit her lip. "Rape? Yes, I suppose that's what it was, although I didn't really think so at the time. I suppose you could say I asked for it. I was feeling miserable after yet another row with Jim, and was looking for a shoulder to cry on. Clearly I was giving out the wrong signals, especially to someone who'd been drinking as heavily as Len had. Anyway, it happened and the rest, as they say, is history." Kathleen stared at him without expression. "So now you have it all, Mr Jordan. I wonder what you'll do with it?"

Mark wondered, too. He'd meant what he said; he wouldn't repeat her tale to anyone, but that meant he couldn't write about it, either.

CHAPTER FOURTEEN

"You were gone ages. What did you do, walk into Harold and back?"

Mark watched Joan serving lunch. He was aware she was speaking but the words didn't register. "Mm – yes," he murmured, and let his mind drift back to the kitchen in the end cottage.

"That was supposed to be a joke, Mark." Her serving spoon clattered into the dish. "I might just as well talk to myself – hello...?" She waved her hand in front of his face. "Hello – Mark?"

"What? Sorry, I wasn't listening, what did you say?"

She raised her eyes heavenwards. "I said... oh never mind what I said. What happened? Two hours ago you went across the road to buy some notepaper, didn't you?"

"Oh, yes - I mean, no."

"Which?"

"No, I didn't go into Harold."

"Good grief, this is like pulling teeth." She tutted loudly. "Did you get your paper, or not?"

"No, I didn't do that either."

"I give up." She thrust a plate of shepherd's pie in front of him. "Here, eat that. It might help focus your mind."

Mark forked the food around absently. "I bumped into Kathleen Abbott earlier. She was in the shop – I carried her bags for her."

"Oh well, say no more. I suppose you managed an invitation to lunch there, as well?"

"No, only coffee. I did have a bit of a chat with her, though. I think she's become a bit isolated in that cottage of hers."

"What do you mean, isolated? She's got the whole village around her. I doubt she can leave her front door without seeing somebody she knows." Joan sounded

94

defensive. "Anyway, I always speak to her when I see her in the shop, and I know I'm not the only one."

"Now don't get all indignant. I didn't mean it like that. Of course she's not short of people to pass the time of day with. It's close friendship she misses. I suspect she hasn't held a meaningful conversation with anyone since losing her daughter."

"Until today, it seems."

"What do you mean?"

"Let's face it, you do have an uncanny knack of getting people to tell you their deepest, darkest secrets. How do you do it?"

"Funny - that's what Kathleen said. Anyway, what makes you think she confided in me?"

"Well, she must have been telling you something interesting. You were in there for a couple of hours, and I doubt you were studying knitting patterns."

"Sometimes it's easier to talk to a complete stranger," he filled his mouth with food. "This is good, Joan." He took another mouthful.

"Did you tell her about your book?"

"I didn't have to, she already knew. She seemed quite amused by it, which is more than I can say for Eve Simpson. I think she'd just as soon see me push off back to London. I could understand her attitude better if I'd been making a nuisance of myself, or if my interest was causing grief to the Abbott family. But I've met them now and I know Kathleen doesn't mind."

"What about Jim?"

"Jim." Mark stopped eating. "Now he's a bit of a worry. The man's ill, that's obvious. As for him knowing about my writing - I doubt it. I doubt if he's aware of anything much."

"Well, give it time, dear." She started to clear the table. "Another couple of days and you'll have him sorted out, too."

"What's that supposed to mean?"

Joan smiled. "There's no need to get all defensive," she imitated his earlier remark. "I simply meant that your arrival seems to have made an impact on certain people. Apart from Kathleen, there's Bob. Since his retirement, he's done nothing but mooch around the village like a lost soul. The only time he seems even vaguely animated is when he's tending his roses."

"So what's changed?"

"He seems livelier, somehow – interested in things. I suppose you've made him feel useful. And, what about Maude? We've all been quite happy to leave her to it up there in her farmhouse, thinking she preferred her own company – boy, did we get that wrong! If nothing else, Mark, you've taken our blinkers off, and I, for one, am glad about it."

Mark was starting to feel uncomfortable. "Oh, give over, Joan. You talk as if I'm the Second Coming. I just happened to be in the right place at the right time, that's all."

"If you say so, dear. Oh, I almost forgot, there's something else for you to sort out. Lionel rang and wants you to call him this afternoon. I expect it's about Crane cottage."

Joan hovered anxiously at the kitchen door. She was too far away to hear the conversation between Mark and Lionel and, to her irritation, could gain nothing from his expression.

"What are you doing lurking there?" George's voice seemed to echo around the kitchen.

"Shhh... don't shout, and I wish you wouldn't creep up on me like that."

"Well, what are you doing?" He peered through the door. "You're eavesdropping - Joan!"

"Will you keep your voice down? Mark's talking to Lionel about the cottage."

"Oh, sorry - what's happening?"

"That's what I'm trying to find out." She pushed him behind the door. "I've completely lost the thread now, look out... he's coming."

Mark entered the kitchen looking annoyingly normal. "Hello George." Then he saw Joan with him. "What on earth are you two doing huddled behind the door?"

George spoke first. "Er... nothing lad. Everything all right?"

Still looking bland, Mark said. "It all depends which way you look at it. From my point of view everything's great, but I don't know about you two."

Mouths gaping, they stood, unable to think of anything to say, until Mark grinned and said. "How do you feel about Carlton having a new resident?"

"Oh, I'm so pleased." Joan couldn't conceal her delight.

"Well done, lad." George clapped him on the back.

Feeling like an eighteen-year-old who'd just passed his A-levels, Mark couldn't help grinning. He'd become very fond of them both, and was touched by their delight in his news.

"What about a drink to celebrate?" George slapped him on the back again.

"It's a nice idea, George, but I think I'd better keep a clear head. I've decided to go down to London this evening; there are several things I need to sort out."

"Surely you could do most of it by phone?" Joan suggested.

"Not really. I need to see my bank manager and the solicitor. I also need to clear my flat. I want to pick up the rest of my clothes, and there are one or two pieces of furniture I'd like to bring back, then I can arrange to let it out."

"You're not selling it then?"

"No, I don't want to burn my boats completely at this stage. If I let it out it'll give me a bit of income, and just in case things don't work out, well, it's always there, isn't it?"

"Very wise. How long will you be away?"

"I can get most of it done in a couple of days. If I leave about six this evening I could be there by ten, have an early night and start first thing in the morning."

Mark spent the afternoon phoning people in London. He secured appointments with both his bank manager and solicitor, then had an irritating conversation with Richard Lumley. The publisher, playing the eternal pessimist, was at first amused then, when he realised it wasn't a joke, turned almost scathing. In the end, he agreed to meet the writer for lunch the next day. Mark knew Richard would do his best to dissuade him from leaving London, but the more he thought about it, the more impatient he became to cut all ties – and start what he viewed as a new life.

It didn't take him long to prepare for the journey. Everything he needed for the next couple of days was already in London. Mark put his head round the kitchen door. "Joan, I'm just going to put a few things in the jeep. I won't be a minute."

"A minute eh? That's what you said this morning."

In the lane, Mark suspiciously eyed a cluster of dark clouds overhead. He tossed his bags in the back of the jeep then, fearing a soaking, ran to the front door. A movement at the end of the lane caught his attention. He turned just in time to see Mary Tyler scuttle across the lane to the footpath. Something in her manner, the way she hurried, head bent, clutching what looked like a large canvas bag, puzzled him.

Curiously, he walked slowly to the junction and watched her as, half walking, half running, she headed up the hill towards the church. Keeping her in sight, he followed at a safe distance, staying close to the hedge so he could duck down quickly if she looked back. The tiny woman scurried along, a hunched figure looking furtively from side to side until she disappeared inside the ruin. The reason for her behaviour was beyond him but, thoroughly intrigued, he followed wondering, not for the first time, if the woman was completely mad.

Treading carefully, neatly side-stepping the fallen door, he negotiated the path leading up to the building. Between them the eerie silence and the darkening sky created a sinister atmosphere. Nothing moved – even the creatures in the woods nearby seemed to have ceased activity. For a moment he considered abandoning the whole thing, but his natural curiosity overcame his unease.

At the porch he stood quite still, listening. At last a sound broke the unnatural silence, but it was nothing he could make any sense of. A faint rhythmic scratching like small claws on a hard surface – maybe a small animal foraging for food. Very slowly he inclined his head and peered around the doorway. It was even darker inside, but clearly empty. Taking a deep breath he stepped through the doorway. The scratching noise was louder, but there was still no movement... nothing. Keeping close to the wall he edged carefully towards the door to the right of the stage. With each step the noise grew more menacing, and seemed to be coming from inside the old kitchen.

Slightly breathless with anticipation, he eased the door open, then stood for several seconds unable to comprehend what he saw. Mary Tyler was on her knees crouching over, of all things, a dustpan and brush. He could hardly believe it; she was frantically scraping every scrap of dust from the quarry-tiled floor. Suddenly he wanted to laugh, partly at the lunacy of it, and partly with relief. In the moments prior to his discovery he had considered just about every horror imaginable, and here she was, the object of his terror, this frail creature wielding nothing more sinister than a broom.

Completely engrossed, she was quite unaware of his presence until he said softly. "Mrs Tyler?"

The cleaning tools fell to the ground with a clatter. Still kneeling, clasping her hands tightly as if praying, she turned her head. The emaciated face appeared disembodied and hideously grotesque in the half-light, and her expression, when she saw who it was, disturbed Mark far more than any foraging animal might have done. Sunken eyes stared at him with childlike curiosity as pale, dry lips, unused to speech, emitted a hoarse whisper. "I haven't finished yet... Reverend Matthews will be here. I have to finish." Her eyes darted around the room. "You can't come in... not until..."

"Mrs Tyler." Mark tried again. "Let me help you."

"No, leave me. You mustn't come in yet - I haven't finished." Suddenly she looked at him like a petulant child and spoke in normal tones. "I can't find the vases... and where are the flowers?"

Realising it was useless, and that she was completely deranged, Mark gently placed a hand under her elbow. "It's all right, Mary. Reverend Matthews isn't coming today. Come home."

Obediently, but still rambling, she allowed him to help her to her feet and lead her out. In front of the stage she stopped to stare at the floor. "Can you see it?" she demanded. "I've tried and tried but it won't come out." Mark looked down and found nothing. "I told them not to play here..." He kept walking her toward the door. "Have you seen the vases...?"

The footpath seemed endless as he led her down. All the while she rambled unintelligibly, but Mark didn't answer, he knew she couldn't hear him.

In the lane, she tried to pull him towards her own cottage. "I must get Len's tea... where are those girls?"

Gently he steered her away. "Len's in the pub, Mary. Come on, we'll go together."

Later that afternoon Mark struggled to come to terms with what had happened. Mary had probably been going up to the church for years, thus far without interference. Now here he was, following, questioning - and all to serve his own curiosity. A curiosity that had first angered Maude, practically reduced Kathleen Abbott to tears and now this poor creature, Mary Tyler, was in hospital. "It's all my fault," he muttered.

Joan knew what he was thinking. "That's quite ridiculous. If you hadn't found her someone else would have. Anyway, she couldn't go on like that, could she?"

"I suppose not, I just wish it hadn't been me. You should have seen her, the expression on her face... like someone startled at life, while staring death in the face."

Joan didn't really understand what he was saying, but she knew he was badly affected. "She's been ill for a long time, Mark. I suppose we always knew that one day she would crack up completely. Do you remember what I said when you first saw her in the garden? I said, she was like a coiled spring and that it wouldn't take much to push her over the edge."

"I remember. You were right, it didn't take much, did it?"

She stared at him. "You're not really suggesting it's because of you?"

"Not directly, maybe. But don't you think it's a bit beyond the bounds of coincidence that this should happen just as I start digging it all up?"

"Digging what up? As far as I know you've been looking into the Christie Abbott thing. Mary's illness has nothing to do with that. I told you, it's because of her husband."

"I know." Mark looked resigned. "I'd still like to know just what it was that set her off today, though."

"Maybe we'll find out eventually. At least she should get some treatment now. Did the doctor say anything about what will happen next?"

"He said they would take her to the cottage hospital in Harold tonight. No doubt they'll keep her under sedation. Then, after assessment, transfer her to Derby for psychiatric analysis tomorrow."

"I feel we should tell someone, Mark, but I don't think she has any relatives other than her daughter, and I haven't a clue where she is."

"Someone in the village must know. What about Kathleen?"

Joan shook her head. "I doubt it. She and Mary and haven't spoken for ages."

Mark stood up abruptly. "There's one person in this village that knows everything - Eve!" He looked at his watch. "It's only five thirty, I'll go over and ask her – that's if she'll speak to me, of course. I won't be a minute."

"That's the third time you've said that to me today," Joan almost laughed. "If you're not here for breakfast I'll start worrying."

Mark smiled. Joan, at least, had lost none of her humour. "No, this time I mean it. I'll have to get moving soon."

True to his word he wasn't long at all. Perching on the edge of the sofa he said. "I would have been quicker if Eve hadn't held me up with all her questions – talk about the tables turning. Anyway, she seems to think Helen lives somewhere near Earls Court."

"Is that near where you live?"

"Not really, but I've got a friend in the Met. I'll see if he can help."

"The Met - isn't that something to do with the weather?"

He laughed. "The Metropolitan Police - Scotland Yard. Actually, he's a forensic scientist so missing persons isn't really his field, but he'll know somebody who can help." He stood up. "Right, I'd better get going. If anything happens while I'm away - make notes, will you?" He leaned forward and quickly planted a kiss on her cheek to let her know he was joking. Before closing the door behind him, he said. "See you in a couple of days, Joan."

"I'd better not hold my breath on that," she muttered to an empty room. "So far your sense of time has been somewhat unreliable, my lad."

CHAPTER FIFTEEN

For Mark the day had started and ended with a nightmare. For Susan, by contrast it had been a turning point, a day when she found comfort and understanding from an unexpected source.

Still smarting from the previous evening, she had prowled around the cottage until she finally lost patience. One sleepless night and a very irritating morning had been quite enough to devote to one man's ego. So, with Lexer in tow, she set off briskly along the Harold Road, intending to reach the next town. But whether through threat of rain or a simple a need for company, she found herself in Maude Brandon's farmhouse.

The old lady immediately sent the two dogs off into the garden to amuse each other, then turned her attention to her guest. She would have liked to attribute this unexpected visit to an act of pure friendship, but she sensed another reason. From the outset she noticed a nervousness in Susan, a troubled look in her eyes. With gentle questioning she urged her to talk, and within a short time had learned all there was to know. The death of Susan's mother and her subsequent feelings of guilt had clearly had a profound effect on the girl's state of mind, but she knew there was more to it than that.

"You mustn't let guilt obscure your objectives, my dear. It's important that you put all this behind you, get on with your life - believe me, I know." The last was said very quietly.

"That sounds like the voice of experience."

"It is," Maude said wryly. "I didn't become a spinster by choice, you know. It's just the way things worked out, or rather the way I let them work out. I had my father to consider, you see. You know my dear, if you don't take control of your own destiny, you'll find someone else will." She smiled gently. "You've simply suffered a temporary loss of direction. Be patient, in time you'll find the right path."

"That's what I thought I was doing now." Susan looked gloomier than ever. "This is the first holiday I've had in years, certainly the first I've taken alone. I really thought a change of scenery would help, but so far it's been a bit of a disaster."

"Well, I can think of better ways to start. Finding a body on your first day is hardly likely to lift the spirits, but that's all behind you now, isn't it?"

"Is it... I wonder?"

Maude felt they were getting to the crux of the matter. "What is it, dear... what's bothering you?"

Susan slumped in her seat. "I don't know. I see shadows moving in every corner, I hear things - perhaps I'm just not used to the countryside, I don't know," she repeated.

"What sort of things are we talking about here? True, the countryside has a sound that city folk find hard to adjust to – or to be perfectly correct, it's usually the silence they can't stand."

"Now, that I can understand. At home, the sound of traffic drowns everything else. In the cottage, at night, you could hear a pin drop. The trouble is it's not pins that I'm hearing, and it's not always at night."

"Could it be animals? Gibson's farm is quite nearby – he keeps geese, among other things. They can be very noisy,"

Susan shook her head. "No, it's not geese, and it's not just noises. I wish I could explain it. There's nothing tangible; nothing I can put my finger on - that's the trouble. I hear sounds when there's nothing there. Occasionally I'll see something out of the corner of my eye. Then, when I turn, it's just the branches of bush swaying in the breeze, or a gate creaking as it swings to and fro. On the surface these things are trivial, but I start to question my sanity when I find there's no breeze, and I distinctly remember closing the gate. At times I'm convinced I'm being watched - and then there's Lexer."

A frown creased the old lady's brow. "What about him?"

"I suppose he could just be picking up the jitters from me, but he's not behaving normally, that's for sure. He goes to the window and growls when there's nothing in sight, and I've found him in the garden barking furiously at the wall. Actually, that's happened a couple of times. Once I'm sure I heard footsteps running away, but again there was nobody there."

"You've got to remember this is a different environment for him, too. He's hearing things he's never heard before. That's probably why he keeps growling."

"That's what I thought, but in the early hours of this morning we both heard something that couldn't be put down to imagination. Someone was trying to open the back door. I heard it a split second before he did. The moment I sat up, he was awake and barking his head off. After that I couldn't hear anything, and by the time I got downstairs, whoever it was had gone. It was just like all the other times, every time I investigate, there's nothing - nobody." Susan laughed nervously. "Perhaps the cottage has a ghost, or maybe we're both going nuts."

"Nonsense. I'm quite sure it's neither. And I doubt someone was trying to break in. Rosemoor is one of three cottages all linked together, is it not?" Susan nodded. "Do you know if either of the other two is occupied at the moment?"

"I don't know. I haven't seen anyone." Susan bit her lip. "You know, I never thought of that. Maybe it was someone from next door – that would explain a lot, wouldn't it?"

"It certainly would." Maude smiled, pleased to see the girl relax a little. "You've had a bad time recently and, quite frankly, I'm not surprised you're overwrought. And you're quite right about Lexer, dogs sense things." She smiled warmly. "Give it time, you'll see. When you relax, so will he." She poured more tea. "Come on, we'll have one more cup, then you can give me a hand in the garden. You need something else to think about."

Maude managed to occupy Susan's next few hours by doing what she did best – teaching. With enormous enjoyment she led the girl around the garden, imparting her considerable knowledge of horticulture to a surprisingly willing pupil. She was pleased to find that her efforts weren't wasted when Susan left the farmhouse later that evening, looking very much better than when she had arrived and with a firm promise to return the next day.

For a long while Maude watched her striding down the lane, concluding that what the girl really needed was the company of people her own age. She immediately thought of Mark and thought how curious it was that these two young people should come into her life at the same time. Somehow she knew that each, in their different ways, would become important to her. At the moment though, it was Susan that worried her most. Things were happening in the village that she had no control over, and something would have to be done about the situation before there was another disaster.

She found Robbie, abandoned by his playmate, sitting forlornly on the back step. Scooping him up into her arms she walked into the kitchen. "No need to look so sad my pet, your friend will be back tomorrow." Rubbing her chin gently on the little dog's head, she smiled. "And so will mine."

CHAPTER SIXTEEN

Two days in London, and Mark was already clock-watching. Two frenetic days of crowds, traffic, screaming cabbies and fume-filled streets had dispelled any lingering doubts he might have had about quitting the city.

Hectic though the pace had been, he had accomplished all he had set out to do. His bank manager, not entirely surprised at his decision to quit the city, had quickly and efficiently arranged to transfer his account to a Derbyshire branch and even supplied the address of a good letting agent for his London flat.

However, Richard Lumley had proved more difficult.

"Why Derbyshire? You've always lived in London, you must be mad! You won't last a year."

Mark had said simply, "We'll see."

"What about your writing, what will you do for ideas... inspiration?"

"Believe me, you're worrying quite unnecessarily. In three days I've seen more life in that little village than I have in three years here."

Richard looked sceptical. "Well at least you're not selling your flat. You can come back when you've had enough."

"Yes I can," Mark agreed. "But look, if it's my work you're worried about, please don't. You know what a hard time I had with the last one? I was struggling at the end."

"I know." Richard chewed his steak with obvious difficulty. "God, this is tough." He put down his knife and fork. "But what makes you think you'll get started out there in the sticks?"

"I already have."

"What, another book? I don't believe it. You've always taken a couple of months off... said you needed to."

"I know, it usually takes me that long, but this is

different. If you remember, I went away to recover."

Richard looked disbelieving. "Two days isn't long enough to recover... or start another book."

Mark sighed. "Richard, trust me. I promise you, at the rate I'm going it won't be very many weeks before I prove you wrong."

At last Richard's engaging smile returned. "All right, all right!" He held up his hands. "I've done my best to talk you out of it. Now can we order something else? This steak is lethal."

To Mark's relief the rest of the meeting passed without further comment, or further references to his sanity.

Shortly after lunch he phoned Scotland Yard and was pleased to find his old friend in good spirits.

"All right, what is it this time... human remains found on a Welsh mining tip, or a headless corpse in the Thames?" All this was followed by a snort of suppressed laughter.

Mark laughed with him. "My books aren't that bad, are they Tom?"

"Don't know old chap, never read one," there was another snort, "but judging by the daft things you ask me, they're pretty gory. How are you, anyway?"

"I'm fine thanks, and I can tell you're as sharp as ever."

"OK, flattery - you know the rest. What can I do you for - is it more research?"

"This is something different Tom, it's not fiction." He went on to explain the events that had prompted his call, finishing. "So you see, we really should try to find this woman's daughter."

"Hmm. I see what you mean. It's not my field as you know, but no doubt I'll find someone to do the necessary. Where can I reach you?"

"Derbyshire." He said with resignation and prepared himself for the inevitable fusillade of questions.

Mark spent the whole of the following day dealing with letting agents, solicitors and, most importantly, his belongings. He was surprised to find that, after living for ten years in the flat, there was remarkably little of such sentimental value that he wanted to take it with him. A reproduction regency desk and chair, together with his computer and all its accessories, were all that interested him. He carefully sifted through old photographs and papers – most, of which he threw in the bin. Yet another testament to his solitary existence.

It made for a tiring day, yet that night he slept fitfully, and for only a few hours. At 5.00 am he was clearing kitchen cupboards, locking windows and double-checking that water and electricity supplies were switched off. He took one last look around before closing the door firmly behind him, and felt nothing but relief - he wanted to get away.

Maude greeted him at the gate of Crane cottage. "You're far too early," she whispered. "We're nowhere near finished yet - and in any case, George said you're to go straight to the pub, Bob wants to see you."

Mark looked past her to the cottage. People were moving about inside, and there was washing on the line. "What's going on - who's in there, and why are you whispering?"

"Shhh... it's only Joan and Susan, we're cleaning the place up for you and it's supposed to be a surprise." She held her hand up to stem further inquiry. "Now get going before they see you. George sounded most insistent and, I have to say, worried. What's more, for some reason, I mustn't tell Susan anything." She glared at him accusingly. "I'll go along with it for now but I shall expect an explanation, you know."

Mark found the two men in the bar. "What's all this about? I've been banned from the cottage and Maude's behaving most oddly."

"Don't look so worried, lad." Bob patted the seat beside

him. "We simply wanted the women out of the way for while, and Maude was the best bet to keep it quiet."

"Why, has something happened?"

"Not yet but... look, sit down and I'll fill you in before Jack gets here."

"Jack - why?"

George joined them. "Just let him start from the beginning, lad. Go on Bob."

"Right. I took Shona up to the meadow opposite the cottage the morning after you spoke to me. I have to say I thought it was a waste of time at first because I could see nothing unusual at all. But Shona kept going back, again and again to the same spot behind a clump of bushes, so I had a good look around."

"And?"

"And, the only thing I can say for sure is that somebody had been there. The grass was flattened and bruised by feet shifting about on the spot. Of course all this means nowt on its own, but I went up again yesterday and... well, that's why Jack's coming later."

"You've found something, haven't you ... What?"

"A knife."

"You're not serious?" Mark couldn't believe his ears.

"I'm afraid I am. The previous afternoon we had a violent storm here that lasted through most of the night, so knowing the ground would be soft, I was hoping to find footprints - something tangible - anything. I wasn't prepared for a knife though."

"What sort of knife?"

"A small paring knife with a wooden handle. Under normal circumstances I would suspect picnickers had left it, but this wasn't normal. It certainly wasn't there the day before, and who would picnic in weather like that?"

"Where's the knife now?"

"I gave it to Jack." He looked at his watch. "He should

be here soon, I've asked him to dig out the file on Christie Abbott as well."

"Have you? Oh Lord!"

Bob smiled reassuringly. "Don't look so worried, it might turn out to be nothing."

Mark shook his head. "I've got a nasty feeling about all this."

Bob leaned forward. "Now look here, Mark, you've had something on your mind for days, don't you think it's about time you told us what it is?"

"I suppose so. It's just that ever since Susan arrived in Carlton people have been saying how much she looks like Christie Abbott. Suppose the murderer has seen her in the village, it could send him, or her, completely mad, maybe think she's come back and – well, it doesn't bear thinking about."

George looked horrified. "If you're right, that lass is in terrible danger."

Bob remained silent, his expression grim. Half expecting the ex-policeman to laugh at his assumption, Mark said. "You don't seem surprised Bob?"

The man shook his head. "I'm not. The same thought had occurred to me but I'd more or less dismissed it. Now you've actually put it into words..."

The three remained silent until Bob continued, "There's something else I think we should consider. If - and I do mean if - we're right, it means whoever murdered that child is someone we know, someone from the village."

"Oh Lord, this is getting worse by the minute." Mark's mind was racing. "What will you tell Jack?"

"The truth of course. If he thinks we're all barking mad, then so be it, but we can't all be suffering from the same delusion, now can we?" He looked at his watch for the umpteenth time. "I just wish he'd get here."

George was still trying to absorb it all. "I can't believe

all this happening," he said.

Mark nodded. "I know, it's all a bit scary, isn't it? This all started as an idea for a book... I just hope we aren't all going off half-cocked."

George pulled a face. "Well I hope we are. Because if we're not, it means this is real. And if it's real, what are we going to do about this young lass, Susan? I don't like the idea of her being in that cottage alone, for a start."

"Neither do I, but we can hardly tell her we think someone's trying to murder her, can we?" Mark ran his fingers through his hair distractedly. "We could take it in turns watching the place, I suppose."

"Nay, lad." Bob started pacing the floor. "We can't go lurking about behind bushes, we'll end up getting ourselves arrested."

George was at a complete loss. "Well I don't know what to say. I'd certainly like to see her out of there, but goodness knows how we're going to manage it. Thank God she's got that dog, that's all I can say."

"True." Mark agreed. "Lexer won't let anyone get close to her without a fight."

Bob couldn't settle. "Aye, he's protective enough, but if it comes to some crazed idiot with a knife, I don't know that he'd cope. It could end up with both the dog and the lass getting..." He stopped, not wanting to voice his thoughts. "Now if it was Shona, she'd know what to do."

"Well that's it then." George suddenly spoke. "Get the lass to look after Shona for you. Of course you'd have to say you were going away or something..." He tailed off wondering why the other two were looking at him so oddly. "What's up?"

Bob grinned. "That's the best idea I've heard yet."

Mark agreed. "Yes, it's a great idea, but would you mind, Bob? After all, it's putting the dog in danger, isn't it?"

"Aye, it's a risk, but somehow I think Shona and Lexer together will be more than a match for anyone. Let's face it, most people would be put off simply by the sight of two seven-stone German Shepherds."

"You know, this could be a case of locking the stable door after the horse has bolted." Mark chewed on his lip. "I mean, there's a chance the problem has already been dealt with."

"You've lost me now." Bob looked puzzled.

"It was something I came up with while putting the plot for the book together. In my mind the villain has always been Mary Tyler."

"Good Lord, how did you manage to come up with that?"

"I thought the motive was jealousy because she couldn't have a child of her own. Add to that the way she's been ever since..."

Bob shook his head. "No, you're barking up the wrong tree there. She didn't go like that after Christie's death. That didn't happen until after her husband died, about year later."

"Hmm, that was something that bothered me a bit. Mind you, at one point I had Len Tyler down as chief suspect."

"No, it wouldn't have been Len. Alcoholic he may have been - murderer no. Anyway, he loved Christie, almost as much as his own daughter."

"Yes, I know he did..." Mark stopped abruptly. He'd almost given the game away, but Bob wasn't listening.

George scratched his head. "Well I don't know what to make of it all. If it wasn't for the link between the two murders, I'd have to say my money would be on this guest of ours."

"Steven Wade? Haven't you sussed him out yet?"

"Sussed him out? I'd be hard pressed to even recognise him. If Joan didn't have to make his bed every morning we wouldn't know he was here."

A pleasant-looking man in his early thirties opened the door. "Hello," he said studying the three men huddled around the bar. "You haven't started without me, have you?"

CHAPTER SEVENTEEN

To everyone's relief, Jack Witchell had come prepared to listen to their ideas without scepticism. He'd also come armed with information Mark had never expected to see. With great interest he watched the policeman shuffle through a pile of papers and then proceed to tell them as much as he could about the fifteen-year-old murder.

"It doesn't make pleasant reading." He said. "You don't want all the details, do you?"

Bob spoke first. "Well I do. I don't know about anyone else."

Mark nodded. "If it's all right for you to tell us, I'd like to hear it all."

"It can't hurt now, It was a long time ago and besides, if telling you helps us..."

"Just get on with it, lad." Bob was getting impatient.

"I don't know why you want to hear all this, you're the one person here that was actually on the case." He gave his uncle an affectionate smile. "You probably already know a great deal more than this file has to tell."

"My memory isn't what it was, and you might mention something I've forgotten." He glared at him. "Go on, get on with it!"

"All right, if you say so. A Mrs Blanche Armitage called the police after hearing Maude Brandon shouting for help. By the time our lot got to the church the whole village was up there." Jack paused to remark to his uncle. "I bet that pleased the scenes of crime officer."

"Tell me about it - people trampling all about made it impossible to check for footprints or anything else." Bob pulled a face. "Anyway, get on with it, lad."

"Right, well the officer-in-charge reported finding James Abbott kneeling in front of the altar table with the child in his arms. Apparently he wouldn't accept the girl was dead, and refused to let the ambulance men take her away. He just kept telling them – and I quote, 'there's no need, she'll be all right in a minute.'"

Bob had been nodding throughout. "Aye, I remember that, they had to give him a sedative in the end."

Jack continued. "After that it was just a matter of questioning all the village people and waiting for the pathologist's report."

"Can you tell us his findings?" Mark asked.

"Yes, she died from a single knife wound to the throat. Not the customary slit from ear to ear, though - it was a single penetration, one stroke right through the jugular." Jack muttered to himself. "My God, it must have been a blood-bath."

"It was." Bob didn't want to dwell on that. "What else does it say?"

"The forensic report states the wound was caused by a straight-bladed weapon, the blade being approximately three inches in length and half an inch wide."

"Like a paring knife." Bob muttered.

"What?"

"Nothing, go on."

"There were no other wounds or marks to the body, and no sign of sexual assault." Jack thought for a moment, then said. "That must have had them puzzled."

"Why?" Mark asked.

"Most child murders are motivated sexually or, in extreme cases, for the sheer joy of sadistic mutilation. This was neither. The deed was executed cleanly and efficiently. Whoever it was simply wanted the child dead."

George has been listening carefully. "Was the weapon ever found?"

"No. A thorough search was made of the church and surrounding area, but it turned up nothing."

At this point George went off to answer the phone,

returning almost immediately. "It's for you Mark, someone called Tom."

"Oh! Good, thanks."

Jack watched him leave. "Nice chap that."

"Yes, a bit imaginative, but then he's a writer." Bob lowered his voice. "Actually, don't tell him, but I've read one or two of his books - they're not bad."

Mark returned looking very thoughtful. "Everything all right?" George asked.

"Yes thanks, George, fine." He turned to Jack. "Were the woods searched?"

Jack read quickly through the papers again. "It doesn't mention it specifically, it just says surrounding area. Any special reason for asking?"

"No, I just wondered." Bob could see Mark was being evasive but decided not to remark on it.

George looked at the clock. "I reckon Joan will be back soon, are we going to keep all this to ourselves, or what?"

"I think, for the time being, the fewer people that know, the better." Jack began gathering his papers together. "Now if you've heard enough, I think it's time I headed back. Look, I don't want you lot blundering around like a bunch of vigilantes, but by all means question and probe. And Mark, you can keep pretending it's all research for a book."

"What do you mean, 'pretending'? This *is* research."

Jack smiled. "OK, whatever you say, just don't do anything dangerous." He turned to his uncle. "Rosemoor is the middle one of those three cottages on the Harold Road, isn't it?"

"Yes."

"Do you know if the other two are occupied?"

"I think they're both empty - why?"

Ignoring the question he spoke to Mark. "Do you think you can find out who this young lady rented the cottage from... I mean can you do it without alarming her?"

"Yes, I think so."

"Good, right I'm off, nice to have met you Mark. Uncle, I'll be phoning soon." Jack touched Bob's shoulder as he left. "By the way, no prints on that knife you found, but I expect you'll have guessed that."

Bob lowered his voice. "I thought as much, though I reckon it'll turn out to be three inches long and half an inch wide though, don't you?"

The rain returned with a vengeance that evening. In his room, Mark stared dismally at the ruin on the hill wondering why he felt so deflated when, by rights, he should be feeling pleased with himself. Soon he would have a very different view to contemplate, especially if Maude had anything to do with it. Not content with finding him a home and cleaning it, she had also found a way to furnish it for him. "The attic is full of furniture that my father made." She'd told him. "It would please me to see it used. When you have time, come up and have look." If only Maude could solve this immediate problem so easily he would feel a lot happier.

At seven o'clock he went down to the bar to find Susan. During the afternoon he'd found time to offer an apology and a tentative invitation for a drink. To his surprise, she accepted both. This time, he vowed, she would get his full attention; he wouldn't mention his work once. But Mark hadn't reckoned on Bob.

As the evening wore on it became blatantly clear that Susan was steadily becoming the worse for drink. Watching Bob refill her glass, Mark whispered. "I think she's had enough, don't you?"

"Trust me." Bob muttered under his breath. "I know what I'm doing."

All was revealed at closing time when Susan stood up to put on her jacket. Swaying slightly, she grabbed Mark's arm. "Oh dear, I think I've had a little too much wine."

"Good job you're not driving, lass." Bob was looking extremely pleased with himself.

"But I am," she mumbled, looking decidedly off colour.

"Well you can't drive in that state, and neither can Mark, he's had more than enough." Bob rubbed his chin thoughtfully. "Look, you'd better stay at my place tonight."

"I couldn't put you to all that trouble..." She stumbled against a chair, then sat down awkwardly. "Oh dear, how silly of me."

"No trouble, come on you two." Bob rounded the dogs up. "Mark, you'd better give the lass a hand."

Joan leaned quietly against the bar watching the proceedings with curiosity and amusement. Something was going on, she was sure of it. She looked suspiciously at George who, having adopted a look of patently bogus innocence, scuttled away to the cellar.

An hour later Mark found him sitting on a barrel reading an old newspaper. "You can come out now, Joan's gone to bed."

George grinned. "Thank goodness. She knows summat's up and won't rest until she finds out what it is. Here, did you know what Bob was going to do?"

"I had no idea, brilliant though wasn't it?" He balanced awkwardly on an upturned crate. "Well that was obviously plan A. Now, I want to talk to you about plan B."

CHAPTER EIGHTEEN

"Why on earth didn't you wake me earlier?" Mark stumbled into the kitchen, his clothes in disarray and carrying a pair of trainers.

"I tried but you were dead to the world, and I could hardly shout, could I?" George watched him struggle into his shoes. "For goodness sake, drink this, I'll do your laces." He thrust a mug of coffee into Mark's hand. "And calm down, will you? You'll need your wits about you if we're to get this right. The state you're in you'll muck it up."

Mark took a deep breath. "You're right - stay calm. What's the time?"

"Just after six, you've got plenty of time."

"Yes, but I've got to get out before him, haven't I?"

"You will, just stop flapping. Now look, I've been thinking, you'd do better to take my car, your jeep will stick out like a sore thumb."

"Hmm. You're probably right. Thanks."

"Here." George handed him a plastic carrier bag. "There's a flask of coffee and some sandwiches in there - should keep you going for a bit. Now, I've watched him leave and he always goes the same way, out of the drive then right. The nearest town in that direction is Castleton, it's about six miles."

"Right, I'll get going, if I park down the end of the lane I might be able to pull out behind him without arousing suspicion. What have you told Joan?"

"Nothing yet, but I'll think of something. It's best if I play it by ear, if I start rehearsing I'll make a hash of it." They both heard a door close. "Quick that may be her, or worse still - him."

"Right, see you later, I'll phone if I can." Mark left through the back door, then immediately returned with his hand outstretched. "Keys..."

"Oh... here." George took a bunch of keys from a drawer and tossed them to him, then breathed a sigh of relief when the door closed. Now all he had to do was come up with something to keep Joan happy. Maybe she'd think Mark was still in bed. He heard another door bang. "Oh gawd," he muttered, and fled to the cellar. He needed more time to think.

It seemed an age since Mark had followed Steven Wade's Ford into the car park at Castleton railway station. He glanced at the dashboard clock. It was, in fact, only thirty-five minutes but nothing had happened, and it seemed longer. In all that time, the man hadn't moved. As far as Mark could see, he was doing nothing more sinister than reading a book.

Another fifteen minutes passed and there was still no sign of movement. Feeling decidedly cramped, Mark stretched as best he could in the confines of George's Rover. He was beginning to feel very silly - and very impatient. This could go on all day. "Right, chum," he said aloud, "it's time one of us made a move." Easing himself across to the passenger seat he got out and, crouching low, made his way between the cars to the road. He prayed that nobody was watching this performance, he was going to look pretty silly if someone asked him what he was up to. In the street he looked about for a suitable shop. The chemist was nearest. Inside, he quickly found enough items to fill a carrier bag, then breezed into the car park swinging it aloft. He whistled loudly while making a business of looking for his car, then, spotting Steven Wade apparently for the first time, tapped on his window.

At first the young man look startled then wound the window down. "Yes?" He looked at Mark as if he'd never seen him before.

"Hello, it's Steven, isn't it?" Mark said cheerfully. "I thought it was you. What's up – have you missed your train?"

Disconcerted, the young man mumbled. "No - not

exactly. I'm sorry..." Clearly he hadn't a clue who Mark was.

"I'm staying at the Royal Oak," Mark reminded him. "We met on the landing the other day."

"Oh yes, of course. I'm sorry, I can't remember your name."

"Mark Jordan." He raised the shopping bag. "Been doing a bit of shopping. There's a limit to what Mrs. Simpson can provide."

"Mrs. Simpson?"

"Yes, you know, the shop opposite the pub?"

"Oh, I've never been in there."

"Really? Well, I'd recommend a visit before you leave Carlton, it's quite an education - here, are you all right?" Mark frowned at the young man's pallor.

"Yes, I'm all right. I just need a bit of fresh air, that's all."

"Look, why don't you get out and stretch your legs for a minute. Better still, we could find somewhere to have coffee and a bite of something."

"No I can't, I have to stay here." His tired eyes were fixed on the station.

"Are you planning to sit here all day?"

Steven Wade suddenly looked very weary. "As a matter of fact, I've been sitting here all day, every day for nearly two weeks... but it seems longer."

Mark could see he wasn't joking. Without a word he walked around and got into the passenger seat. "Do you mind?" He asked, while trying to make himself comfortable amid a litter of empty cigarette packets and sweet wrappings.

Steven shrugged. "Please yourself."

"Look, you can tell me to sod off if you like, but there's obviously something wrong and I'd like to help, if I can."

Without averting his gaze from the station forecourt the young man said, "Thanks, but there's nothing you can do. I'm just tired, that's all."

It was clear that Steven Wade didn't really care one way or the other whether Mark stayed or not, and might even prefer him to go, but he was determined to get to the bottom of it. "Who are you waiting for?" He asked quietly.

"My girlfriend." he said simply.

Mark nodded. "I thought so, Helen Tyler."

At last he got a reaction. Steven Wade turned on him. "How do you know that?" He demanded. "Have you been checking up on me?"

"Not you - her. Helen's mother has been taken ill and we've been trying to trace her."

"And you found she was living with me, right?"

"Right, and we also found that she's been missing for three or four weeks. It's important that we find her, Steven."

"Yeah, well I hope you have better luck than I've had." He laughed bitterly. "She's a headstrong girl, is Helen. Clearly the feelings of others don't come too high on her list of priorities."

Mark remained silent. Every word Steven Wade uttered just confirmed his suspicions. Someone was going to have to shatter this young man's illusions, but he didn't want it to be him. "Why are you waiting here, Steven?" He asked, at last. "What makes you think this is where you'll find her?"

"It's my last resort," he said simply. "I should have given up after the first week, but I kept thinking, maybe just one more day…" Steven leaned back heavily in his seat. "Oh, I don't know what I was thinking – or even why I'm bothering."

"Do you want to talk about it? It might help."

"Might as well," he mumbled. "I was on the verge of giving up when you arrived. Telling you this much has made me realise how stupid it all is." The young man looked resigned and depressed. "We've been living together for over a year, you see. I thought we had something worth hanging on to."

"A year is a long time," Mark said quietly, "not easy to let go."

"Helen didn't find it too difficult, did she?" Steven snapped. "And there was me thinking all sorts. I even thought about marriage... but..."

"But what?"

"But nothing. She's left me and I just have to accept it."

"What happened – did you have a row?"

"Sort of... we were getting on fine until that last night. She'd found out she was pregnant, you see. That's what started it all off." There was a long pause, and then he added defensively, "It wasn't as if I didn't want the baby. I was delighted about it, and told her so. I even said we'd get married straight way." He sighed. "It was the wrong thing to say, she went potty, started shouting and screaming. She didn't want to have the baby, said something about not wanting to bring another brat into the world. We had a terrible row, which ended up with her saying she was going to get rid of it. I pleaded with her, but she was adamant. In the end I managed to persuade her to think about it, not to do anything immediately. Eventually, she agreed to sleep on it – said we'd talk about it in the morning - but the next morning she was gone."

Mark had been watching him very closely. Steven was very close to breaking point. "Look, you don't have to tell me all this, you know."

"I want to tell somebody. I've been going nuts sitting here thinking about it."

"Steven, just why are you sitting here?"

Steven laughed mirthlessly. "I suppose it does seem a bit odd, but it's all I could think of. Helen didn't exactly go without a word, you see. She left me a note saying she was going to visit her mother. Said she wanted time to think, and promised not to do anything without telling me first."

"And you haven't heard from her since?"

Steven shook his head. "She phoned once, the day after she left. She said she was at her mother's house and was going to stay for a couple of weeks. Apparently there was someone she had to see - a friend in the village, someone who'd helped her a lot when she was a child. She promised to call again in a day or two but when I didn't hear from her, I decided to come up here and see her. I called at her mother's cottage as soon as I arrived, but the woman got into a terrible state, didn't speak, just kept shaking her head and pushing me away. I called again the next day but she was worse than ever - to be honest she scared me a bit. There's something seriously the matter with that woman. Anyway, it occurred to me that Helen may have gone off to have an abortion, and would come back to her mother afterwards. Helen can't drive so I knew she'd have to travel by trains and buses. It wasn't difficult to work out which station she'd arrive at - so here I am." He finished simply.

"And you've been sitting here every day... waiting for her?"

He nodded. "I knew I had to see her before she reached her mother. Once she'd got inside the cottage that woman would never have let me anywhere near her."

"She may have gone back to Earls Court, did you think of that?"

"We've got friends living next door. I've phoned once or twice but there's been no sign of her. Anyway, they've got the number of the pub, they'd have called if there was any news."

Mark wasn't sure what to say to all this. One thing was certain though; he couldn't let him go on like that. "Why don't you come back with me? Helen's mother is in hospital now so you don't have to worry. If Helen does turn up, the cottage is empty."

Steven looked at Mark for the first time. "Thanks for listening."

Joan was in her usual place at the kitchen sink as they came in. She took one look at Mark's face and all the questions she'd been saving up froze on her lips. Instead she asked. "Are you both here for lunch?"

Steven went up to his room, and once out of earshot, Mark said. "I'll explain everything later. I've just got to have a quick word with Bob, is he in the bar?"

Joan wiped her hands. "He is - and so is Susan. Now, don't you tell me there's nothing going on, Mark. There's Bob wandering about after Susan like a mother hen, frightened to let her out of his sight. Then you disappear in the early hours with George's car. As for George, every time I turn around he's disappearing into the cellar. And now here you are, back with this chap who hasn't been seen around in the hours of daylight since he got here - what is he, a vampire?"

Mark suppressed a smile. "I promise Joan, all will be revealed soon. Meanwhile, go easy on Steven, he's had a rough time and, if I'm not mistaken, he's about to hear some very bad news."

The next few hours were difficult for everyone. Jack sent one of his men from Harold police station to talk to Steven - and ultimately take him to identify the murdered woman's clothing. When the phone rang later that afternoon, no one was surprised to hear that the body found in the woods had been positively identified as Helen Tyler. Steven had virtually collapsed, so someone was coming over to collect his things, and Jack was making arrangements to send the lad to his parents.

Bob and George elected Mark for the task of explaining the day's events to Joan and Susan. "If I do it, Joan will see right through the whole thing, George complained, "and we don't want her asking questions, do we?"

"He's right." Bob backed him up. "We've still got the business of keeping an eye on Susan, and the less Joan knows about it the easier that will be. She'll believe it if you tell her you were just following up on an idea for your book."

And she did. Careful to omit their fears of a prowler with a knife, Mark managed to convince her his behaviour that day was entirely due to curiosity. With that important hurdle behind them, the men began to relax until Susan announced she was going back to the cottage.

"But it's only six o'clock." Mark protested. "Why not stay here for the evening, have a drink?"

Susan grinned wickedly at Bob. "I'm not sure I'm completely over last night's little episode yet, and beside that I've got things to do."

"What - can't they wait?"

"No they can't, there's some ironing for a start and then I'm going to pamper myself. After a long hot soak I'm going to wash my hair and then..."

"All right, I've got the message. I'll drive you up there, then."

"Thanks, but I'd rather walk... Lexer needs the exercise."

Mark was getting desperate, there's was no way he could keep her there, short of tying her down. Thankfully Bob came to the rescue.

"Actually, lass I'm hoping you can do me a favour. I'm going over to Kerridge to see my brother tonight, and he's bound to insist I stay. I wondered if you could take Shona with you."

"Of course I will, but will she be all right? I mean, she's never away from you, is she?"

"She'll be fine. I usually leave her with old Sam but she's a bit too boisterous for him these days. I thought, seeing as she gets on so well with your chap... that's if you don't mind?"

"Of course I don't mind, in fact I'll enjoy it. These two can keep each other company while I get on with my chores."

Mark and Bob watched as she walked up the lane with the two Shepherds. "Well, she should be all right with those two on guard." Mark turned to the man at his side. "Thanks Bob." Then seeing his anxious expression, asked. "You're not worried about Shona are you?"

"Lord bless you no, that dog can look after herself. It's me I'm worried about. I've landed myself with an evening in front of the telly haven't I?" He managed to look thoroughly depressed. "I can hardly go in for my usual pint with Joan thinking I'm over in Kerridge."

CHAPTER NINETEEN

The Harold Road, like so many lanes around the village, had no street lighting. Susan reined the two Shepherds close to her and, avoiding the meadow side of the lane, quickened her step. It would be dark soon, and she wanted to be home.

Seen in silhouette at dusk, Rosemoor Cottage presented a welcoming sight. A warm light from the front window flooded the garden, illuminating the whiteness of the picket fence that surrounded it. Susan stopped dead in her tracks – welcoming or not, there should be no light. The sun had been shining when she left the cottage that morning, so there was no need to put a light on – unless Bob had done it.

She reached the front gate slightly breathless - more from anticipation than exertion, she knew. Suddenly she thought of Maude. The farmhouse wasn't far away; perhaps she should go there. The old lady's reassuring voice seemed to echo in her ears. 'More ghosts, Susan? Take control, my dear. Face up to your fears.'

"Right!" Susan threw the gate open and marched up the front path, making sure the dogs were close behind. At the door, with the key in her hand, she faltered. It might be prudent, she thought, to look through the window first – just to make sure.

Side-stepping quietly, and crouched low under the sill, she picked her way through the shrubbery and along the front wall. The room inside was exactly as she had left it. "Stupid," she muttered, and straightened up. "What did you expect?" She went back to the door, opened it and pushed the dogs ahead. "OK, troops, the coast's clear. In you go." She flung the door open wide, wondering why she hadn't done this in the first place. If anyone had been in the cottage, the dogs would certainly have sensed it.

An hour later, her ironing done, she prepared a meal for

the dogs and heated some soup for herself. She viewed her entry into the cottage that evening as the first step towards normality. A couple of days ago she would have fled to the farmhouse in search of sanctuary – but she'd overcome her anxiety. Granted, it was a very small triumph, but she felt stronger for it. Now all she had to do was figure out why everyone else was behaving so oddly.

She had sensed a subtle change in the last twenty-four hours, although there was nothing she could put her finger on. People were still friendly towards her but they seemed to be watching her every move – almost as if they were expecting something to happen.

It surprised her to find it was Bob that occupied her thoughts most. It had all started that morning when she found herself, a little the worse for wear, in Bob's spare bedroom. She knew she hadn't imagined the sheepish look on his face when, having finally dragged herself downstairs, she complained of a headache - and that was another thing. It was Bob who had plied her with wine and got her drunk in the first place. If it had been anyone else she would have been highly suspicious of his motives, but he had treated her with the utmost courtesy all day.

On reflection she rather wished she'd been a bit more receptive, for he proved a very entertaining companion. He'd insisted on accompanying her back to the cottage, 'so that he could exercise the dogs,' then, after she'd showered and changed, he'd suggested a stroll around the village ending with lunch at the pub. Carlton boasted a limited number of historic buildings, but he managed to fill the hours until opening time with sufficient to entertain her.

"The oldest buildings are the pub and Blanche Armitages's thatched cottage." he told her. "Blanche says her ancestors built it. Now she's the one you should talk to about the history of the village, though mind you, make sure Maude isn't around at the time. Those two never agree on anything."

Susan smiled as she put her book away and prepared for an early night. Maybe he was lonely, she thought, or perhaps he was just being kind. Either way, it was pleasing to know she had made yet another friend.

After relaxing in a bath of warm, scented water, Susan sat at her dressing table studying her complexion critically. She looked better, she decided, the dark shadows under her eyes were barely visible, and there was a hint of colour in her cheeks. Maybe this holiday hadn't been such a bad idea after all.

Just as she was debating the benefits of a face pack, both Shepherds jumped up barking in unison. "Quiet!" she yelled as she opened the bedroom door, then laughed when the two dogs tumbled over each other in their race to get downstairs. It wasn't until she reached the kitchen and found the door open and the dogs gone that she felt the first twinge of alarm. She was sure she'd closed the door before going upstairs.

In the darkness she could see very little. One of the dogs was barking furiously at the far wall... but which one? On bare feet she walked further into the garden. "Lexer, come here!" she commanded, and waited for the patter of feet. "Lexer!" she called again, but there was no response. She continued in the direction of the noise until she could see it was Shona who was barking and running up and down the length of wall. Her coat, a lighter colour than Lexer's, gleamed in the moonlight. "Come here, Shona," she called. The dog came to her side immediately but continued to growl menacingly at the wall. "What is it, girl?" Susan moved towards the raised shrubbery and carefully climbed up. Peering over the wall she could see something, a furry mass, lying in the grass. "Oh God... no." She wasn't aware she'd spoken aloud until Shona, now beside her, whimpered anxiously. "Stay here, girl." She climbed up onto the wall then jumped, almost falling onto the prostrate animal as she landed.

Her heart pounded painfully in her chest as she gently ran her hands over the unconscious creature. Anxiety turned to panic when she felt a warm sticky substance oozing through the dog's soft coat. Frantically she tried to lift him, but the dead weight was too much for her. Shona, aware something was very wrong, whimpered pathetically. "Stay with him, girl."

Susan clawed her way painfully back over the wall. Everything seemed to hinder her, loose bricks fell away, she tripped on her gown, and stones dug into her feet. By the time she reached the phone she was breathless with fear and she couldn't think what was the number. She ran back to the kitchen - where had she put her jacket? She rummaged through the pockets and breathed a sigh of relief when her fingers touched the crumpled card Joan had given her.

It seemed ages before anyone answered, then Joan's familiar voice said. "Hello?"

"Joan, I need help, Lexer's hurt, he's bleeding, I... I think he's dead..."

"What?" Joan heard the tremor in the girl's voice. "All right, we'll be there straight away, try to stay calm, dear." She ran into the bar. "Mark!" she shouted. "Quick, it's Susan..."

Mark didn't wait to hear any more. Instantly on his feet he called, "George, go and fetch Bob. I'll get the jeep out."

Seconds later they were speeding up the Harold Road. "What did she say Joan?" Mark was crashing gears and cursing the jeep. "Come on..."

"Just that she thought Lexer was dead, nothing more."

All three were silent when they lurched to a halt outside Rosemoor. The front door gaped open but there was no sign of Susan. Mark was out first. "It's too quiet, they must be at the back." He ran through the cottage and into the garden. "Susan, where are you? Susan!"

"Here, I'm here, behind the wall. Shona's with me."

Within seconds he was over it and standing in front of her. She knelt on the grass, her white robe stained darkly with

Lexer's blood. The dog's beautiful head lay silently in her lap. Mark knelt beside her as she raised her stricken face. "He's dead, Mark."

In the darkness he could see her tears glistening as they slid slowly down her face. He didn't know what to say - what could he say? Swallowing hard, he looked up as Bob joined them. There was no boisterous greeting from Shona this time. Her ears flattened against her head, she sloped away to stand close to her master, pressing herself against his legs.

Putting a steadying hand on her head, Bob stared sadly at the Shepherd's lifeless body. "Listen to his chest, lad." he said quietly.

Mark pressed his ear to the damp fur. "I think he's still breathing." he whispered. "Yes, I can hear something – quick, Bob, we must get him to a vet."

The following couple of hours were intolerable for Susan. Joan did her best, but nothing she said could reassure her. Eventually she persuaded the girl to go upstairs to shower and dress. "And while you're up there you'd better pack a few overnight things," she said.

"Pack, why?"

"Because you're coming back with us. Whatever happens, I don't think you should be alone tonight. Come on, I'll give you a hand." More than anything Joan wanted to keep her occupied. She glanced out of the window wishing the men would come back, or at least phone. She too, felt uneasy. Whoever had done this could still be lurking somewhere outside. Her eyes fell on Shona; thank goodness Bob had left her with them.

They were in the kitchen when the men returned. "He's going to be fine." Mark grinned. "He's taken a hell of a whack on the head so they're keeping him overnight, but all being well, we can collect him tomorrow."

Susan looked disbelieving. "Really?

"Really." Mark put his arm around her. "He's also got a

134

nasty stab wound on his rump, which is now stitched up, and he's lost a bit of blood. Actually, the vet was more concerned with the concussion, but Lexer came round during the examination - and then we knew he was all right. You've never heard such a racket."

The scenario that followed was becoming almost monotonously familiar. Everyone involved in the day's activities, sitting in Joan's lounge holding a post-mortem.

"The first thing I want to know is..." Joan's voice included them all, but her eyes settled determinedly on Bob, "why the devil aren't you in Kerridge?"

CHAPTER TWENTY

By 10 o'clock the following morning, curiosity had enveloped Carlton like a shroud. Nothing disturbed the stillness – not even a curtain twitched. All eyes were on the Royal Oak.

'She's in there, that girl from London – and summat's happened.' Hushed whispers broke the silence as, one by one the village folk centred on Eve Simpson's shop. A police car had been stationed outside Rosemoor Cottage for most of the night and they wanted to know why. This time she had to disappoint them, for once she knew no more than they did.

Inside, Jack Witchell carefully positioned himself with his back to the light. It was a trick he'd learned from experience. Not that he intended to treat any of the three other people in the room as suspects. It was simply procedure – and for him, procedure had become a way of life. Once he was satisfied no one could read his expression and react accordingly; he directed his attention to Susan. "You haven't had a very happy time since you arrived in Carlton, have you?"

"I've had better weeks." Susan smiled weakly at the man who'd come to question her, and tried to remember where she'd seen him before. It was recent, she knew that much – but where?

Jack Witchell watched her with concern. He knew about stress and its many effects, and Susan was showing classic signs. Her outward calm, with a touch of wry humour didn't fool him. Just one more thing and she'd crack - but which way? She'll either withdraw completely, he thought, or get boiling mad and do something stupid.

"I've seen you before, haven't I?" She asked at last.

"You have, last Monday - the woods on the hill."

"Of course, you're the man in the suit. And I understand you're Bob's nephew?"

"Right again, but don't let that worry you." He grinned wickedly at his uncle. "Insanity isn't always hereditary, you know."

Susan relaxed visibly. She'd felt nervous about being interviewed by the police, but Jack Witchell had diffused the tension with a grin that transformed his grim expression, and reminded her she was amongst friends. He would probably be quite handsome if he smiled more often, she thought.

He leaned forward in his seat. "I know you're probably tired, but do you think you're up to answering a few questions?"

"I'm fine, but I doubt I can tell you anything you don't already know. What I would like to know is why all this is happening - is it something to with the body – that woman?" Jack opened his mouth to answer, but she continued. "Or is it because of that child, Christie, and my resemblance to her?"

"No, well certainly not all of it. The body you found had been in the woods for several weeks - long before you arrived. As for the child..." he shook his head, I really don't know." Jack sat back. He was more used to asking questions than answering them, and she'd made him feel uneasy. He leaned forward again. "Have you remembered anything else about last night?"

Susan shook her head. "No, nothing. I didn't see or hear anything until the dogs sounded the alarm. The only thing that struck me as odd was the back door. I'm absolutely certain I closed it, but when I reached the kitchen, it was thrown wide open - that's how the dogs got out." She looked across at Bob who sat quietly on the sofa with Mark. "Lexer must have gone straight over the wall, but Shona didn't... why?"

"Training." He said simply. "She wouldn't give chase without a command, much as she might like to." He stroked the dog's head. "That's why I wanted her with you. Lexer's a brave enough dog and will always try to protect you but, without training, instinct will take over and he'll go after

137

anything."

"Have you heard how the dog is?" Jack asked.

"Not yet, I think I'll ring now." Mark stood up. "Have you been up to the cottage Jack?"

"Yes, I went up there last night after leaving here, then again first thing this morning. I didn't find anything though, just a lot of tyre tracks."

Mark's jaw dropped. "Oh God, that was me. I drove the jeep round the back to save carrying the dog through the cottage - I didn't think."

"It's all right." Jack reassured him. "I'd have done the same thing myself." He watched Mark leave, then turned to Susan. "I want you to try and think back, has anyone reacted strangely to you, or mentioned your resemblance to Christie Abbott?"

"Maude Brandon was the first to mention it, but I couldn't say she reacted strangely. It was Mary Tyler that worried me; she seemed terrified and tried to speak. I just wish I'd been able to make sense of what she was saying."

"Well you can rest easy there, we've checked with the hospital and Mary's still under sedation - and will be for some time."

"Do you really think somebody stabbed Lexer deliberately? I thought he might have landed on some glass or something."

"I wish it were that simple." Jack didn't want to alarm her but she had to know the truth. "I spoke to the vet last night, in fact soon after Uncle Bob called. He's in no doubt that the dog was stabbed and possibly kicked or beaten. He was certainly hit on the side of his head with something hard enough to render him unconscious."

She was suddenly enraged. "If I find out who did it..."

"You'll do nothing." Jack looked at her sternly. He could see the crack in her facade widening as her anger mounted. "I don't want to alarm you, Susan, but this whole matter must be handled with extreme caution, and for the foreseeable future I would rather you weren't left alone."

"You don't think it's somebody from around here, do you? I mean, surely I can go round the village on my own? The people I've met so far have all seemed perfectly normal, except Mary Tyler of course."

"People don't necessarily look disturbed Susan, in fact some of the most notorious murderers in history have seemed, on the surface, as normal as any of us here."

Mark returned grinning. "The vet says we can collect Lexer, he's fine."

In the back of the jeep Susan stroked Lexer's ears and silently thanked God, and the vet for his survival. "He was lucky," the vet told her. "The blade missed all the vital organs and hit tough muscle tissue in his rump. He'll be a bit sore for while, and make sure he has these antibiotics. As long there's no infection, he's in the clear." She hardly took her eyes of the sleeping dog until Mark switched off the engine.

In daylight Rosemoor Cottage looked a picture of serenity. The police had gone – everything looked normal, but Susan knew she would never feel comfortable in there again. "Why have we stopped here?" She asked.

Mark got out and opened the rear door. "We're going to pack up the rest of your things, you're staying at the pub until this thing is over."

"But, I don't think…"

"Well, I do. You heard what Jack said this morning, he doesn't want you left alone and, in any case, Joan's already getting the spare room ready."

Quietly relieved that someone else was making the decisions, Susan made sure the dog was comfortable and followed Mark though the gate.

They entered the cottage together. Susan started upstairs. "I'll get my clothes, would you get Lexer's food out of the fridge for me?"

"Right, give me a call when you've finished and I'll bring your case down." He watched her go up, then walked into the kitchen. He saw the broken glass and splintered wood at the exact moment he heard Susan's stifled cry.

He found her in the doorway of the front bedroom. She was unnaturally still, frozen almost. Her hands covered the lower part of her face leaving only her eyes visible - eyes wide with fright. He moved past her into the room and felt the hair on the back of his neck stand up.

At first glance it looked like any other rag-doll propped against the pillows. Dressed in a pale blue smock, white ankle socks and black button shoes it was a pretty toy, but this had been cruelly mutilated. The almost severed head lolled drunkenly to one side, its face crudely painted with a hideous grin. A deep incision in the throat oozed a dark red, sticky substance that had dripped onto the pillow.

"Dear God," he muttered, and turned away. Susan hadn't moved. Placing his hands on her shoulders, he said. "It's only a doll Susan." He shook her gently at first, then more firmly. She couldn't seem to tear her eyes away from the pathetic toy. "Look at me." He spoke louder. "Look at me, damn it!"

Suddenly she sobbed. "Why is this happening...?"

"I don't know." He sounded angry. "Come on, let's get out of here, we'll worry about your things later."

Bob was in his front garden when they pulled up. Calling Shona he went to greet them.

Mark said, grim-faced. "I think you'd better call Jack again, someone's broken into the cottage."

Without a word Bob went into the pub. "Joan, you'd better go out to Susan, the lass looks as if she's just about reached the end of her rope." He looked around. "Can I use your phone?"

For the second time that day Jack Witchell paced the floor in Joan's sitting room. He didn't like the way things were going at all. "Mark, did you touch anything - leave your prints anywhere?"

"Probably, the front door handle for sure, and possibly the stair rail."

"Nothing in the bedroom?"

"Definitely not, as soon as I saw it I just got her out of there."

"Hmm. It wasn't blood on the doll's neck you know, I'm pretty sure it was nail polish, the face as well - that awful grin. I suppose it could have been lipstick though. Either way it looks as if it was all Susan's stuff, the dressing table was a bit of mess."

"The doll's hers as well." Mark told him. "She says she's had it since she was a baby. One of those things you keep forever."

Jack rubbed his temples wearily. "We're dealing with a maniac for sure. I meant what I said this morning; I don't want her left alone for a minute. Where is she now?"

"In bed, sleeping I hope. The doctor gave her a sedative."

"Oh I almost forgot." Joan made them both jump. "I rang Maude, Susan asked me to. It seems she promised to go and help her with the garden today and didn't want her to worry. Now of course she's worried to death, so I said you'd go and fetch her Mark, I hope you don't mind?"

"Of course not, I'll go now."

Maude was waiting at the gate with Robbie. "You took your time young man." She settled herself firmly in her seat. "Now, I want to know exactly what's been going on, and no pussy-footing around - I got enough of that from Joan."

In spite of everything Mark found himself smiling.

"Maude, you're priceless."

CHAPTER TWENTY ONE

Anybody else would simply walk away and let the village return to its former state. It would be easy enough; all he had to do was say he'd changed his mind. Lionel wouldn't be too happy, and he could just imagine the sort of ridicule and abuse Richard would hurl at him, but that would be a small price to pay to be rid of the guilt he felt.

None of them blamed him, he knew that - they didn't need to, he was doing just fine all by himself. His thoughts kept returning to the day he'd arrived in Carlton - peaceful, quiet, a place where nothing ever happens, that's what he'd thought - how wrong could you get! Maybe it would be best to just go, and take Susan with him. Between them, her looks and his interference, they had created mayhem.

"This really is too much....it has to stop!" Maude's voice, strident as ever, brought him back with a bump.

"What - sorry?"

"We've got to do something Mark, that is, if you can tear yourself away from examining the carpet."

"The carpet?"

Clearly losing patience, she glared at him. "You've been studying the pattern on it for twenty minutes and, fascinating as it may be, there are more important things to dwell on."

"Sorry, I was thinking. What did you say?"

"I said, don't you think we should do something?"

"About what?"

"Oh for heaven's sake, about Susan of course."

"Oh, right - what do you suggest?"

Mark discovered what was meant by a withering look. Maude's eyes positively bored through him. "Let me know when you've finished thinking Mark, and maybe we'll get some sense out of you." She turned away from him. "Now Joan, you're right of course, on no account must Susan be left alone. Is she asleep?"

"She was when I looked in half an hour ago."

"In that case," Maude got to her feet. "I'm going over to the shop, there are one or two things I need and I might as well do it now. Can I get you anything?"

They both looked at her in amazement. Shopping at a time like this? Joan shook her head. "No thanks, Maude."

When she'd gone, Mark and Joan sat back, glad of some peace, but it was to be short-lived. George pushed the door open and announced. "Kathleen's in the kitchen, shall I bring her in?"

Joan sat up with a start. "Oh Lord, someone's got to tell her about Mary - and Helen."

"Well, don't look at me," Mark jumped to his feet. "You do it Joan, you're much better at this sort of thing, anyway I'd better go and check on Susan."

He returned to the lounge an hour later and flopped on the sofa. "She's still sleeping. How did Kathleen take the news?"

"We had a few tears, but on the whole she wasn't too bad. She was far more upset about Helen than I expected her to be, though. Apparently she befriended the girl after her father died and they subsequently got very close. It was Kath who persuaded her to get away from Carlton and make a new start. She said Helen had always kept in touch, and she couldn't understand why she hadn't heard from her lately."

"Well that's another mystery solved then. Steven said Helen wanted to see a friend in Carlton, someone who helped her a lot when she was a child. Must have been Kathleen. Is Maude still at the shop?"

"No, she came back to leave her shopping and now she's gone up to see Blanche Armitage. She's up to something, but I'm blessed if I know what."

"I expect she'll tell us eventually." Mark rose, intending to join George in the bar.

"Oh no you don't, you just sit there a minute." Joan's voice had a firmness to it he hadn't heard before. "Now, are you going to tell me just what's going on in that head of yours?"

"What do you mean?"

"Earlier, when you were so absorbed in the pattern of my carpet - and don't give me that look of pure innocence either. You were miles away and, it has to be said, you looked as if you wished you were."

Returning his attention to the carpet, he tried desperately to think of something to say - and couldn't.

"So I was right," she said more gently, "You were thinking of leaving."

"Yes."

"I thought so. But you've changed your mind again, haven't you?"

He stared at her. "Have I?"

She smiled. "Of course you have. You couldn't possibly go without seeing it through, and you know it. I know you think all of this is your fault, but you're wrong. Susan is the main factor here, not you. Her likeness to Christie, the effect of it on Mary, the break-in at the cottage, and even the attack on Lexer - all this would have happened whether you were here or not. Quite frankly, I for one am very glad you are here, and I think I'm right in saying Susan is too." Before he could respond to all this, she placed a gentle hand on his shoulder. "Go on, go and have that drink with George, and stop brooding." She turned to leave him, then at the door, paused to stare at the carpet. "Funny - it's never had that effect on me."

Beads of perspiration glistened on her forehead. She struggled to free herself from the heavy weight on her chest - can't breathe, it hurts and - my legs won't move. She heard a cry and tried to sit up - if she could just move her shoulders. Something held her down, pressing hard on her chest - hot breath fanned her neck. Her eyes felt heavy, as if weighed down. Someone had told her once they put weights on your eyes when you're dead, to hold them shut. But I'm not dead - can't they see that?

Suddenly her eyes opened, but the darkness blinded her. Oh dear God, they've buried me - I'm buried alive! She sensed movement, somewhere above a draught of warm air wafted over her, it came and went like something swinging pendulously to and fro. Back and forth it went, like heavy breathing - panting, if only she could see. It was getting nearer, closer and closer to her face, as it swung in an arc over her head. From side to side it went, first left, then right - left, her head swayed in time, right - left. Abruptly it stopped, directly above her, a luminous sphere suspended in the darkness. A twinge of terror shot through her body, but still she couldn't move. The dolls severed head hovered over her, grinning hideously, eyes bulging in the tortured face while blood dripped from its neck. Without warning, it altered its path. Now it reeled away from her. Tendrils of hair, matted with blood, flew out like tentacles towards her, then back it swung again, its insanely grinning face almost touching hers. She tried to move her head away, but an icy hand held her down. The grotesque head widened and split, almost into two, as the mouth opened – and then it screamed, a sound so dreadful it seemed to echo in her ears, all around, enveloping her. Must get away - someone held her shoulders. Please let me go... The screaming grew louder, almost deafening in its agony....

"Susan! Wake up."

"Shall I get the doctor?"

"No wait, I think it's only a nightmare."

Someone tried to shake her - couldn't they see it was useless - couldn't they see she was dead? The screaming stopped, someone lifted her, and she heard a whimper. Lexer! Oh please, don't hurt him... Suddenly a voice penetrated the confusion, a voice she knew.

"Susan! Wake up this minute! Do you hear me?" The voice, stern at first, subsided to a calming whisper. "There, there, it's all right, it's only a dream."

She was sitting up, her head on Maude's shoulder. The old lady rocked her gently as she sobbed. "That's right, my dear," she crooned. "You have a good cry – it'll do more good than anything else."

"Who was screaming?" she asked at last.

Maude smiled. "You were - you frightened the life out of us."

Susan was aware of Joan and Mark standing in the doorway. "I couldn't move... there was something heavy on top of me, it was awful."

"That was Lexer." Joan spoke now. "He was frightened, I think."

"That was some nightmare." Mark moved to the other side of the bed. "We heard you down in the kitchen. You've never seen such chaos, we three collided with George coming out of the bar, then the four of us tried to get up the stairs at once."

Susan began to laugh, more from relief than anything else, but it seemed to set them all off. George arrived to find the four of them in a state of hysterical collapse. "Come on, boy," he signalled to the dog, "you'd best come downstairs with me. They've all gone barking mad up here."

CHAPTER TWENTY TWO

Susan checked her watch. Six thirty, it was still too early to go downstairs. Standing at the bedroom window she watched the rain splash onto the roof of her car. Thank goodness Mark had collected it from Rosemoor last night, without it her plan would never work. She glanced across the street to the shop. Eve was the most important part of this. Susan had sown the seed in the shopkeeper's mind in the bar, just before closing time last night. All she had to do now was let the woman do what came naturally to her.

She spent the next hour checking and re-checking; nothing must go wrong. Of the five of them Joan would be the easiest to deal with, it was Maude and the three men that posed the biggest problem but, quite unwittingly, the old lady had cleared the way with one simple remark.

"Why don't the three of you come up tomorrow afternoon and sort out the furniture for the cottage?"

Feigning indifference, Susan had held her breath while they debated the possibilities, but she needn't have worried - Maude had insisted. Susan smiled; how it would annoy the old lady if she knew!

All she had to do now was get through the morning without arousing suspicion, and think of an excuse to leave the pub after lunch. This last phase of the operation bothered her most - getting out was one thing, getting out alone was quite another.

The solution to the problem revealed itself around mid morning. She was helping Joan prepare lunch when the door burst open. A sudden gust of wind whipped around the kitchen as Kathleen Abbott almost tumbled in. Throwing her hood back she laughed. "I'm like a drowned..."

The two women stared at each other in astonishment. Susan knew who she was immediately. "You must be Kathleen," she said pleasantly. "I hope I'm not too much of a shock for you?"

Realising she was gaping, Kathleen managed to smile. "It's amazing, I'm glad Mark warned me though, if I'd bumped into you in the village I'd - well I don't know what I would have thought."

"Is she that much like Christie then?" Joan took her dripping raincoat.

"Yes, in a way. Of course, Christie was just a child but I imagine she would have grown up to look much like Susan." She studied the girl critically. "Christie's hair was a lighter colour, but it would probably have darkened as she got older anyway. Oh I'm sorry, I'm staring. I don't mean to make you feel uncomfortable."

The two women talked until Kathleen insisted she had to leave. "I'd better get back ... Look, why don't you pop over this afternoon, Susan? I've got some photographs that might interest you. Come about three o'clock, Jim will be busy in his shed by then. I don't want to be rude but I don't think he should see you just yet, not until I've had plenty of time to prepare him anyway."

Susan agreed readily. This was just the excuse she needed. Of course there was always a chance that when she didn't turn up Kathleen might come looking for her, but by then it would too late - it would all be over.

Shortly before the pub shut for the afternoon, Susan went to her room to get things ready and to await the men's departure. As the time for action drew near she felt the first twinge of unrest. This had better work - all she needed was one look at his face, and to do that she'd have to be alone.

While she was pacing the floor of her room, a conversation that would have certainly halted her plans was taking place in the lounge downstairs.

Bob peered around the lounge door. Mark was engrossed in writing. "Psst!" He tried to get his attention.

"Psst... Mark," he whispered.

Startled, Mark looked up. "What's up?"

"Where's George?" Bob asked, still whispering.

"Right here." George boomed behind him.

The man nearly jumped out of his skin. "Don't do that, you fool." Bob put his hand on his chest. "You could have given me a heart attack!"

"Well, what are you whispering for?"

"Because I don't want the women to hear of course." He grabbed George's arm. "Get in here." He pulled him into the lounge and closed the door. "I've just had a call from Jack - things have started moving. Young Steven Wade has sent him a sort of diary that he found among Helen's belongings."

"What do you mean, a sort of diary?"

"Jack says it's more like a story, reckons the girl was trying to write a book about her life."

Mark was all ears. "This is interesting, did he give you any idea what she's written?"

"No, he says it's all scribbled in longhand, and most of it's illegible. A handwriting expert is trying to sort it out and, with a bit of luck, he'll have a typed version later today." Bob pulled a face. "I've got a feeling he knows who it is now, but I couldn't get it out of him. All he would say was, if things went as he expected, he would be coming to Carlton later this evening."

"To bring the journal?"

"I think it's to make an arrest."

At last it was time. Susan appeared in the kitchen dressed for a deluge.

Joan put her iron down. "Goodness me, you're not taking any chances, are you?" She studied the Wellingtons and heavy waxed jacket. "Kath only lives across the lane, dear."

"I know." Susan tied her hood firmly under her chin. "It does seem a bit excessive, but seeing how wet Kath got this morning, I thought I'd be prepared." Susan opened the back door. "I'll see you later Joan."

Praying it would start, she ran to the car. People had been around her all day and there'd been no opportunity to try it. The engine roared into life, first turn of the key.

Silently giving thanks she pulled out of the drive as slowly and quietly as the little car would allow. The next worry was, would it get up the hill and was the footpath wide enough? Wishing she'd checked that before, she eased her way slowly up the lane to the junction. Here she paused for a moment, to debate whether or not to make a quick detour to Rosemoor. No, best not, she decided, better stick to the original plan. Turning left onto the footpath she was immediately struck by how narrow it was. This wasn't going to be as easy as she'd thought.

Keeping the car in first gear she nosed it through the narrow gap, holding her breath as branches from the hedgerow brushed against the windows on each side. The rain was heavier now, or so it seemed. The sharp pattering on the roof and the monotonous click of the wipers somehow emphasised the gravity of what she was doing. All she needed now was a crack of thunder and she had the makings of a Hammer Horror movie. At the top, where the path was wider, she switched off the engine and looked to either side. To the right, the woods where she'd found Helen's body, to the left, the church. For several minutes she sat trying to ignore a twinge of foolishness. It was quite possible that she could sit there all afternoon and have nothing happen. How would she explain her actions to Joan? She switched the engine on so she could use the wipers - if she could just see who it was, there would be no need for explanations. Peering through the rain she stared at the desolate ruin while drumming her fingers on the steering wheel. "Come on... come out if you're in there." She stared at the doorway, where nothing moved except the rain dripping from the lintel. Of course it was possible that Eve hadn't done her bit. Susan had put great faith in the assumption that the woman could keep nothing to herself. It would be too ironical if Eve had suddenly developed a conscience. Susan released a pent sigh of impatience. It was no good; she'd have to get out. If she left the car unlocked she would be able to run back, get in quickly, then at the push of a button, lock herself in. Better still, turn the car round ready for a quick getaway.

Carefully making her way along, she neatly side-stepped puddles and the door lying awkwardly across the path. At the entrance she stopped. If someone were inside they would expect her to come in this way; there must be a back door. Edging her way round to the right of the porch and keeping close to the wall, she trudged the length of the building, wincing at the sound of her boots squelching loudly on the sodden grass. Rain ran down her face and into her eyes and for the first time she seriously doubted her sanity. Maybe this was foolhardy - supposing he could hear her? He might be waiting at the back, so she'd better be ready to run - but supposing she fell? But no one was waiting; there was nothing but a gaping hole in the wall where a door had once been. She peered in cautiously, the room was empty, a door in the far wall, shut. "Oh God, this is madness." Taking a deep breath she tiptoed across the stone flags.

Rivulets of rain-water ran off the waxed coat, leaving a trail of dark, damp stains in the dust. At the door she stood still, listening for the slightest sound. Aware of nothing but an eerie stillness and the sound of her own heartbeat, she pulled the door slowly towards her. It creaked loudly in the silence. She gasped, feeling her heart thudding painfully in her chest. Stupid, stupid! She mouthed the words silently. What did you expect - oiled hinges? Her eyes scanned the large, bare room - there was nothing. Then, suddenly, she sensed rather than saw a movement on her left. Turning quickly, she saw the door which, unbeknown to her, led to the kitchen. That's odd - she hadn't noticed it before, was it open when she came in? Surely she wouldn't have missed that?

While she was debating this, the door moved fractionally... or did it? Yes, it moved again. Suddenly she was frozen with fear. Oh God! - The door swung back, crashing loudly against the wall. At first she thought she was looking at a mirror image of herself, the figure in the doorway was dressed identically, green waxed coat and Wellingtons, the only difference was the hood, left untied it fell forward completely shadowing the face. They stood facing each other for what seemed a long time, and then with great speed the figure took a step forward - it was then she saw the glint of steel.

Susan stifled a scream, then, before she had time to think, began running through the church to the front door. As she went through the doorway she glanced behind her, the figure stood motionless near the stage, the knife clearly visible in the right hand - and something else in the left. Her breath caught in her throat - how could she have been so stupid? She watched, petrified, as the hooded figure raised its arm - dangling from the bony fingers were her car keys!

Spinning on her heel, she made a dash for the car. Please, let it be open. She grabbed the handle - it opened easily. Whoever it was might have had the sense to take her keys but not to lock the door. Kneeling on the driver's seat panting, she rummaged frantically in the glove compartment for the can of hair spray she'd brought with her. Suddenly the whole thing seemed ridiculous - what on earth was she thinking about? This wasn't some mugger on the streets of London; this was a crazed murderer hell-bent on making her his next victim. She'd brought the can with her, intending to spray it into her assailant's eyes, but now, in the midst of panic, logic somewhat belatedly, surfaced. If she got close

153

enough to use the spray, she would certainly be close enough to be stabbed. Looking up, she saw the figure coming out of the gate. She had to run, but not to the woods - certainly not there. Back to the village, yes - and if necessary, screaming blue murder all the way.

She started running. "Help... help!" She looked behind her; the figure was running now - and to her horror, gaining ground. She tried to quicken her pace but the rain had turned the path into a river of mud. She looked back again, and then - the thing she'd most dreaded - she fell.

She struggled to her knees but something hard thudded against her shoulder - then her face was in the mud. She tried to raise her head but a searing pain in her shoulder almost made her black out. Suddenly her head was jerked sharply back, someone had hold of her hair - then she felt herself being lifted backwards, onto her knees, as an arm wound round her neck and forced her chin up. She tried to turn her head, if this was to be her last moment she wanted to know who this evil creature was, but her eyes were caked with mud.

Just as in her dream, they felt weighed down, she could see nothing. The murderer's head must be very close, she could hear the rasping breath - then the voice.

"There, there, it'll be all right. Open your eyes, my darling, let me see them one last time." The voice, barely a whisper, was almost caressing. "Why did you come back Christie?" The breathing grew more rapid. "There's no place for you here - or for Helen..." The voice grew louder. "She knew, you see." The hand gripping her hair tightened as the pressure on her neck eased. "Open your eyes." he commanded. "Look at me and remember..."

With a supreme effort, she forced her eyes open to see the blade of the knife, glistening with droplets of rain and blood - her blood. She tried again to turn her head, wanting to see him too, but he held her too tightly, she was forced to stare as the skeletal hand raised the knife in the air, the tip pointing towards her throat. "Go back Christie, you must go back - Oh God, forgive me!" She watched in horror as the fingers tightened around the hilt, then closed her eyes, awaiting death. Suddenly she was face down - she couldn't breathe, mud filled her nostrils. A deafening noise exploded above her head - odd, she felt no pain. Had she been shot, stabbed - did it matter?

Her head was lifted again, but gently this time.

"Susan? Someone wiped the mud from her lips. "Susan, listen to me - you're all right."

It was that voice again, that dear familiar voice that had saved her from her dream. She spluttered and coughed. "Maude?"

"Yes, it's me." Using her scarf, the old lady tried to clean the mud from the girl's eyes.

"Where is he?

"There." Maude moved aside so Susan could see the body. It lay face down on the path.

"Is he dead?"

"I think so." She stared sadly at the lifeless form. "I would never have believed it if I hadn't seen it with my own eyes."

"Who is it, Maude – tell me?"

"It's Jim Abbott, Christie's father."

Susan stared at the body in disbelief. "I heard a shot - Maude did you ..?"

"Heavens no, I just clouted him over the head, I think he fell onto the knife. The shot came after... that was to let Blanche know. By now she'll have phoned the police, Joan, the men - and probably the rest of the village."

"You and Blanche - how did you know?"

Maude smiled. "I saw your face last night when we were making the arrangements for the furniture. I knew you were plotting something, and it had to be today. I've been sitting in Blanche's cottage since mid morning."

"But you're supposed to be at the farmhouse."

"I left Mark a note saying I had to go out, I didn't say where though, in case I was wrong." She watched the blood seeping through the cut in Susan's jacket. "How does your shoulder feel?"

"Oddly enough, it doesn't hurt."

"Hmm. Probably just a flesh wound. It will later." She stood up and looked down the hill. "Ah, here they come now, brace yourself, Susan, we've got some explaining to do."

CHAPTER TWENTY THREE

Jack Witchell faced a silent audience. "This," he said, holding a sheaf of papers out. "is the typescript of Helen Tyler's story. Whether she wrote all this as a personal journal, or whether she intended it for publication, we'll never know." He leafed through the pages. "As you can see, it's very long and much of it has no bearing on what has happened. The first chapter is the most significant and the most poignant." He read aloud:

"My earliest memory is of Christie. During her short life she was to become my only true friend... in death, my torment. I was an unpleasant child, yet - in those early years, she understood me as no one else ever did, or has since. She understood my feelings of inferiority and shyness, even the consuming, impotent jealousy I would feel whenever she had something that I wanted. Her answer to this was simply to give it to me. It was this generosity, together with my greed, that brought about the destruction of my adoptive family. But is that really true? After all this time, I still don't know. Was I responsible for those two dreadful deaths, or is my guilt a product of my mother's insanity?

For the most part my existence has been plagued by feelings of guilt, mistrust, and fear. By writing down the events of my life, I hope, somehow the whole tragic episode will become clear.

My involvement in Christie's death began the day after her seventh birthday. As soon as I saw the pretty gold crucifix her parents had given her, I wanted it. It was no surprise when, on my birthday five weeks later, she gave it to me. It was to be our secret, she said.

'You mustn't tell anyone, mum and dad will be cross and take it back.'

I never wore it, it wasn't necessary. It was enough simply to own it. The delicate piece of jewellery lay at the bottom of a drawer in my room only to be taken out and admired in secret.

Christie's murder and the events surrounding it have never been entirely clear to me, but I remember what I heard and what I saw as if it were yesterday.

I should have gone to the dentist that morning, but Mr Couchman's assistant called to say he was ill. Mum said I could go and play with Christie so, knowing where she would be, I ran up the hill to the woods. I found her, as I knew I would, collecting caterpillars - our favourite game. We would spend hours looking for the pretty furry creatures to see who could find the most, only to let them go before we went home. On this particular day she'd had enough of caterpillars. 'Let's play hide and seek instead.' She said. 'You count to twenty and I'll hide.' She ran off laughing. 'And no cheating.'

That was the last time I saw her alive. I searched for what seemed ages, but in reality, it was probably only five or ten minutes. Eventually I went back to where I'd last seen her; all that remained was her caterpillar jar, which lay on its side empty but for the remains of a lettuce leaf. I remember staring at the church with growing impatience. Surely she wouldn't be in there - we weren't allowed, but it was the only place left to look. I went around to the back of the church feeling frightened, if we were caught I would get the blame - I always did. At last, I plucked up enough courage to go in through the kitchen. What I saw that day has haunted me ever since.

Uncle Jim was kneeling by the stage with Christie in his arms. At first I thought she was sleeping, then I saw the blood on her neck, her shoulders, it was even oozing from the corner of her mouth. All the time Uncle Jim kept talking to her quietly. I tried to hear but I only caught snatches of sentences. 'It's all right - not your fault - that Tyler...'

I was terrified - what had I done, what did he mean? Suddenly Miss Brandon came in carrying a big basket of daffodils. I knew, if she saw me, she would say it was entirely my fault, so I turned and ran out through the vestry and around the side of the church. I remember struggling with the gate, Miss Brandon must have closed it, and the latch was stiff. At last I was out and running down the path to home.

I hid in dad's shed trying to decide what to do. From my hiding place I could hear sirens and bells, people shouting, the village was in an uproar. At last, when it was quiet, I crept into the house and up to my room. I don't know if I fully realised then that my friend was dead, but I knew something was dreadfully wrong. For comfort I took out the gold crucifix and sat on my bed praying for everything to be all right – and that was how my mother found me.

At first she was relieved that I was safe, she hugged and kissed me - then she saw Christie's crucifix. 'Where did you get that?' She no longer sounded relieved, she was angry and, I think, frightened. She shook me hard and fired questions at me. 'Where did you get it - have you seen Christie today? Tell me the truth, have you seen her?'

I shook my head. 'I couldn't find her.'

'Don't lie to me Helen, where did you get this?' She held the cross in front of me.

'Christie gave it to me.' I sobbed.

For the first time in my life, she hit me, a resounding smack on my face. She was quiet for a long time, then suddenly she spoke. 'Now, listen to me carefully Helen. If anyone asks, you were at the dentist this morning, do you understand?'

I didn't, but I nodded anyway. I just wanted her to stop being angry.

'Even your father,' she said. 'If he asks, you went to the dentist.' She became very quiet. 'We will never speak of this again, never - do you hear me?' She walked to the door very slowly. Her voice sounded strange when she said. 'If you ever tell anyone, Helen, they'll take you away from me and lock you up, remember that.'

Jack paused, all eyes were on him but no one had anything to say. "There's quite a lot in here about the following year in Helen's life," he said. "Apparently her mother became more and more withdrawn, at the same time, her father became more drunk. The only one she mentions with affection is her Aunt Kath." Jack shook his head sadly. "Without Kathleen I don't know how that child would have coped." He flicked through the pages. "This is the next relevant part, it's about her father's death."

"The day my father died is also the day I lost my mother forever. I played truant from school that afternoon, something I did quite often. I avoided the village, for obvious reasons, and spent my time picking wild flowers in the meadow behind our cottage. Often, at these times, I'd pretend Christie was with me, although I never went to the woods again, nor did I look for caterpillars.

It seemed unusually quiet that afternoon - until I heard the shot. I knew instinctively that something dreadful had happened and started to run home. As I got nearer to our back gate, I saw uncle Jim coming out of dad's shed, he was running and almost fell trying to get over the fence. Thinking he might see me, I crouched in the long grass until I saw my mother running down the path. When she went into the shed I jumped up and ran to the gate. I met her coming out. 'I've been sent home early,' I lied.

Mother's mouth opened and closed but nothing came out. She looked strange, very pale, her eyes were staring but she didn't see me.

'Mum! What's wrong?' I cried, but it was useless.

Very frightened, I looked inside the shed. My father was sitting at his workbench, his head hung forward onto his chest. I moved closer quietly, thinking he was asleep, then I saw it, a gaping black hole where his eye had been - and blood splattered over the wall behind him. I ran out to my mother, who stood where I'd left her, still staring, still opening and closing her mouth soundlessly.

Suddenly she looked at me. 'This is your fault Helen... it should have been you.' Those were the last coherent words she ever said to me."

Jack Witchell looked up from the neatly typed pages. His eyes settled on his uncle's face. The look that passed between them spoke volumes. Only Bob would understand his feelings of inadequacy. A brief smile of gratitude touched his lips before he looked away, to the couple who had allowed their home to be used for this meeting. George studied the carpet, deep in thought, while Joan tried, in vain, not to cry.

Jack swallowed with difficulty; the passages from Helen's journal had moved them all. He was glad Kathleen wasn't there. One day, when she was stronger, he would let her read Helen's journal – but not yet

His gaze rested on the neatly tied shoulder-strap supporting Susan's arm, then to Mark who perched protectively on the arm of her chair. They were lucky these two, Susan to be alive, and Mark for not losing her. It was clear to all that this was more than a holiday friendship. Perhaps now their relationship could develop.

Finally he studied the old lady sitting quietly in an armchair by the fire. Their eyes met, his filled with admiration, hers with reassurance. With surprise, he realised she also knew how he felt. She knew of the guilt that had plagued him since the incident at the church. He should have known - could have stopped it.

It was Maude who spoke first. "That's the saddest story I ever want to hear." All eyes were on her. Sitting up straight in her chair she looked at each of them in turn. "But it's over now. It's time to forget."

Jack nodded. She was right, there was no sense in

dwelling on what might have happened. Carefully he placed the papers in his briefcase as the others began to stir. At Joan's suggestion, she and Maude went to make tea and sandwiches, while George made tracks for the cellar. Then Mark suggested he and Susan take Lexer for a gentle stroll along the lane before supper.

Alone with his uncle, he relaxed. No need to put up a front with this man, who knew him so well.

Bob spoke quietly. "She's right you know, lad, it's time to forget - and we will in time."

One by one the others returned, and over supper the first steps towards normality were taken. Nobody mentioned past events, but two members of the group were making silent resolutions. Jack vowed to be more aware, and Mark determined to stick to fiction.

CHAPTER TWENTY FOUR

Sunday 23rd September 1990

"I think it all went rather well, don't you?" Susan stretched out on the sofa. "And it was so nice to see Kathleen again."

"I'm just glad she arrived after the caterpillars. Can you imagine the impact that might have had on her? Whatever was Maude thinking about?"

"Mark, sometimes you're impossible. You're the only one making a fuss about it."

"No I'm not."

"Oh yes you are," she insisted. "And it's not just caterpillars either. Every year, come the autumn, someone only has to mention the woods, the church or those unmentionable furry creatures, and you shoot back to 1984 and relive the whole sorry story."

Looking remarkably like his four-year-old son when scolded, Mark said nothing. What she said was true but he certainly wasn't going to admit it.

"Why can't you get beyond it Mark?" She asked at last. "Nobody would argue that it was a dreadful time, but it's over, and has been for six years."

"For the rest of you maybe." He looked directly at her. "I wish I could explain it, Sue, it's something that's always there, unfinished and incomplete."

"Are you talking about the situation, or that wretched book?"

"Both." He smiled ruefully. "Sometimes I think, if only I could write that last chapter I'd be free of it, but I've just never come up with a suitable ending."

Susan sighed. "I simply don't understand. Of all the books you've written, 'The Carlton Murders' is the only one based entirely on fact, so why try to manufacture an ending -

what's wrong with sticking to the truth?"

"In this case the truth was too - sudden. There was no aftermath, no explanations. Oh let's drop it, just thinking about it gives me a headache."

"I suppose you could always talk to Kathleen." Susan persisted. "After all, the last chapter should be hers, don't you think?"

"I agree." Maude came into the sitting room. "Especially as she's in the process of exorcising the past, but you'll have to look sharp, she's only staying with Jamie for a week or so."

"Jamie? I thought she was staying with you?"

Maude stared at him in exasperation. "Sometimes I wonder why I bother. I told you yesterday, I met Jamie in Ashbridge last week. He's married now and lives there with his wife."

"I thought he was in the RAF?"

"He had to come out, something to do with a back injury. I'm sure I've told you all this."

"You haven't – really Maude, I'd have remembered."

The old lady looked as if she didn't believe him. "Well, anyway, Kathleen lives in Derby now with Rebecca. She's doing very well for herself according to Kathleen, she's qualified and has a good job in a salon there."

Susan interrupted. "It was me you told all this to Maude, I don't think Mark was there."

"Oh." Maude looked confused. "In that case, I'm sorry Mark, I must be getting forgetful in my old age." She stood up. "Actually I'm feeling a bit tired, I'll just go up and say good-night to Tim, then I'll be off."

Susan waited until the door closed, then said. "I'm starting to worry about her, you know. She seems so preoccupied all the time."

"I know, she hasn't been herself for weeks. I think it's to do with this forthcoming funeral. The whole thing has got her down. Mind you, it's hardly surprising. This will be the third funeral she's had to attend in as many months. I suppose when you reach a certain age it's all you can expect, but it must be damn depressing watching your friends pop off one by one. Having said that, this one is a bit different."

"In what way?"

Mark looked surprised. "Hasn't she told you?" Susan shook her head. "This one was suicide."

"Are we talking about the same funeral – over in Ashbridge?"

"Yes, it's that woman she used to work with, Eleanor Mayling."

"Good heavens, suicide! I wonder why Maude didn't mention it?"

Mark shrugged. "The state she's in at the moment, she probably thinks she has. The trouble is, Maude won't believe it - she reckons there's something suspicious going on."

"Did you know this friend of hers, Eleanor?"

"I only met her once, when I took Maude over to Ashbridge last Christmas. You must remember, that dinner she went to at the vicarage?"

"Yes, I remember. At least, I remember all the fuss we had about what Maude was going to wear. What was she like?"

"Eleanor Mayling? I liked her. She was like a younger Maude, you know - no nonsense."

"What about her family?"

"There's only Alex, her son. He was working abroad when it happened. What a shock he must have had! Anyway, I've told Maude I'll drive her there tomorrow, do you want to come?"

Susan heard Maude coming down the stairs. "We'll talk about it later, let's not upset her again."

Later that evening, when Maude had gone, Mark broached the subject of Kathleen again. "What did Maude mean, Kathleen's exorcising the past?"

"Precisely that. Now she's come to terms with what happened, she feels she can face people again."

"Surely she didn't think anyone in Carlton blamed her for what her husband did?"

"I think she did. It's sad really, in different circumstances, she and I could have become good friends. I tried to persuade her not to leave Carlton, did you know that?"

"No, when?"

"Shortly after it all happened. I went to her cottage. We had quite a long talk but nothing I said could deter her. I remember she was very confused about things. She said she accepted that Jim was responsible for what happened to me, but she would never believe that he murdered Christie or Helen."

"Really? But she must have read Helen's account of it in that journal, didn't that persuade her?"

"Apparently not. Anyway, she said she knew that everyone in the village believed it was Jim and that was why she had to get away. I suppose she couldn't face people, and she did say she would always feel partly responsible for Jim's actions against me."

"Well, that's ridiculous."

"I know, and I told her so, but she said every time she looked at me she would remember how close I'd come to being killed. I can understand it in a way, she needed to start a new life, get away from the memory of it all - me, Christie, Helen - everything."

"So today was the first step. Do you think she wants to come back here to live?"

"Not to Carlton, maybe somewhere nearby, where she won't feel so cut off. But first she has to lay the ghost."

Mark looked at her dubiously. "Yes, but which one?"

CHAPTER TWENTY FIVE
Ashbridge
Monday 24th September 1990

"Which one is Alex Mayling?" Mark whispered.

Maude inclined her head towards a young man standing quietly by the side of the grave. "I'll introduce you later, when we get back to the house." She took his arm. "Come on, let's go, perhaps if we move off the others will follow. I suspect Alex might like a moment or two alone."

Mark watched him curiously as they walked away. On the surface Eleanor's son appeared unmoved by the occasion. "He seems very calm," he remarked.

"Don't be fooled by his outward appearance." Maude urged him away. "There will be a lot more going on beneath the surface than you can possibly imagine. Alex, like his mother, will do his crying in private."

In fact, Alex Mayling was experiencing a strange kind of detachment, as if he were watching the whole performance on an ill-lit stage. Oh that he were, that presently the final curtain would fall, and he would rise from a moquette-covered seat, buttocks numb, knees stiff, and leave the smoke-filled theatre to join the real world outside.

He grasped a handful of soil; it felt dry and slightly gritty as it slipped through his fingers. The hollow rattling as it fell on the coffin made him wonder, irrationally, if she really was in there.

Lines of concentration formed deep crevices across his brow as he stared intensely at the casket. Suddenly he wanted to look inside - he needed to see her – make sure that it was his mother. He knelt to study the brass plate that adorned the lid. Six feet down and shadowed from the autumn sunlight he could still see the boldly etched inscription. Alex closed his eyes. Good Lord, am I going mad, or is this illogical sort of thinking another symptom of grief? Alex knew grief could do strange things to the mind, hadn't he lectured about it often enough? One might feel guilt, anger, and disbelief – well, he could certainly attest to the latter. Oh, he believed his mother was dead, but he couldn't believe she had killed herself. Beyond that, he wouldn't allow himself to think - not yet.

Aware someone was speaking to him, he raised his head to stare into clear grey eyes.

"May I offer my condolences, Mr. Mayling? Eleanor and I were friends, you know." The black-suited gentleman spoke softly.

"I'm sorry, have we met?"

"No, but I've heard so much about you, I feel I know you." He offered his hand. "I'm David Latham, I was your mother's doctor."

"Oh I see. I didn't know she was seeing a doctor, or that she was ill." Now the guilt, Alex thought - I suppose he's going to tell me she'd been ill for years, and hadn't told me.

"She wasn't, I mean she wasn't ill, that's why it was such a shock." The doctor put a reassuring hand on Alex's arm and glanced around. "Look, we must talk sometime, about Eleanor. Not now though, people are beginning to move off. I'll call you"

The Reverend Cross came to Alex smiling sympathetically. "Alex, my dear boy, it's a sad day. How are you coping?"

"Oh, I'm all right." Alex tried to smile, and thought, I suppose I'll have to listen to this sort of thing all afternoon. Of course I'm sad, what do people expect? Damn fools! Christ - now the anger. He felt his jaw tighten as he forced himself to say. "Thank you Reverend, that was a lovely service." As the white-haired man walked away, Alex tried very hard to subdue his seething emotions. Lovely - what was he saying? How could it possibly be lovely watching one's mother being lowered into the ground – ridiculous! Oh dear, he really must stop this.

Watching the mourners leave he knew he was in no fit state to deal with the inevitable gathering at the vicarage, not just yet anyway. Hannah would cope, she always did.

The vicarage was all that remained of the original village church and buildings and had once been the home of his grandfather, John Wakely the vicar of St. Michaels. Built in the early part of the fourteenth century, the church itself no longer existed. Having suffered severe damage through several wars it was eventually pronounced unsafe and razed in 1920. A new church, with a smaller vicarage had been built at the southern end of Ashbridge. One very important reason for the relocation was to extend the graveyard. The original had become overcrowded and funerals were rare. Only the occasional addition to a family plot brought mourners to this small, but beautifully maintained burial place. Fortunately the old vicar, using his wife's money, had been able to purchase the vicarage and convert it to a private residence. Both Alex and his mother had been born there

Separated from the vicarage garden by only a small copse known as Folly Wood, the graveyard had become part of his play area as a child. It had always struck him as odd that his mother didn't mind him playing among the graves, but absolutely refused to allow him to enter the copse. He wandered among the ancient gravestones studying the familiar inscriptions until he'd achieved a measure of calm.

He reached the gate that led to the road. Nothing much had changed while he'd been away, maybe one or two new inscriptions on family gravestones, but the one that had fascinated him most as a child was just the same. Right on the edge, near the copse, a plain stone cross still leaned crookedly at the head of a tiny mound. There was no inscription and there were never any flowers. Alex had always felt tremendous sympathy for the unknown child beneath and, on occasion, had robbed the vicarage garden of a few blooms to lay there. Today, the sight of the solitary cross saddened him more than ever. Offering a silent promise to bring flowers next time he turned back to the house.

Feeling guilty, he quickened his pace when he reached the drive. Hannah would forgive his truancy, but he could not. Poor Hannah, it was easy to see how his mother had come to rely on her so much, now he was doing it himself. As he understood it, Hannah had lived at the vicarage since his parents' marriage and, since his father's disappearance the women had become very close. In all Alex's twenty-seven years he'd never thought of her as anything but a member of his family.

The lounge at the vicarage was large by anybody's standards, and today it was full. Alex stood in the doorway scanning a sea of unfamiliar faces and realised he was completely out of touch with his mother's life, her friends and her activities.

Somehow he got through the afternoon, smiling and mumbling polite responses until the crowd began to disperse. As the last few stragglers made their way to the door he spotted an elderly woman sitting in a chair by the window, talking to a young man in his early thirties. Alex had never seen him before but the woman reminded him of his mother. He watched as she rose from the chair, then moved towards her assuming a polite smile, ready to say for the umpteenth time, 'Thank you for coming.' But she saved him the trouble.

"Alex, dear, I really think that now it's all over, we could do with a nice cup of tea." Then, seeing his puzzled expression, added. "Of course, you don't remember me, do you?" Her eyes twinkled impishly.

Something about her bearing, her voice - long-forgotten memories of his childhood... "Aunt Maude?"

The old lady smiled. "Oh you do remember, good, that

saves a lot of explaining. Alex, this is a friend of mine, Mark Jordan. He very kindly drove me here today." The two men shook hands then Maude took Alex's arm. "I should think you've had quite enough by now dear but," she paused for only a second. "I really can't accept this business of suicide."

Mark, quite unprepared for this, interrupted quickly.

"Maude, I don't think..."

"Mark, will you leave this to me?" The old lady threw him a stern glance. "If you're offended by my bluntness Alex, I'm sorry but, unless I'm very much mistaken, you won't believe it either."

Alex looked from the discomfort on Mark's face to the grim determination on Maude's and, for the first time that day, smiled with genuine warmth. "Thank God, at last someone who really knew her. Everyone else seems to have simply accepted it."

As they crossed the hall to the kitchen the doorbell rang. Alex opened it to find a man in his early sixties anxiously clutching a wreath. "I hope I'm not intruding, I wanted to pay my respects."

Alex stood back. "Come in. I'm afraid everyone else has gone, but you're welcome..."

"Oh no, I just wanted to put this on her grave. I can't tell you how sorry I was to hear about Eleanor. I've been away and only heard about it this morning."

"You were a friend of hers?"

"Yes, well sort of, my name's Tom Field." He smiled at Alex. "You probably don't remember me, you were only about eight or nine when I last saw you. It's been a long time, your mother may have mentioned me?"

Alex shook his head. "I'm sorry, but I hadn't seen my mother for a while. Look, are you sure you won't come in?"

"Yes, but perhaps I could call again - when you're less busy?" The man glanced past Alex to the couple waiting in the hall. "I'll just take this to the grave then." He turned to leave.

"There's a short cut there, through Folly Wood." Alex pointed to a break in the hedge. "It'll save you walking all the way round."

"Yes I know, thanks. I'll see you again then."

Alex frowned as he watched him walk away. "How odd." He closed the door and turned back to his guests. "Seems I'm not the only one with a phobia about Folly Wood, that chap's just taken the long way round." He smiled warmly at Maude. "Come on, let's have that tea."

He watched Hannah and Maude greet each other with raised eyebrows. "You two know each other?"

"Of course we know each other, Hannah's been with your mother a long time." Maude kissed Hannah's cheek.

Alex stared at his shoes. "Yes, and I haven't been around much have I? I barely knew anyone that came today... I feel I've missed a chapter somehow."

"Well, I can soon tell you who everyone is but I don't think you'll find it very edifying." Maude studied him closely. "You don't mind talking about her, do you?"

"Not at all, in fact I'd welcome it, but maybe another time." He looked at Mark. "This must be very tedious for you, especially as you don't know anybody."

Mark smiled. "I met your mother last year, I liked her." He said simply. "This must have been a dreadful shock for you."

"It was, it's the last thing I would have expected."

"You were in the States when it happened, weren't you?"

"Yes, we were on an exchange programme. I'm a prison counsellor."

"Really? How interesting."

Maude was helping Hannah with the tea things. Her voice carried across the room. "Alex, be careful what you say to Mark, next thing you know it'll end up in a book."

Alex raised his eyebrows. "You're a writer?"

Mark gave Maude a withering look. "I wish you wouldn't do that." He scolded. "She does it every time - puts people on their guard."

Alex laughed. "How irritating for you. What sort of books do you write?"

"Crime fiction." Mark muttered. "But only fiction, don't worry I'm not likely to quote you on anything."

Maude snorted loudly. "You've been warned, Alex. Mark has an uncanny knack for coaxing people into telling him their life histories, so if you've any skeletons..."

Alex suddenly stopped smiling. "I don't, but I'm beginning to suspect my mother did."

An uneasy silence followed. Maude, impatient as ever, was the first to speak. "Hannah, you were probably the last person to see Eleanor alive."

"And the first to see her dead." Hannah spoke bitterly. "I found her, you see." She sniffed loudly. "You were going to ask if I'd suspected anything, or noticed a change in her behaviour, well the answer is no. She seemed perfectly normal, ask Dr. Latham, after all he was here that last night."

Alex looked puzzled. "Really? He didn't mention it when I spoke to him earlier. I suppose that's why he said he wanted to talk to me."

Mark cleared his throat. "Er... could I ask - how did she do it?"

"Pills." Hannah told him. "She'd had trouble sleeping these last few months. She said they were just mild relaxants - anyway she took the lot. I found the empty bottle on the bedside table."

"How she did it isn't really important." Maude could see Hannah was getting upset. "The question is why? Did she leave a note?"

"No." Alex answered. "I even checked with her solicitor to see if she'd left anything with him, but she hadn't. Apparently there's only the will and that's relatively straightforward."

"When did she make her will?" Maude asked.

"What's that got to do with anything?" Mark was starting to feel embarrassed by Maude's forthright questioning.

"I should have thought it obvious. If she only made the will recently, or changed its contents, it could mean she'd planned all along to bump herself off."

"Maude!" Mark almost wailed.

The old lady brushed aside his concern. "What do you think Alex?"

Alex shook his head. "I just can't believe she did it on purpose."

Mark spoke quietly. "I suppose someone has to voice the obvious. Unless it was an accident, which seems highly unlikely, and no one can accept suicide - there's only one other possibility."

CHAPTER TWENTY SIX

Unknown to those at the vicarage, Tom Field's thoughts were closely akin to theirs. He'd known Eleanor Mayling since before Alex was born – knew everything about her, or so he thought. He stared at the abundance of flowers surrounding her grave, and pictured Eleanor as she had been when he first met her. Twenty-eight years to the day, almost - could it really be that long? How different things had been then! Driving home on that September night he couldn't have known how the woman he was to meet in such strange circumstances would change the course of his life.

The speedometer touched seventy. That's pushing it a bit, Tom thought. He eased his foot off the accelerator and opened the window. Only another four miles - God he was tired. Stifling a yawn he tried to shake off the drowsiness that had threatened to overwhelm him for the last half hour. He'd become dangerously mesmerised by the endless miles of unlit lanes, with nothing to distract him but the monotonous twinkling of catseyes caught in the glare of the headlights. Impatient to get home, he'd forgone his roadside nap. It was a dangerous thing to do, but Louise would never forgive him if he missed this anniversary. Tom chewed on his lip and increased the pressure on the accelerator. He knew that wasn't true, of course Louise would forgive him – it was forgiving himself that was difficult. Seven years they'd been married, and how many events had she spent alone? The Christmases, birthdays, anniversaries that he'd missed were countless. Ferrying haulage might a lucrative job, but was better suited to a loner, he thought. Someone with no obligations. But they needed the money, and that was the crux of it.

Only two more miles, nearly there. "Jeez!" He slammed his foot on the brake as a dark shadow ran into his path. All eight tyres screamed as maps and papers flew forward into the foot well, together with Harley, his dog. He switched off the engine and grabbed the scruffy mongrel who, still half asleep, tried to get his bearings. "All right boy, stay there."

He'd stopped so abruptly, he couldn't be sure whether he'd hit anything, or not. He rummaged amongst the rubbish littering the cab until he found a torch, and jumped down into the road. At the back of the lorry he walked around, prepared to find something unpleasant. He even crawled on his hands and knees between the great wheels, but, to his immense relief, the road was clear.

That might have been the end of it – he might have continued the last few miles and spent the rest of the evening in the comfort of his home – but Harley had other ideas. As Tom opened the cab door, the dog, thoroughly awake, jumped down and loped off into the woods. Tom sighed with resignation; this was all he needed. "Harley!" he bellowed into the darkness then climbed into the cab and waited for the familiar patter of feet.

Tom drummed his fingers on the steering wheel, Louise would be starting to worry. A glance at the dashboard clock increased his irritation. Nine o'clock - he'd said he'd be home by eight.

Eventually, impatience got the better of him. He reached for his jacket and jumped down, shouting. "Harley! Get back here now, or I'm coming in there after you." He slapped his hand against the door to make more noise. It was then he noticed the blood on his hands. Using the torch he cast the beam across the tarmac. Spots of blood, glistening darkly on the road, formed a steady trail leading into the woods. "Oh, hell!" He must have clipped a fox, or something. "Harley!" He pushed his way through the trees. Stupid name for a dog, he thought for the umpteenth time. "Harley!"

He'd walked about twenty yards from the road when he spotted the wayward mongrel. He was backing out from the bushes with something in his mouth. "What have you got there?" He took the object and held the torch to it. "Where did you find this, boy?" He examined a leather shoe, turning it in the light. It was clearly a woman's, and not very old. Bit of shame really, he thought, it looked like the sort of shoe Louise would wear. He was about to toss it into the bushes, when a sound reached his ears. It was a pathetic noise, a kind of whimper. "Bloody hell! I really have hit something." In spite of the late hour, Tom was unable to bear the thought of anyone, animal or human, left injured and in pain, or worse, dying. He pushed on through the damp bushes until he heard it again. That's not an animal - he stood still, trying to pinpoint the direction of the sound. "Who's there?" He called.

The dog bounded off into the bushes again. "Come back here... " There it was again, this time unmistakable, someone was crying. He moved further on until the beam fell on the huddled figure of a woman. She was on her knees, head bowed, her face obscured by a tangle of dark, unruly curls. She held both arms tightly about herself as she rocked back and forth.

"Are you hurt?" Tom's boots squelched on the damp leaves as he inched towards her. "What's happened to you?" He squatted down and put a hand on her shoulder. She recoiled as if she'd been stung. "It's all right," Tom said. "I'm not going to hurt you - was it you that ran out in front of my lorry?"

"Please don't – please, leave me alone," she sobbed.

"Don't be frightened," he spoke softly. "Who did this to you?" He could see clearly that her injuries weren't the result of a road accident. Her clothes were in tatters. The front of her dress had been brutally ripped apart. There were deep scratch marks on her shoulder, and blood oozed from the corner of her mouth.

Tom took off his jacket and gently placed it around her. She sat, completely motionless, while he shone the torch on her face. He carefully studied the cuts and scratches - and the makings a black eye, and satisfied himself there was nothing life-threatening to worry about. Underneath all this, he saw an attractive woman of about thirty, and realised his initial assessment was wrong. This was no farm-girl who'd had a barney with her lout of a boyfriend. Nor was she one of the girls who pedalled their charms in the city. This was a lady. Even with her battle wounds, she oozed class. "I think I'd better get you to a hospital," he said gently.

She jumped in alarm. "No, no hospital. I just want to get home."

"OK, where do you live?"

"Just through there," she nodded to her left.

"That's the old vicarage, isn't it?"

"Yes, I live there with my - with my husband." She winced as she tried to stand

"Look, perhaps I should go and fetch him?"

"No!" She practically shouted the word. "He won't be in, he's at a meeting."

"Well, somebody must be home?"

She was on her feet and leaning heavily on his arm. "No, there's no one - but I'll be all right, really I will." She tried to walk in the direction of the house.

"Here," he caught her arm. "This must be your shoe."

"Oh, yes it is. Thank you."

"What about your doctor?" Tom persisted. "Maybe you should call him out - just to check you over."

"No, no really." She carried on walking.

He could see there was no point in arguing. "OK, but I'll come with you to your door, which way is it?"

"Here." She moved to her left. "There's a path here."

"What's this, some sort of short cut?"

"Yes, that's it - a short cut. I always use it."

"Did you see who did this to you?"

"No." She walked ahead. "It was too dark. Look we're here now." Tom could see the house lights through a break in the hedge. Suddenly she stopped. "Look, thank you so much for your help, but I'll be quite all right now."

"Well, if you're sure?"

"Yes quite sure - there's just one thing," she looked up at him. "I'd be most grateful - it's my husband, you see, he won't understand."

"What do you mean, he won't understand?"

"My husband is Reverend Mayling." She announced this as if it explained everything. "I'm afraid he has rather Victorian ideas. I shouldn't have been out, you see."

Tom saw very clearly, and wondered why a woman like her was married to a drunken Bible-puncher like him. "Yes, Mrs Mayling, I understand what you're saying. I know your husband. He was the vicar at my wedding - though I doubt he'd remember it." He finished quietly.

Suddenly, she smiled sadly. "Oh dear, well in that case you'll understand why I'd prefer he didn't know about this."

"Don't worry, he won't hear of it from me. My name's Tom Field, by the way."

"And I'm Eleanor Mayling. Look, to save you going through the Folly again, why don't you go out through our front gate?"

"Yes, if I can find my dog, I will. Goodbye."

Tom whistled for Harley, who wasn't far behind, and headed for the road. At the gate he turned to wave farewell, but Eleanor Mayling was nowhere to be seen.

It wasn't until much later that night, having made his excuses to Louise, and been forgiven as usual, that two puzzling thoughts occurred to him. Where had the blood on his hands come from? The scratches he'd seen on Eleanor Mayling wouldn't have produced the quantity of blood he'd seen on the road. And why on earth would she be trudging through the thickly wooded Folly at night, when her front gate was only yards away? And she'd called it a short cut.

The sound of an engine running drew him from his reverie. Glancing quickly at his watch he was shocked to find he'd been staring at Eleanor's grave for nearly half an hour. Taking one last look he turned away. Louise would be wondering where he was. Lengthening his stride he headed for the road, unaware that he was still subconsciously avoiding the Folly.

CHAPTER TWENTY SEVEN

Mark drove slowly through narrow lanes to the north end of Ashbridge. As soon he'd turned onto the main Harold Road, he put his foot down.

"What are you thinking about?" Maude had been watching him for several minutes.

"I was just hoping we weren't a bit too outspoken."

"Hmm." Maude agreed. "Maybe we were a bit, but someone had to say it. After all, if people keep insisting it couldn't be suicide..."

"Yes, but I still wish we hadn't said it aloud."

"We didn't, did we?"

"Well, somebody did."

"Maybe we just thought it."

He glanced across at the old lady. "Did you see Hannah's face?"

"Yes, she was quiet horrified, wasn't she?"

Mark nodded and fell silent again.

The old lady tried to assess his mood. Over the last six years she had come to know him well. She was able to recognise the signs, and could establish when conversation would be welcome and when it would not. Deciding to risk being ignored, she asked. "Are you writing at the moment?"

"No."

"You're dragging your heels a bit aren't you, it's months since you really got into something. What's wrong?"

"Nothing, there are just no new ideas coming through, that's all. I think I've reached my limit as far as crime fiction is concerned."

"Nonsense," she snorted. "You just need a little inspiration."

Mark's jaw set firmly. "No, Maude, don't even think about it. The last time you inspired me it almost ended in tragedy - and left me with an unfinished manuscript."

"I must admit, I'm surprised you haven't laid Christie to rest yet. Do you really believe it's because it's a real life story?"

Mark grimaced. "Not really, that's just my excuse. I never intended it to be absolute fact; I just based it on what happened. Most of it is pure fiction and it's only the ending that's got me stumped."

"What's wrong with the truth?"

"Now you're sounding just like Susan, have you two been talking?"

Maude didn't answer.

"Silly question, eh? Right, well I'll tell you what I told her. In comparison to what I've written so far, the true ending seems rather limp, which means I have to invent a final chapter that lives up to the story without being melodramatic."

Maude looked confused. "Well, as excuses go I suppose it's not bad. A little convoluted, but not bad."

Mark laughed. "Good, because it's the only one you're going to get."

"Do you ever talk to Susan about it?"

"Only in literary terms. We never discuss what actually happened that day."

"Well, I think that's all about to change now Kathleen's returned, don't you?"

"Why should it? I'd imagine it's the last thing Kathleen would want. She's just spent six years trying to get her head around it, why would she want to drag it all up again?"

"Because it's not really over - not for her, anyway."

"So you have been talking to Susan."

"Not at length. She just told me that Kathleen never believed Jim killed Christie." She gave him a sideways glance. "Do you?"

Mark eased off the accelerator, "Oh Maude, do we really have to get into all that again?"

"Not if you don't want to, dear. Mind you, it might just

help you with that last chapter."

"I doubt it, and no, I don't want to get into it again. I really don't think Susan should either - please don't mention it to her, especially now."

"Why ever not? She's pregnant, Mark, not mentally deranged."

"I know that. It's just that she gets a bit overwrought these days, and I don't want her fretting and imagining all sorts of horrors."

"Well that's a strange reversal, it's usually you imagining things." She remained silent until they reached Cherry Lane, then said airily. "Did you know that Eleanor's husband disappeared in rather mysterious circumstances?"

Mark smiled wryly. "Nice try, Maude, but nothing doing." He pulled up outside Crane Cottage. "Fact is something I have to live with every day - fiction is my escape, and that's what I'll stick to."

"We'll see," she muttered quietly, then smiled when she saw Susan coming to meet them. She was secretly quite proud of the part she'd played in the lives of these two young people. It was she who'd helped to bring them together, she who'd suggested this cottage, and she who'd instructed Susan in the art of gardening and helped her transform the once rather neglected little patch into something of a horticultural miracle. The Jordans were her family now, and nobody was more delighted than she that it was expanding.

Susan reached the gate followed closely by her faithful Lexer. At the sound of an excited whine, everyone stood back while Maude braced herself against the gatepost. "Slowly, Max." Susan called in vain to the younger Shepherd, as he raced up the path and hurled himself first at one, and then the other. Satisfied with the greeting, and ignoring all commands, he then scampered away into the cottage and up the stairs.

Everyone took a deep breath, and Maude straightened her hat. "It's like being hit by a tornado," she grumbled, then smiled at Susan. "Hello dear, have we kept you waiting?"

"No, I just wanted to make sure Mark didn't take you straight home. Tim flatly refuses to go to sleep until you've been up to see him." She linked arms with the old lady. "Was it awful - the funeral I mean?"

"Actually, it wasn't. Alex was very calm, and nobody stayed too long, except us. Anyway, how's Tim?"

"Much better, the doctor says it's a sinus infection and gave him some antibiotics. You'd better go up and see him or he'll never get off to sleep."

In the pretty sitting room Mark stretched out on the sofa. "Sorry we were so long, Sue, we got talking."

"It doesn't matter, anyway I had some company. Kathleen was here this afternoon."

"What again? What did she want?"

"Well, now she's broken the ice, she wants to see more of her old friends in the village and asked if I'd go with her. She's still not a hundred percent confident, you know."

"That's hardly surprising, but most of the village were here yesterday - who's left?"

"Eve, for a start, then Blanche, and she wants to try and trace Mary Tyler, although how we'll do that I don't know. Nobody's seen or heard from her since she went into hospital."

"I'm not sure that's a good idea." Mark looked worried. "Mary may not want to see her."

"I thought the same, but I could hardly say that. Anyway, how was Maude? She seems a lot brighter than she was yesterday."

"She's fine."

"Good. Perhaps now it's over she can stop thinking about it."

"I wish," Mark said dryly. "She's doing her best to persuade me to investigate the disappearance of Reverend Mayling, but I rather suspect she's hoping I'll dig something up about Eleanor at the same time."

"Well why not? You've been grumbling about having nothing to interest you. The Mayling family could be the answer."

"Maybe - maybe not. It would be just my luck to find they're all related to the Abbotts."

CHAPTER TWENTY EIGHT

Mark reached the junction at the start of the Harold Road shortly after nine o'clock. Unaware, as always, that he was doing so, he ignored the footpath to his right. He paid no attention at all to the upward-sweeping meadows or the ruined chapel at the top of the hill. Instead he gave his full attention to the lane. With a critical eye, he studied the row of flint-faced cottages on the right hand side. The leases had expired on one or two of them during the last six years, and new owners had moved in – new owners with new ideas. Surprisingly, he had worried more than most about the effect this might have on Carlton, and actually had argued the point about certain proposed changes at the town council meetings. The reward for his efforts had been twofold. The old locals had at last begun to accept him as a fully paid-up member of the community, and the cottages had been saved from certain destruction. Any alterations that had subsequently been made to the buildings had, if anything, enhanced the character of the village.

He paused as he reached Eve Simpson's shop, wondering if for once he could pass it without being seen. Eve and the shop, (impossible to separate the two) were the heart of Carlton. Nothing could happen; nobody could say anything or do anything, without Eve somehow knowing about it first. She was everyone's friend and advisor, and in Mark's case, after a shaky start, his most ardent critic. Today, impatient to see Bob Witchell, he walked quickly past with his head turned studiously away. If he were lucky she would be busy with a customer. He paid great attention to the forecourt of the Royal Oak, and waved cheerily at its blank windows. He had no idea whether George or Joan was inside or whether they could see him waving – he just wanted to look busy.

"Hello, lad." Bob stood back as Mark pushed past. "What's the hurry?"

"Quick, shut the door. I don't want Eve to see me. I really can't face another re-write this morning."

Bob grinned. "She won't be happy until you've named her co-author. Anyway, what are you doing here this early, there's nothing wrong, is there?"

"No of course not. I just wanted a word."

At the kitchen door, Bob stood with his hand on the doorknob. "Are you ready for the onslaught?"

Mark braced himself against the wall. "Hasn't that dog settled down yet?

"She's gradually calming down, but when people call she forgets all her training - ready?"

Two great paws pinned Mark to the wall. "All right Cassie, I'm pleased to see you too." There followed a great deal of grunting and groaning while he wrestled the great Shepherd to the ground where she rolled onto her back kicking her legs in delight. "She's bigger than Shona was." Mark managed to untangle himself at last.

"Aye, and dafter. Come on girl, that's enough." Bob grabbed her collar and led her out to the garden. "How are your two?"

"Lexer's no trouble at all, and quite fit for his age. Max is as bad as Cassie, all legs, ears and energy."

Bob nodded to a large framed photograph on the wall. "I think we kept the best of her pups."

Mark studied the picture of Shona. The dog's beautiful eyes seemed to follow him as he crossed the room. "Yes, but neither of them seem to have her intelligence."

"She was a one-off - still..." Bob cleared his throat. "Now, are you going to come straight to the point or are we to dance around it for half an hour?"

"What makes you think there's a point?"

"Come on - I've known you long enough to recognise the signs. What is it, research for another book?"

"Sort of, but this is a bit different. It's something Maude

said after Eleanor Mayling's funeral yesterday, but don't let her know I'm probing into it or I'll never have any peace. It's something that happened twenty-odd years ago. Something you might have first-hand knowledge about."

"This sounds interesting. What's it all about?"

"Richard Mayling."

"Richard? Oh, you mean the vicar of Ashbridge, Eleanor's husband?"

"Yep. What can you tell me about him - or her? You knew Eleanor, didn't you?"

"In a professional capacity. I had to see quite a lot of her when her husband ran off. I suppose that's what you want to know about?" Bob smiled. "He hasn't come back, has he?"

"No, nothing like that. Maude was going on about Eleanor, wanted me to write a book about her, and naturally she told me about the vicar's disappearance, and well..."

"Your curiosity is aroused." Bob finished for him. "And you want to know what I remember about it all?"

"Exactly. You do remember it then?"

"Aye, I remember it all right, even though it was more than a quarter of a century ago. Funny how I always remember the unsuccessful ones, isn't it?"

"What do you mean - unsuccessful?"

"Maybe I should have said unsolved. We never found him, and not for the want of trying, mind, he'd just disappeared into thin air."

"Did you know the man?"

"I knew of him - that was enough. I don't think too many people were upset about his departure, not even his wife."

"Maude said he drank a lot."

"Like a fish, and he had an eye for the ladies, too."

"So you think he just upped and left of his own accord then?"

"Well, that's what it says on his file, but I have to say it was all a bit unsatisfactory. Most of us thought there was more to it, but we had absolutely nothing to go on. The locals weren't falling over themselves to be helpful either. As I said most of them were glad to see the back of him. I reckon if we'd ever found a body the whole village would have been under suspicion."

"That bad, eh?"

Bob nodded. "Yep, there weren't many he didn't manage to upset in one way or another. He'd turn up drunk at weddings, christenings and funerals. Fell out with most of the local shopkeepers, mostly over unpaid bills. The general feeling was that someone had bumped him off, probably a jealous husband, but with no corpse - we eventually had to abandon it." Bob suddenly smiled. "This is a bit like old times, isn't it?"

"That's what Susan said." He grinned and looked knowingly at the ex-policeman. "I don't suppose...?"

"I could get my hands on the file?" He chuckled. "I'm even finishing your sentences for you again."

"Well someone's got to." Mark pulled out his notebook "Was there any indication that he might have just walked away?"

"There was no indication of anything." Bob began counting off items of information. "Firstly, all his clothes were still there, in the wardrobe where he'd left them. Secondly, his money - still in the bank. Everything pointed to his being dead."

"How long did the investigation go on for?"

"I can't be precise without the records, but it was several weeks as I recall. I know just about every copper in the vicinity was called in, and some of the villagers took part in a mass search of the surrounding area. We had all the dogs out and eventually dug up parts of the garden." Bob shrugged. "There was nothing. Not one clue as to his whereabouts."

Mark chewed on his lip. "Makes me wonder if this is

such a good idea after all. It's twenty-eight years, Bob, nothing new is likely to surface now, is it?"

"Are you sickening for something? It's not like you to give up so easily."

Mark sighed. "I know, but to be quite honest I don't really know where to start, and there can't be many people left who remember anything about it."

"I agree, it won't be easy. But what else have you got to do with your time?" Bob grinned impishly.

"Huh, you're right about that. I think Maude has planted this particular seed because she knows I'm struggling for material at the moment. Susan's getting cheesed off with me mooching about the house – in fact, I'm beginning to think it's a conspiracy between the two of them." He suddenly looked suspicious. "You're not in on it, too, are you?"

Bob chuckled. "Since when did Maude ever let me in on anything? No, of course I'm not. Look, if you fancy having a dig around – count me in. I'll help all I can."

"Right, let's do it then. Even if we come up empty, it might help to get me started again. Where do you reckon we should start?"

"Well, I could give Jack a ring and make some enquiries about the Mayling file. But before we get too carried away, I suggest you talk to young Alex about it. It's his father we're going to be working on, after all. You never know, he might have a few objections about it."

"No need, I spoke to him last night and he's quite keen to help. Mind you, he thinks I'm considering a biography of his mother. How he feels about his father, I don't know. We'll have to sound him out when we get there."

"We?"

Mark grinned. "That's why I'm here. I'm going over to see him this afternoon, do you want to come?"

"Try and stop me!"

"I was rather hoping you'd say that."

Hannah heaved the great oak door open as they pulled up outside the vicarage. "Hello Mr. Jordan, oh..." her smile became curious when she saw Bob. "I'm sure I know you. Now, where have I seen you before?"

Bob advanced a few paces. "The last time you saw me, I was in uniform."

"Of course, you're from Harold police station, aren't you?" From her tone it was clear she was still puzzled.

"Not any more Hannah, I'm retired now. It's been a long time, hasn't it?"

"Great heavens! It's Sergeant Witchell," she announced with a radiant smile. "I knew I'd seen your face somewhere. Yes, it has been a long time, but how very nice to see you again. Come in both of you, Alex is on the phone at the moment, he won't be long."

They followed her into the drawing room. "Did Alex tell you what we're here for?" Mark asked.

Paying unnecessary attention to the cushions on a large, chintz-covered sofa, Hannah answered absently. "He did mention something about a book you want to write - something about Eleanor?"

"That's right. Maybe you will be able to help, as well. You probably know the family better than anyone."

Hannah looked at him blankly. "Don't see that I can tell you much. Nothing very spectacular happens in a little village like this - it didn't to Eleanor anyway. We've lived a very quiet life here Mr. Jordan." She turned to face him. "I really can't think of anything that might be interesting enough for a book."

Mark tried not to look disappointed. He had hoped for a little more enthusiasm. "What about the disappearance of Reverend Mayling? That must have been quite spectacular at the time?"

At fifty-seven, Hannah presented a plump unattractive figure, and was apparently happy to remain so. Fine, mouse-coloured hair, which might have improved her appearance considerably, was allowed to hang limply, cut bluntly to the earlobes in a straight, unbecoming line, which emphasised the heaviness of her jaw. Even her most attractive feature, small but vividly blue eyes, were obscured by heavy, unevenly shaped eyebrows. Now her thin, colourless lips pressed into a tight line of disapproval. "Hardly spectacular, Mr Jordan. For those involved it was tragic."

Mark bit his lip. As usual he'd jumped in feet first. "I'm sorry Hannah, I didn't mean to sound callous. Did you know the Reverend well?"

"As well as one gets to know an employer." She sounded slightly bitter. "I can't say I'm sorry either. Eleanor suffered greatly at that time and I suppose I'm still rather sensitive where she's concerned." She pulled a handkerchief out of her pocket and dabbed clumsily at her eyes.

Feeling extremely uncomfortable, Mark focused on a vase of dried flowers on a table by the window. This was a good start, he hadn't even begun probing, and already there were tears. Relieved to hear the door open, he looked round as Alex came in.

"Hello again." The young man crossed the room directing his greeting at Mark then, turning politely to Bob, held out his hand. "You must be Bob Witchell, I'm Alex Mayling."

Bob shook his hand warmly. "I was so sorry to hear about your mother, dreadful shock."

"Thanks, sit down both of you. I'm sorry I've kept you waiting, I've just had one of my mother's friends on the phone. He wants to come round this evening, says he's got something important to tell me. I must say, he was being very cryptic – didn't want to talk about it over the phone. Do you remember him, Mark? He called when you were here with Maude."

"Do you mean the chap with the wreath?"

"Yes, Tom Field. I must say I'm quite fascinated." Alex

settled himself in an armchair opposite the two men. "Now, what can I tell you Mark?"

"Anything and everything, whatever you can remember, Alex."

Alex surprised them by coming straight to the point. "Are you sure it's my mother you want to write about? I would have thought my father's disappearance would be more up your street?"

Slightly disconcerted, Mark decided there was little point in hedging. "I have to admit it's an intriguing tale - no disrespect, Hannah," he added quickly.

With a disapproving sniff she went to the door. "I'll get the tea."

Alex watched her leave. "Oh dear, it looks as if Hannah's been crying again."

"I'm afraid that was my fault," Mark apologised. "I'd just mentioned your father before you came. I think I was a bit heavy-handed about it."

"Don't let it worry you. I've been treading on eggshells for days, everything I say sets her off."

Mark felt uneasy. "Look Alex, maybe we should leave this until another time, it's a bit soon..."

"Good grief no, I'm only too pleased to talk about things. I'm following my own advice you see. After all, that's what I tell other people to do." He smiled ruefully, "Now I can see first-hand whether it works or not."

"Well, if you're sure, but listen, if you get fed up with us, just say so and we'll push off."

"Agreed. Now, where shall we start? I, for one, am more interested in my father. Years ago I tried a bit of sleuthing myself, but came up with nothing. I suppose it was a bit ambitious to think I could succeed where the police, and everyone else, had failed."

Mark silently agreed he had a point there. For the second time that day he wondered if they had embarked on a wild goose chase. "I thought we'd start by trying to get hold of some old newspapers, Bob and I have planned call in at the library on the way back."

"I've already done that, in fact I think I've still got the cuttings upstairs." Alex rose as Hannah came in wheeling a tea trolley. "I won't be a minute Hannah, I'm just going to get something. Do you know if there are any photos of my father anywhere? I've only got one, and it's not very good."

"Have you looked in the album?"

"Yes, ages ago - there weren't any. Oh well, I might find some among mother's things when I get around to sorting them out."

"Yes, maybe," Hannah said quietly, but Alex had already gone.

Mark watched her as a cat watches a mouse. She was the only one in the room who had known Richard Mayling, and he needed to find a way of questioning her without causing distress. In the end, he said, "I say, these look good Hannah." He looked with admiration at an array of cakes she'd placed on the table. "Did you make them yourself?"

"Yes, they're fresh today. It makes a change to have someone to bake them for. Eleanor was always watching her waistline, and cakes were forbidden fruit as far as she was concerned." She handed him a small plate and napkin. "No fear of that with Alex, though. Of course, I used to do a lot more cooking when he was a baby. We entertained quite a lot in those days. Lately, it used only to be the ladies from the Women's Guild. Eleanor let them hold their meetings here twice a month." She passed him the plate of cakes. "I don't know what they'll do now. I suppose they'll have to go to the new vicarage."

"Thanks." He selected and transferred a chocolate and cream concoction to his plate. "Wouldn't you like to carry on with the Guild yourself?"

"Certainly not. I never had anything to do with it apart

from the catering. Can't be doing with all that business - arranging fetes and jumble sales. Eleanor was very good at that sort of thing, but I'm not." She offered the plate to Bob.

After some thought, Bob selected an iced bun and spoke for the first time "Reverend Cross lives in the new vicarage, doesn't he?"

"Yes, but his wife died some years ago. That's why Eleanor took over organising a lot of the church functions." She smiled rather sarcastically. "I doubt Eleanor's passing will have much effect there though. He'll have plenty of offers of help from the other ladies in the Guild."

Alex came in carrying a large manila envelope. "This is all I could find." He tipped the contents onto the table and sifted through the bits of paper. "Ah, here it is." He picked up a rather battered black and white photograph. "This is my father." He passed it to Mark.

Bob moved nearer to peer over his shoulder. "You don't look much like him, Alex."

"Mother always said I take after her side of the family. What do you think Hannah?"

She studied him critically. "You certainly look more like a Wakely than a Mayling." She craned her neck to look at the photograph. "He was a nice-looking man, though, your father."

"Meaning I'm not?"

"Oh, you know what I mean!"

Mark was the only one who hadn't passed comment. The photograph, taken in harsh sunlight, was hardly flattering. Richard Mayling had probably been handsome in his youth, but deeply etched lines around his eyes and an unattractive puffiness to his skin, indicated too little sleep and too much to drink. "How old was he when this was taken?"

"I don't know - Hannah?" Alex looked at her hopefully.

She thought for a moment. "He must have been about thirty five, I suppose. I can't say for sure."

Mark thought he looked a lot older but said nothing. He placed the photograph with the other papers on the table. "Are these the news clippings?"

"Yes, help yourself." Alex pushed them nearer.

"I didn't know you had these Alex, where did you get them?" Hannah squinted through her tiny eyes trying to read the faded print.

"Some of them came from the library, and Mother gave me the rest, why?"

"No reason." She shrugged. "I thought she'd thrown them all out. They don't tell you much, do they?"

"Unfortunately not." Alex handed the envelope to Mark.

"Here, put them in here and take them with you, if you like. You can browse through them when you have the chance."

"Thanks, I will." He finished his tea. "Well I think we've taken up enough of your time today."

Bob hurriedly swallowed the last of his cake and mumbled an agreement. He wouldn't have minded another but clearly Mark wanted to get away. "That was delicious, Hannah," he managed at last.

Mark got to his feet. "Before I left home Susan insisted that I invite you both to lunch tomorrow, can you come?"

"We'd love to." Alex answered immediately.

Hannah looked disconcerted. "Do you mean me as well?"

"Of course." Mark started to make his way out before she could think of an excuse. "Will twelve o'clock be all right?"

"Twelve will be fine." Alex followed them into the hall, leaving Hannah looking perplexed. "You've made her day," he whispered to Mark, "Mother's friends always excluded Hannah when offering invitations. Much to mother's annoyance, they would insist on treating her as a servant."

"But isn't that exactly what she was?"

Alex shook his head. "Not for years. Mother looked on Hannah as her closest friend. That's probably why Hannah's so distressed. She'll be lost now, without her."

They were almost at the front door when Mark paused to admire an ornately carved gun cupboard. "This is interesting, I didn't see it on the way in." He peered through the polished glass at a neat line of shotguns. "This cupboard must be an antique - and the guns look pretty old, too."

"The cupboard has been here for as long as I can remember. Most of the guns belonged to my grandfather, though I don't think he ever used them. The two on the far end belonged to my father. Apparently he enjoyed hunting."

"There's one missing." Mark indicated a vacant notch in the retaining shelf.

"That's the one he had with him when he disappeared." He lowered his voice. "It seems he went off shooting one evening, apparently his usual practice, and never came back."

"Curiouser and curiouser," Mark muttered, and stepped out onto the porch. His eyes followed the curve of the gravel drive until a cluster of trees obscured it from view. "Alex, that copse over there, is it part of the vicarage property?"

"Yes, funny little place stuck bang in the middle like that. I think it was planted there originally as some sort of boundary between the old church and the vicarage house. Bit of a waste really. I once suggested to mother that she have it all cleared away and incorporate the land into the garden, but she wouldn't hear of it."

Mark smiled. "Well, I imagine this is all yours now, Alex. It's yours to do with as you like."

"That's true, but first I have to convince Hannah."

It started to rain as they drove into Harold. "I suppose you'll tell me what's bothering you before we get home." Mark finally got through to his companion.

"What?"

"You haven't said a word since we left Ashbridge, what's up?"

Bob drew on his lip thoughtfully. "Nothing's up, it's just that one or two things have got the old nose twitching."

Mark waited. "Well, are you going to tell me?"

"I can't be sure until I check the records but, as I recall, nobody ever said anything about a gun before. You'd think it would have been mentioned, wouldn't you? And that I'd have remembered it if it was."

"Well yes, I suppose so, but twenty-eight years is a long time."

"Yep.. I've probably got it wrong."

"There's something else, isn't there?"

"Not much gets past you, does it?" He pulled a face and quickly changed the subject. "Here, I don't remember Susan mentioning anything about them coming to lunch tomorrow?"

"She didn't, but I want her to meet them both. She always senses things in people that I tend to miss. Anyway, I got the distinct impression Alex wouldn't open up all the time Hannah was around him, so Susan can keep her occupied while I talk to him - of course, that's if Kathleen let's her."

"Kathleen?"

"She's been a constant visitor these last few days. She's gradually going round the village, picking up the threads of her old life and taking Susan with her for moral support." He looked across and was surprised to see Bob looking worried. "What's the matter?"

"How long is she staying?"

"Only another couple of days, why?"

"You know what she's up to, don't you?"

"What?"

"She's trying to find Mary Tyler."

"I know that, what's the problem?"

198

"I had a long talk with Kathleen at Tim's birthday party. She accepts what Jim did to Susan, but she's absolutely convinced that Mary's responsible for Christie, Len and, would you believe it - Helen."

"How on earth has she managed to come to that conclusion?"

"Well, as she puts it, she's had a long time to think it all out and has gone over every detail of what happened during those fifteen years, and no matter which way she looks at it, she always comes back to Mary." Bob released a long sigh. "Loath as I am to drag the whole thing into question again, in some ways I think she could be right."

"Oh Christ, here we go again!" Mark muttered under his breath.

"You don't seem very surprised."

"Are any of us? You know as well as I do, none of us could really believe it at the time. Jim did what he did to Susan because he was insane. But he wasn't like that before Christie's death - only afterwards. I have to say, I've often wondered about it. Did we all settle for the obvious six years ago, and make him the scapegoat? Now there's a thought to keep you awake at night."

CHAPTER TWENTY NINE

Lunch at Crane Cottage was eaten in tense silence. Maude did her best to relax the atmosphere, but had to give up in the end. In her opinion, everyone was behaving very oddly. Susan, usually quite relaxed when entertaining, fussed and fiddled around, adjusting this and tidying that until Maude felt like slapping her wrists. Hannah, completely out of place and unpractised in the art of socialising, stared rigidly at her plate and made a production of every mouthful. Bob was the only one who seemed unaware of the tension. He consumed every course with relish, and in silence - unlike Alex, who seemed to be having difficulty just sitting still. Maude got the impression that he'd sooner forget the meal altogether. There was something important on his mind, and he'd burst if he didn't spit it out soon.

Maude eventually turned her attention to Mark and was surprised to find him watching her. Their eyes met - both with the same questioning expression. As usual, their thoughts were perfectly attuned.

As soon as the meal was over, Susan persuaded Maude and Hannah to join her in a stroll around the village. She badly needed some air but, more importantly, she knew Hannah had to be out of the way if Alex was to talk freely.

Both Mark and Bob listened in silence as the young man related all he had learned from Tom Field. The words tumbled out as he told them how Tom had met Eleanor in the woods twenty-eight years ago, and how, over the years, the friendship had grown and extended to include Tom's wife, Louise. He knew all about Richard Mayling's disappearance, and the effect it had on everyone, especially as Eleanor was expecting Alex at the time.

Tom's theory was that the errant vicar, unwilling or unable to face the responsibility of fatherhood, had run off in search of greener pastures. None of this had come as any surprise to Alex, and at first he'd felt a certain amount of disappointment that this big man, Tom Field, had so little information to offer. The bombshell had finally dropped when Tom revealed the secret he'd sworn to keep until Eleanor's death.

Alex discovered that when he was only five years old, his mother had left the village and gone to live in London with Louise. The reason given at the time was that Louise was ill and needed specialist treatment in a London hospital and, as Tom was working abroad at the time, it had fallen to Eleanor to accompany her friend. The truth was quite different, and kept secret from everyone, even Hannah. Eleanor was expecting another child. Louise took her to stay with some relatives of hers in London, and five months later was present when Eleanor gave birth to a girl, Alex's sister. After a great deal of agonising the child was put up for adoption, a decision which left Eleanor racked with guilt and suffering from depression. Louise kept her in London until she'd recovered sufficiently, then they both returned to Ashbridge, and it was never spoken of again.

As Alex reached the end of the tale, Mark tried to assess the young man's state of mind. The news had clearly shaken him but his manner betrayed an underlying excitement.

After nobody had spoken for several minutes, Mark asked. "Why has Tom Field decided to tell you all this now?"

"My mother lodged a letter for him with her solicitor. Her instructions were that it be passed to Tom upon her death. He let me read it. It's largely personal stuff, she thanks them for their friendship and all the help they gave her over the years, and finally she releases them from their promise. Her words were, 'If you think it will benefit Alex to know the truth, you have my permission to tell him.'"

"What about the child's father, does Tom know who it is?"

Alex shook his head. "She never told anyone. Apparently she thought it would serve no useful purpose for anyone to know. Tom said she only spoke to him about it once. It was a few years after it had all happened and apparently mother had somehow found out who had adopted her daughter. She told Tom that she was happy in the knowledge that the baby was being brought up by good people. She even liked and approved of the name they'd chosen for her - Caroline."

"Did this letter you saw give any indication that she might take her own life?"

"Absolutely not, but as I said, it was written years ago."

At last Bob found something to say. "So, Alex lad, you have a sister?"

"Yes." He said. "Now all I have to do is find her."

At last everyone had gone. Susan had made a light supper while Mark walked the dogs then, with Tim fast asleep in bed, they settled in the lounge.

Unable to make sense of his jumbled notes, Mark tossed his book aside and looked across to his wife. He was about to suggest a drink, but hesitated when he saw her expression.

She had that look again, a kind of sadness in her eyes. In six years he'd only seen it maybe three or four times, but whatever caused it, in every case her fears had been confirmed.

She had tried to explain it to him once. 'It's just a feeling, a fear of impending disaster. The first time it happened was when my father was killed. I was only ten years old at the time, but I remember waking that particular morning feeling anxious and depressed. I knew something was wrong but, as always, I didn't know what it was - just that it was very sad. When the police came that night to tell mother that father had been knocked down and killed on his way home from work, I felt no surprise. I was heartbroken, devastated even, but unsurprised. I knew instinctively, it was why I'd felt so unhappy all day, it was like experiencing the grief before the loss.'

Mark had tried to sum it up into a single word. "You mean, you had a premonition?"

"No, I didn't. I didn't know what was going to happen. I just knew, with tremendous certainty, that something was. That's the worst part, you see - not knowing.'

She hadn't stirred for several minutes. Unsure whether to interrupt her thoughts or not, Mark watched as her eyes moved beyond the pages of the novel she was holding and settled on a spot just above the fireplace. He wished he could see it too, whatever it was that made her look so sad. Eventually he whispered. "What is it Sue?"

She hadn't heard, for now she was staring at the copper coalscuttle. A watery sunlight streamed into the room, throwing a bright, blinding yellow off the metal; she didn't even blink.

"Susan." He spoke louder. "Susan, what's wrong?"

Blinking like a child waking from sleep, she looked at him in surprise. "Sorry, what did you say?"

"I've spoken to you twice, you were miles away." He gave her a lop-sided grin. "Are you going to tell me?"

"Tell you what?"

"It's happened again, hasn't it? What is it this time?"

He grinned when he saw her jaw set stubbornly. "Come on Sue."

She shrugged. "What can I tell you? As usual it's all very unclear, but it seems to centre on that woman, Hannah. Something about her − something quite tragic, I think, but don't ask me what it is." She frowned at him. "Why on earth should I be worrying about someone I hardly know?"

"Did you like her?" he asked.

"I'm not sure. At first I didn't think I did, but I overheard her saying something to Maude that made me think again. Maude was telling her about us and how we met, and how we have become her family. Suddenly Hannah said, 'Be careful Maude. Don't rely on it too much. I've spent thirty years, or more, thinking I was part of a family – only to find I was wrong.' She made me feel quite sad for her.

"She is a bit dour, isn't she?" He chuckled. "I think, for some reason, she rather disapproves of me, and I'm quite sure she'd prefer it if Alex wasn't quite so forthcoming with his family history. She's very possessive about him, don't you think?"

"Yes, and that's another thing. If I hadn't known better, I'd have thought she was his mother, not his mother's companion. I'm sure Alex is very fond of her – I just hope he lets her know it now and again." Susan sighed. "Poor old Hannah. Her whole life has been turned on its head. No wonder she's so lacking in humour." She rubbed her chin thoughtfully. "You know, we really don't have any idea what sort of mother Eleanor was, do we? Maybe she wasn't the maternal type - perhaps she left it all to Hannah – now, that would explain a lot, wouldn't it?"

The phone rang making them both jump. "I'll get it." Mark jumped to his feet and left her gazing thoughtfully into space again.

Susan concentrated on the pages of her book, trying to forget Hannah's forlorn face. There was nothing she could put her finger on; nothing the woman had said or done, but as the afternoon had worn on Susan had become more and more uneasy. She'd found herself studying her until, at one point, Hannah had caught her staring. They had locked eyes for a moment but, shocked by the depth of sadness in the vivid blue gaze, Susan had immediately looked away. After that, she had tried not to look at Hannah again; it made her feel too uncomfortable.

Grinning broadly, Mark returned to his seat. "That was Jack Witchell, he's got the file on Reverend Mayling. Bob and

I are going to meet him at the pub tomorrow night, do you want to come?"

"I'm not sure that I can. Kathleen's coming over again in the afternoon and she might stay for dinner."

"Well, bring her too."

"She might not want to come, Mark, her head is too full of other things at the moment. Today, she was going to the cottage hospital hoping to find someone who remembers what happened to Mary Tyler - what's the matter, why are you frowning?"

Mark pulled a face. "I don't have premonitions - or the benefit of that strange insight of yours, but something about this search for Mary makes me feel very uneasy."

Only a few miles away, in Ashbridge, Alex was embarking on a search of his own. He found himself wishing he had Mark's investigative skills. It wasn't going to be easy searching for his missing sister. All he had to go on was her place of birth and a single name - Caroline.

CHAPTER THIRTY
London
September 1990

Sarah Younger smiled at Ricco's head waiter. "I'm meeting someone, Henry. Is Miss Denning here yet?"

"Yes she is, madam. Please come this way."

Some of the diners looked up as Sarah followed Henry's swaying coat-tails across the room. She knew their eyes were following her, and could sense the curiosity they reflected. Sarah was used to it. She knew that, at almost six feet without her shoes, she presented a formidable figure, and one that could never fail to attract attention. In her youth her height had been a constant source of embarrassment, but once out of her teens she had discovered that it could confer many advantages. She had learned to use her height well, and in a variety of ways. As a weapon to instil fear into underlings, for instance - but it wasn't going to work this time. Caroline was one of the few people she knew she couldn't intimidate. Sarah took a deep breath; she wasn't looking forward to this meeting. Somehow she knew her friend was about to deliver bad news.

Sarah slid gratefully onto a seat opposite her friend. "Sorry I'm late, or were you early – oh, no matter." She turned to the waiter. "It's all right, Henry, we'll order later - no wait." She grinned at Caroline. "Shall we have a drink first?"

"Yes, if you like." Caroline pulled a face. She really didn't want a drink but thought her friend might well need one before long.

Sarah rummaged in her bag and extracted a gold cigarette case. "You don't mind, do you?" She waved the case. "I know I shouldn't but I've had a hell of a morning." She took a moment to light a cigarette, then directing a stream of blue smoke towards the ceiling, said. "I've got some great news, dear. You won't believe it... "

"Sarah!" Caroline tried to interrupt.

"No, listen. You won't be able to say no."

"Sarah, shut up for a minute."

Sarah glared at her. "Oh, all right. I can see there's no stopping you. Come on, let's have it then."

Caroline took a deep breath. "You're not going to like this, but before you start reeling off what you have lined up for me, I'd better tell you I'm going away for a while."

"Are you going on holiday?"

"No - well yes, in a way I suppose I am."

Sarah frowned. "But what about this job? It's just what you've been waiting for."

"I'm sure it is, but I've thought it over carefully and I really want to do this."

"Do what?"

"Go in search of my ancestors. I want to find my mother." She leaned forward excitedly. "Sarah, I think I'm finally on the right track - I spoke to this woman..."

"Oh Caroline, the job has to be more important. This is your career."

Caroline studied her patiently. Sarah had been a good friend during the last couple of years. As a struggling artist, with talent but no direction, Caroline had almost given up hope of ever earning a living from her skills. Sarah had taken charge and pushed her relentlessly towards illustrating. She'd found work for her and introduced her to the right people. She owed Sarah a lot, but this was something she had to do. At last she said. "I know I'm letting you down, but this isn't permanent. I'll only be away for a while. Let's face it, I may be running up another blind alley, in which case, I shall be back within a few days. Anyway, I finished that last commission ahead of schedule, so I've got a few days grace, haven't I?"

"Yes – but..."

"Well, there you are then." She sipped her sherry. "I

really don't want to take on anything else at the moment. I've got so close now, I just need to do this last bit."

Sarah's shoulders rose and fell imperceptibly "Where are you going?"

"Derbyshire."

Sarah feigned indifference. "Really - why there?" She picked up the menu and studied it absently.

"Do you really want to know?"

Sarah put the card down and smiled ruefully. "Yes of course I do, I'm just a bit miffed - this really is a good commission, Caroline."

"I'm sorry. Don't be too angry with me, I'm really grateful, you know, for all you've done."

Sarah waved this aside. "It was nothing. Caroline, promise me you'll think about it, at least." She watched Caroline shake her head and knew she'd lost. "I wish I had your determination - what is it that's driving you?"

"It's the mystery of it I suppose. It's just as if this woman, my mother, never existed. I really thought once I'd got a surname it would be easy, but there's not a trace - not until yesterday, that is."

"What happened yesterday?"

"Actually it all started a couple of weeks ago. I went to an address I got from the hospital. It was pure chance really, I found a woman who remembered her - well sort of remembered her."

"It's all a bit vague, isn't it?"

"I suppose it is, but at least she gave me a lead. She remembers a young woman who stayed there about the time I was born. She couldn't remember much, and she hadn't heard of the surnames that I've already found. She only knew that she was called Lucy and came from a village in Derbyshire, a place called Harold."

"Funny name for a village."

"That's what she said. She remembered it because it was

her husband's name, Harold."

Sarah sighed. "So you're dashing off to find her."

"Not exactly. First I wrote to the records office. They found no trace of the name, but suggested I contact the local minister, Reverend Stanhope at St. Peter's Church. I wrote to him last week, and yesterday I got a reply. He too, can't trace the name but suggested a visit to the area might prove more revealing. It seems a search of the surrounding village churchyards and cemeteries might offer more information than his records can. Evidently there are lots of little hamlets around Harold, each with their own parish records."

"I have to say I admire your fortitude. I just hope you're not off on some wild goose chase." Sarah sighed with resignation. "How long will you be away?"

"Can't say for sure. As I said, it may only be days – but if I'm lucky, who knows?" She grinned. "You know, I've never been up that way before. If nothing else it'll give me a chance to explore the countryside. I understand it's very beautiful."

"So I believe." Sarah picked up the menu again. "I don't know about you, but I'm ravenous. What shall we have?"

Caroline rose wearily from another eroded gravestone. Staring reproachfully at the ambiguous inscription, she admitted reluctantly that Sarah might have been right when she'd said it was a wild goose chase.

It was six months since she'd begun her search. Endless hours of scouring record books at St. Catherine's House, letters to registry offices around the country, and numerous visits to the Public Record Office at Kew, had finally brought her to Derbyshire. One sympathetic archivist had advised, 'Take yourself off to the cemeteries, that's all you can do. You'll need to go armed, though, with a strong wire brush and a grim determination.'

He'd been right on both counts. After five days her wire

brush was holding up pretty well, but her determination was beginning to flag. Five solid days trailing doggedly from one village to the next, and she knew as much now as she had before she left London. She had a choice of three names to look for, Lucy, Ellwood and Grey, and not one of them had emerged. All she could do now was ask around the villages in the hope that someone had heard the names before.

She flung the wire brush aside and rubbed her wrist. For more than an hour she'd crouched, convinced she'd finally found something this time. It had taken considerable effort to scrape enough lichen from the headstone to reveal the name – and there it was – Elmwood. It was enough to make you weep.

Caroline began gathering her things together. She'd had enough. As she stuffed the brush into her bag, she smiled wryly to herself. The archivist might have been right about the wretched thing's worth, but he hadn't warned her of the physical strength required to use it. She flexed her shoulders and felt the muscles tighten in protest. At this rate she would be returning to London looking more like a Russian shot-putter than an artist. It was all so much harder than she'd imagined.

A small sound caught her attention. Caroline looked up and was surprised to see a woman about ten yards ahead of her. How odd, there had been no one about when she arrived and, as she was directly in line with the entrance, she couldn't see how anyone could have passed without her noticing. Caroline watched, with a certain amount of amusement, as the stout, middle-aged woman stooped to place some flowers in a stone vase, then proceeded to talk, at some length to the headstone. Her head began moving rapidly back and forth, as she wagged a stern finger at it - as if berating a small child.

When the woman turned away from the grave, Caroline saw her chance. "Hello," she called, and began walking quickly between the graves. "I wonder if you can help me."

The woman turned so quickly, she had to grab the

headstone for support. Caroline ran the last few yards. She didn't like the look on the woman's face at all. She was deathly white and there was a bluish tinge to her lips. Caroline took her arm and spoke calmly. "Look, why don't you sit here on the grass for a minute?"

Vivid blue eyes, clouded with fear and confusion, glared at her. "I'm all right now, I just felt a bit dizzy." She still seemed unsteady and appeared to be having difficulty breathing, but she withdrew her arm from Caroline's firm grip. "Did you call me?"

Drawing back slightly from the woman's stony stare, Caroline repeated. "I was wondering if you could help me, I'm looking for a particular grave. I'm trying to trace my family."

She eyed Caroline with interest. "Your family - are they from Ashbridge?"

"They may be - that is, I don't really know." She stopped and smiled ruefully. "Oh dear, I'm not making much sense, am I?"

The furrows on the woman's forehead deepened. "You're not from around here, are you?"

"I'm from London, but I've discovered my mother came from Harold. I've spoken to the vicar at St. Peter's and he seems to think she may not have actually lived in Harold, just nearby."

"Well, that could mean almost any of the surrounding villages, couldn't it?" The woman sniffed loudly. "What's your mother's name?"

"Ellwood-Grey." She studied the plain, rather serious face, hoping for some sign of recognition.

"Don't know it." The reply was quick and decisive. "Have you tried the church in Kerridge?"

Caroline nodded wearily. "I think I've tried just about everywhere now. The trouble is, Ellwood-Grey could have been her maiden name. If she married, it would be different now, wouldn't it?"

The dry colourless lips pressed together. "Hmm. An unmarried mother then, was she?"

"So it would seem." Caroline didn't much care for the look of condemnation on the woman's face.

Tutting loudly as if to emphasise her disapproval, the woman stood back and cast her gaze beyond Caroline to the road. "You could try the Lamb, it's the pub at the other end of the village. The landlord there has been around these parts for a number of years, maybe he'll know someone of that name." She turned away. "I'm sorry, I can't help you further."

"Thanks anyway." Caroline called after her, but she was already disappearing into the woods that skirted one side of the graveyard. So that's how she got in. It must be a short cut to somewhere.

Curious to see what lay beyond the woods, Caroline left the graveyard and drove slowly northwards to two ornate iron gates on the other side of the trees. Without leaving the car she took a few moments to study the rambling building, which stood at the end of a gravel drive. It was draped in old roses and tangled clematis through which she could see mellow brick that glowed warmly in the sunlight. Over the years the severe lines of the roof had been softened by lichen, so that from a distance the house merged gently into the backdrop of upward-sloping meadowland. What a beautiful place to live, she thought, and what a subject for a painting. Wondering if she could match that particular glow on canvas she drove on, vowing to try before returning to London.

At the northern end of the village, looking for the inn the woman had mentioned, Caroline was astonished to find yet another church and - another graveyard. Staring gloomily at the cluster of headstones and wondering if she had the energy to do any more, she was startled by a man's voice.

"Hello, are you looking for something in particular? Maybe I can be of assistance?"

Caroline turned quickly to find a man dressed casually

in a tweed jacket and grey flannel trousers. At first glance he looked like any other local, but his clerical collar left her in no doubt as to his profession or the reason for his presence in the graveyard. She was puzzled by the curiosity in his benevolent eyes, and the smile of recognition on his lips. "It would be nice if you could," she replied wearily. "I'm looking for a specific grave, you see."

The smile faded momentarily, and was replaced by a look of bewilderment. "I'm sorry, how very rude of me to stare like that. I thought you were someone I knew, you see..." Creasing his brow, he asked rather stupidly. "Do I know you?"

"I don't think so." Taking in the portly frame she watched as he tried, rather unsuccessfully, to button a well-worn waistcoat across an unbecoming paunch. "My name is Caroline Denning."

"Denning...hm. It's not a name I recall hearing before - but my memory isn't something I can rely heavily upon these days." The vicar abandoned the stubborn button and instead clasped his hands in front of him. "No matter – now how can I help you?"

Taking a deep breath, Caroline spoke as one who had rehearsed a speech. "I'm trying to trace my ancestry and I'm looking for anyone with the names Lucy Ellwood or Grey or both."

An amused grin creased his round, podgy face into a mass of wrinkles. "My goodness, you've said that a few times by the sound of it."

"I'm afraid I have, and it's beginning to sound very boring."

James Cross scratched his head absently, disturbing the few remaining white hairs. "I can't recall anyone named Lucy, but Ellwood-Grey ... that rings a bell. I'm sure I've heard that before. Your family come from Ashbridge then?"

"That's the trouble, I don't know. My mother lived in

this area and she was known as Lucy, that's all I've managed to find out." She went on to tell him about her search, finishing weakly, "So you see, I don't even know if she was married."

The vicar listened patiently, then said. "Six months you say, and all that has brought you here. Well, at the very least, I can offer you some refreshment, come to the vicarage, my dear. We'll see if Emma will make us some tea." Without waiting for a reply he strode off, carefully picking his way through the graves to the path.

Caroline had to run to keep up. "Emma? Is that your wife?"

"My wife, bless her, died some years ago. Emma Tucker is my housekeeper." He stopped. "Now why didn't I think of that before?" He spoke to himself giving Caroline the distinct impression it was something he did quite often. "Yes, Emma's been around here longer than I have, she might well know the name." They reached a large wooden gate, which was almost concealed in the hedge that bounded the church. Opening it and allowing her to pass through, he added. "If anyone will know, she will."

Caroline trailed after him through a chaotic but colourful garden to a cottage almost hidden by shrubs and trees. A copper beech tree to the side of the front door created a patchwork of shade from the afternoon sun. "This is lovely," she murmured.

"It's mostly Emma's work," he said, opening the door. "She's the gardener, I just do the donkey work." A door opened at the far end of the hall. "Ah, there you are, Emma. We're going into the study. When you get a minute would you come in, there's something you might be able to help us with."

"Me?" The wiry little woman ran her fingers through a shock of unruly white hair.

"Yes, you." James Cross pulled a face at her and laughed. "We're in need of your memory."

214

"Oh, well in that case I'll come in now." She looked beyond the vicar to the slender girl standing tentatively behind him. "Hello, would you like some tea?"

Before Caroline had a chance to speak, the vicar answered. "We'll have tea later, Emma. Er...this is er... Miss er..."

"Denning." Caroline finished for him. "Caroline Denning."

Chuckling good-naturedly, the housekeeper came towards her. "I'd better introduce myself or we'll be here all day, I'm Emma Tucker and, as I don't suppose he's mentioned it, this is the Reverend James Cross." She urged Caroline into the study.

A heady aroma of lavender polish enveloped her. Looking around the comfortable room with its old-fashioned mahogany furniture and net curtains, she felt a rare sense of security. It reminded her of her childhood and happy hours spent at her grandparents home in Devon - but that was another family, another life. Dragging herself back to the present she smiled at the man seating himself behind the desk.

"Now." He tried unsuccessfully to straighten an untidy stack of papers and books on the desktop. "Let's see if we can find your mother. The only thing we know for sure is that she lived in this area once - how long ago?"

Realising just how little she knew, Caroline began to feel extremely inadequate. "Well, I'm twenty two, and she was here then."

"Where did you get the names, Ellwood and Grey from?"

"From my original birth certificate. It shows my mother's name as Ellwood-Grey. Father unknown," she added quietly

"Ellwood," Emma shook her head. "I can't say I've ever heard it before, but I did know someone by the name of Grey."

215

James Cross leaned forward. "Who are you talking about Emma?"

"Nobody, I mean nobody important. The lady I remember was Miss Grey, she was a Sunday school teacher when I was a child." She shook her head again, dismissing the subject. "She's dead now anyway."

"How long ago did she die?" Caroline was immediately interested.

Emma looked at her sadly. "I'm sorry my dear, I hope I haven't raised your hopes. Miss Grey, had she lived, would be old enough to be your grandmother." She looked back at the vicar. "She eventually married your predecessor."

"Reverend Wakely?"

"Yes."

"Then she was Eleanor's mother?"

Emma nodded. "That's right. She died giving birth to Eleanor. Such a sad time, Reverend Wakely was shattered. The whole village seemed to go into mourning. She was well loved - Lucy Grey

"Lucy?" The vicar and Caroline spoke in unison.

"What have I said?" Emma looked from one to the other.

Caroline felt the colour drain from her face. "That was my mother's name - Lucy Ellwood Grey."

"Well, how odd." Emma frowned. "It must be a coincidence though, she died such a long time ago. Let me see, I was about eleven." She started counting on her fingers. "Yes, she died - must have been 1931." She shook her head. "And I don't ever remember hearing the name Ellwood before."

The vicar stood up. "Well there's one way to find out." He crossed the room to a large bookcase. "It'll be in the records."

"What will?" Emma asked.

"A record of the marriage of course." He ran his fingers

along a row of heavy leather bound tomes and eventually pulled one out. "Here we are. 1920 to 1930."

Several minutes later the three sat in stunned silence. "Well I'll be blowed." Emma was the first to speak. "Her name was Ellwood-Grey. She must have chosen not to use Ellwood, for some reason."

"Probably thought it too pretentious." The vicar offered.

Caroline was thoroughly confused. "I don't know what to make of it. The name is right but this woman was dead long before I was born - twenty six years before." She noticed the vicar looking at her oddly. "What is it?"

Ignoring the question, James Cross glanced at Emma. "Who does this young lady remind you of?"

Emma shifted her gaze to the young woman beside her. "There is a resemblance, but surely not...?"

"What?" Caroline looked quickly from one to the other. "What is it?"

Emma and the old vicar eyed each other, then Emma muttered. "Eleanor Mayling."

CHAPTER THIRTY ONE

Mark watched Kathleen Abbott breeze through the gate at Crane cottage. It was hard to believe this was the same woman he'd bumped into in Eve's shop six years ago. He'd thought her attractive then, in spite of the strain she was under. Today he saw a different Kathleen, a woman who walked with an air of assurance, who looked good - and knew it. He smiled as he opened the door. "Nice to see you Kath, come in."

Her eyes fell on the raincoat over his arm. "Oh, you're not going out, are you?" She still spoke with the soft country burr that had first fascinated him.

"I'm afraid so, I'm going over to Ashbridge."

"Oh, do you have to? I've hardly seen anything of you this week." She smiled up at him in a way that made him feel a little uncomfortable. "I'm beginning to think you're avoiding me."

Dear God, she was flirting with him! He took a step towards the front door. "Of course I'm not. Sorry, Kath, it's just been one of those weeks." With relief he saw Susan emerge from the kitchen. "Look who's here!" he said.

"I thought I heard voices, hello Kath." The two women kissed and Mark was reminded again how alike they were.

"Right, I'm off." he said. "I'll be back for dinner Sue. Are you staying, Kath?"

"If I'm invited." Kathleen grinned.

Mark touched her arm. "That goes without saying. Good, I'll see you both later then - must dash, I've got to pick Bob up."

Wet gravel crunched under his wheels as Mark pulled into the drive at the vicarage.

"I still don't know why we're here." Bob muttered as he struggled to unfasten his seat belt.

"I told you, Eleanor's doctor will be there. I think Alex simply feels the need of some support."

"Yes, but if this doctor wants to talk to Alex about his mother, you'd think he'd want to do it in private, wouldn't you?"

Mark nodded. "I'm sure he would, but this is Alex's idea. I think he's prepared to expose all the family skeletons if it will help him to discover the truth about his mother's death. Of course, there's every chance that suicide is the truth, it's only Maude and Alex himself that believe otherwise." He steered Bob towards the front door. "Anyway, I've said we'll be present and that's all there is to it."

Bright yellow chrysanthemums, skilfully arranged in a pottery jug, did little to brighten the atmosphere in the vicarage sitting room. If Mark hadn't immediately sensed an air of gloom, the expression on Alex's face would have been enough to suggest that all was far from well.

A smartly dressed man rose from his seat as Mark crossed the room. "Hello, you must be Mark Jordan. How's that young son of yours?"

Mark was about to apologise for his tardiness, instead he said, "You know my son?"

"I'm his doctor - your doctor, in fact. You must enjoy very good health Mr Jordan, as we've never met." The doctor smiled. "It's a sad fact that I only get to meet people when they're sick."

Alex looked on, smiling rather stiffly Mark thought, then belatedly said, "This is Dr. Latham."

"So you're Paddington." Mark laughed, then apologised. "I'm sorry, it's my son's pet name for you. He says you look just like his teddy bear."

David Latham smiled good-naturedly. "I've been told that before."

Looking around for somewhere to sit, Mark silently

agreed with Tim. David Latham did look like a big friendly bear. It was something to do with the way his mouth turned up at the corners, and the deep cleft in his top lip. He looked as if he was perpetually smiling.

"And here's someone else I don't see very often." The doctor shook hands with Bob. "It must be the air in Carlton, you're all such a healthy lot."

"Goodness, I'm forgetting my manners, please sit down." Alex headed for the sideboard. "What would you all like to drink - Dr. Latham?"

"Scotch please - and it's David."

"Right." Alex looked at Mark then Bob. "What about you two?"

"The same please." Mark answered.

Bob, who'd been watching Alex carefully, nodded. "Yes, scotch for me too, Alex. Are you all right, lad?"

"Yes, I'm fine, just a bit shaken, that's all." He handed them their drinks, then taking his own, dropped heavily into an armchair. "Dr. – I mean David, has just given me some rather unexpected news." He gulped down half the contents of his glass, then taking a deep breath, said. "It looks as if we were all wrong about my mother. It seems she had a very good reason for taking her own life... she had cancer."

"Oh, Alex." Mark's dismay was evident in the simple statement. "And you had no idea?"

"None at all." The young man stared into his glass.

"If it makes you feel any better, Alex." The doctor leant forward. "Neither did I."

Alex's eyes darkened. "But you've just told me..."

"I think I'd better start from the beginning." David Latham placed his glass carefully on a low table in front of him. "I'm afraid Eleanor had me fooled along with everyone else." He looked at Alex with understanding. "If you think you're feeling badly about this, imagine how I feel? I was her doctor, the one person that should have known." He shook his head. "It's rather made me question my judgement, I can tell you."

"But I was her son." Alex almost wailed. "I above everyone should have known something was wrong."

Mark could see emotions were running high in these two. Before long, both would be lost to logic and clear thinking. He attempted to defuse the tension. "Look, David, why don't you start at the beginning as you suggested?"

"Yes, you're right, no good blaming ourselves this way." He took a sip from his glass. "Eleanor and I practically grew up together, we were of the same age you see."

"Did you go to school together?" Mark breathed a sigh of relief; things were getting back to normal.

"No, her father sent her off to boarding school, but we always met up during the holidays. There was quite a crowd of us in the village then, but Eleanor was always set a bit apart from the others because of the different schooling. Somehow though, we hit it off straight away. We formed a friendship that was to last a lifetime - her lifetime, that is."

"Did you keep in touch after her marriage to Richard Mayling?" Mark asked, keen to steer him away from the subject of the woman's death.

"Just the usual things – cards at Christmas and birthdays."

"What about her husband, did you know him?"

"Only by reputation." The doctor glanced quickly at Alex.

Alex nodded. "Go ahead, David, don't worry about me. I don't think there's much you can say that would shock me just now."

The doctor continued. "Well, sufficient to say, the man didn't exactly generate much affection in the village."

Mark nodded. "When did Eleanor first come to you as a patient?"

"Just this year, at the beginning of June. She wasn't ill,

at least that's what she told me. She said she was having a bit of trouble sleeping, but apart from a natural tiredness as a result of it, was feeling quite well. I remarked that she'd lost a little weight, which seemed to delight her. She said she'd been dieting and was pleased her efforts were beginning to show." He finished his drink. "I told her off then, explained that dieting should be done sensibly."

"So what happened after that?" Mark tried to move on.

"I prescribed a fortnight's supply of Nitrazepam capsules – only five milligram. I told her to take one each night, and come back when she'd finished them."

"And did she?"

"Yes. She wasn't very impressed though, she said they hadn't helped at all. I thought it was a bit odd and wondered if she had some kind of resistance to them. However, at least it showed she'd had no unpleasant side effects."

"Could she have done?"

"It's possible, everyone reacts differently to drugs. Whenever I prescribe sleeping pills I always start with a short course just to see how the patient reacts."

"And she was all right?"

"Yes, quite all right, in fact, she said she'd have got more effect from a couple of aspirin. On the strength of that, I suggested that she might take two each night, and gave her a month's supply."

"And that did the trick, did it?" Mark thought he'd exhausted the topic.

"Actually it didn't. Eleanor came back a month later saying the pills were useless and demanded something stronger. I put my foot down at this; in fact we had a row over it. I tried to explain that she had to give herself time, that her sleeping pattern was disturbed and that it might take a while to level out. In the end she agreed to try it for another month, but I told her if things hadn't improved after that, I was going to insist on some tests."

"And she never complained about anything else - just difficulty sleeping?"

"She didn't even complain about that again. The following month Hannah came in with a note for a repeat prescription, so I naturally assumed she was beginning to get some benefit from them."

"When did you next see her?"

The doctor was silent for a moment, then said quietly. "The night before she died. She invited me to dinner, something she would do maybe six or seven times a year." He smiled. "It was always on the understanding that we could talk on any topic except health and medicine. She always said the surgery was the place for that... dinner was to be enjoyed." He sat back heavily. "Then, when Hannah called the next morning to say she couldn't wake her – well, it's a day I won't forget in a hurry."

"And there was nothing in her manner the night before to indicate what she was about to do?"

"Nothing at all, in fact she was in good spirits. I suppose that could have been the sherry though. She didn't normally drink, you see. I think she only had one glass, but for a non-drinker it was enough to make her appear happy."

"Who called the coroner in?"

"I did. Oh, it all looked like a classic suicide, nothing out of place, no struggle, a couple of empty pill bottles on the bedside table. Perhaps it was because I knew her so well, or thought I did, anyway, I wanted a post-mortem."

"How many of these pills would she have had to take?"

"On their own, about two hundred. With a large quantity of alcohol, much less - why?"

Mark was mentally calculating. "So over a period of what - three and a half months, she acquired almost what she needed, two hundred pills."

Alex suddenly spoke. "This whole thing is unbelievable."

Mark nodded. "Unbelievable and unnecessary."

"Unnecessary? What do mean by that?" Alex was almost shouting.

"Calm down, Alex." The doctor's voice was gentle but firm. "What Mark means is, Eleanor went to a great deal of trouble over a period of time, when a handful of paracetamol would have had the same effect, and more immediately."

Alex ran his hands through his hair. "None of this makes any sense."

"I couldn't agree more." The doctor frowned. "I can't believe Eleanor would lie either. Lying was something she abhorred in others, and wasn't particularly good at herself."

Mark was as bewildered as the others were. "What about the post-mortem, have you seen the report, David?"

"The report is the only straightforward part of all this. They found the presence of a minute amount of alcohol, almost one gram of Nitrazepam and, oddly enough, the equivalent of a couple of paracetamol." He paused for a moment. "The shock result was the carcinoma. A malignant tumour of the breast."

"Surely that could have been treated?" Alex questioned.

"If she'd done something about it sooner, yes. She must have noticed the changes in her body some time ago, but sadly, like so many women; she tried to ignore it. You see, in many cases there is no pain, not until the last stages. In Eleanor's case the disease had progressed far beyond the bounds of surgery, the lungs were already affected. She wouldn't have lived for more than another six months or so."

"So, that's why she took her own life." Bob spoke at last.

The doctor pulled a face. "The decision at the inquest was death by suicide while the balance of the mind temporarily disturbed."

"Do you agree with that?" Bob asked.

"I was hoping you wouldn't ask that. If we'd been

talking about anyone but Eleanor I would have accepted it without question, but I have to say it's entirely out of character."

Alex nodded. "My feelings exactly."

Mark at last found himself without a question to ask, which left the four to sit and reflect.

The door opened and Hannah put her head round. "I've made some sandwiches, is anybody hungry?"

Alex jumped up. "Bless you, Hannah. I'm afraid I've been a very poor host, these gentlemen are all sitting here with empty glasses." He smiled at her affectionately. "Sandwiches would be very welcome." His smile faded as she left for the kitchen. "Do you think Hannah knew mother was so ill?"

The doctor shook his head. "I haven't a clue, in fact I'm completely at a loss where Hannah's concerned."

"Isn't she a patient of yours?" Mark asked.

"No. According to Eleanor, Hannah doesn't believe in doctors. She prefers to treat herself."

When Hannah returned Alex rose to take the tray of food from her. "Sit down Hannah, there's something I'd like to ask you."

Hannah looked puzzled. "Really, what?"

"It's about mother. Did you know she had cancer?"

She stared at him as if he'd struck her. After several seconds she opened her mouth to speak but nothing came out.

Alex went quickly to her. "I'm sorry, Hannah, that was not the most delicate way of putting it." He went on to explain the findings of the post-mortem. "We wondered if mother had confided in you," he finished.

Gradually the colour returned to Hannah's cheeks and her stricken expression was replaced by one of bitterness. "It seems Eleanor didn't confide in me about anything at all." She struggled to assume a normal expression. "No - I didn't know. Is that why she..?"

"Probably." Alex patted her arm. "You know how

independent mother was, she wouldn't have wanted to become a burden, would she?"

Hannah rose with some effort. "No, she wouldn't." She walked slowly to the door. "I've left something on the stove - excuse me gentlemen."

As the door closed behind her the four men stared at each other in silence. At last Alex said. "Poor old Hannah, she's had one shock after another lately."

Mark nodded in agreement but for once could think of nothing to say.

The doorbell broke the silence. Alex was the first to move. "I'd better get that," he said, "Hannah's probably sobbing in the kitchen."

It was some minutes before he returned. He stood in the doorway looking almost as stunned as Hannah had. "Gentlemen, we have visitors." He pushed the door open wider. "I believe you all know Reverend Cross." He stood aside to allow the vicar into the room. "And this is Caroline Denning, she's..."

The three men rose simultaneously as the vicar made his announcement. "This young lady, we believe, is Eleanor's daughter."

That evening over dinner, Mark related the afternoon's events to Susan and Kathleen. "You should have seen the three of us, all standing there with our mouths open."

"Do you think she really is Alex's sister?" Susan asked.

"No doubt about it as far as I'm concerned. For a start, she's the image of Eleanor."

Kathleen looked thoughtful. "This poor chap, Alex, must be in state of utter confusion."

Mark nodded. "He is. He doesn't know whether to be sad for the loss of his mother, happy at finding his sister, or worried to death about Hannah."

"How did Hannah take it?" Susan asked.

"I don't know. I'm ashamed to say we left it to Alex to tell her. The news about Eleanor seemed to knock her sideways... goodness knows what effect this latest lot has had." He looked at his watch. "Good grief, I'd better get going or I'll be late."

"You're not dashing off again, are you?" Kathleen looked crestfallen.

"Sorry, Kath. I'm sure we'll get a chance to chat before you go back to Derby, but not tonight. I've promised to meet Jack at the pub."

Susan sensed Mark's discomfort. "You see what I have to put up with, Kath? When he's researching for a book he's impossible to pin down. You might as well try and catch dust in the wind."

CHAPTER THIRTY TWO

"I hear you're turning detective again." Jack Witchell sat at the bar grinning broadly at Mark.

"Nice to see you again, Jack. I'm not late am I?"

"No." He waited while Mark shrugged out of his wet coat. "It's still raining then?"

"It's in for the night I think." He made his way to the bar. "What are you having?"

"This one's on me." George pushed two glasses generously filled with scotch across the bar. "Now, do you want me to push off while you talk or can I listen in?"

"What makes you think we're going to talk about anything you shouldn't hear?"

George assumed his 'you can't fool me' expression. "First of all, it's not often we get the pleasure of the Chief Inspector's company. Secondly, he's got his briefcase with him."

"Oh well that's it then. The briefcase will have to go, Jack. Dead give away."

George looked stubborn. "Well you're up to something, that's for sure."

Mark smiled at the big man. "It's all right George, stay with us. In fact..." he looked around, "all we're short of is Bob. Where is he?"

Jack eased himself onto a barstool. "The last time I saw him he was struggling to put Cassie through her paces - training." He rolled his eyes heavenward. "I left him trying to get her to sit and stay in the kitchen while he went into the lounge. Every time he turned round to call her, she was already right behind him."

Mark snorted. "I think Cassie's proving to be a bit of a handful. She's not a bit like her mother, is she?"

"There'll never be another Shona. Bob says he thinks this one's retarded. She's not of course; she's just a normal boisterous Shepherd, and he's not as firm with her as he was with Shona." He opened his briefcase. "Anyway, I think this is what you're interested in."

Mark's eyes were on the manila folder in Jack's hands. "What have you got there?"

"Exactly what my uncle asked for. What is it precisely that you're after?"

"Didn't he fill you in?"

"He said you're writing a book about Eleanor Mayling, but what the vicar has to do with it, I don't know. He's been out of the picture too long to be of any interest. As for Eleanor - I must say I was a bit surprised. I didn't think there was anything particularly remarkable about her."

"I don't think there was, apart from this questionable suicide - that some seem to think more sinister."

"Really - why?"

"Several reasons, but I'll come to that later. Right now it's her missing husband that intrigues me most. At first I was reluctant to get into it but he's become too much of a mystery to ignore."

Jack handed Mark the file. "Well there he is. Everything we have on Richard Mayling is in there. I hope you won't be disappointed."

"That sounds ominous. Does that mean there's nothing in here?"

"There's not much. I've sifted through it all, and as far as I can see it's just a few statements all saying pretty much the same thing."

Mark took out a sheaf of papers together with a neatly folded map. "What's this?" He smoothed out the thick waxy paper and spread it across the bar.

"Search areas, those bits shaded in red are where they dug the ground over. Needless to say, nothing was found. If it wasn't for his belongings at the vicarage and his bank account still intact, there was nothing to suggest the man ever existed."

Mark rubbed his chin thoughtfully. "It's the money that puzzles me. Surely nobody goes off leaving a substantial bank balance behind?"

"Not unless they're suffering from amnesia," George offered.

Jack nodded. "That's one possibility, but after twenty-eight years you'd think he'd have surfaced, wouldn't you?"

"I suppose so. Then again, if he's dead..."

"No corpse." Jack leaned across and sifted through the papers. "Look they even dug up part of the garden as well."

"There's always the chance he ran off with some wealthy woman, thereby not needing his money." George was fast running out of ideas.

"Goodness knows. Anyway, Mark, you can keep this for a bit if you like, as long as you don't lose it." Jack turned as the door opened. "Oh, at last."

Bob came in looking flustered. "That dog will be the death of me, she thinks everything is a game. Have I missed anything?" He directed his question at Mark

"No, nothing. Jack's given me the Mayling file, that's all."

"Oh good, let's have a look."

Mark handed it to him. "Jack, I was wondering if you could help me out with something else?"

"You know, Mark, I'm beginning to experience a very strong feeling of deja vu. What is it now?"

"Eleanor Mayling. Did you know there was a post mortem?"

"I didn't, but I'm not surprised. A sudden death, suspected suicide, it's not unusual, you know. Anyway it must have been straightforward or they wouldn't have released the body."

"I know, but what are the chances of having a look at the coroner's report?"

Jack stared at his uncle in mock amazement. "Can you

believe this chap? Six years and he's still as pushy as ever."

Bob held up his hands. "Don't blame me. I warned you he had the bit between his teeth again."

Jack shook his head. "I still can't understand why you didn't join the force instead of writing all that make-believe stuff."

"Oh, that would be no good at all." Bob chipped in. "He's too impatient and far too tenacious. He never knows when to let go. Can you imagine, Jack, if he'd been around when the vicar went missing, he'd still be fretting and worrying about it twenty-eight years on."

"He's right," Mark agreed. "At least with fiction I can manufacture a suitable ending - well, most of the time anyway."

Jack laughed. "If you come up with a suitable ending in this case, I might just put you on the pay-roll as my advisor. Now, what do want with the coroner's report - have we got ourselves another mystery?"

"Maybe - maybe not," Mark hedged. "There's a number of people who find it difficult to accept Eleanor's suicide, people who knew her well. Even Bob finds it hard to swallow."

"Not half as hard to swallow as two hundred pills." Bob muttered.

"Two hundred - is that what she did?"

"Apparently." Mark looked sceptical. "Hard to believe, isn't it?"

"Well, if nothing else it proves she was determined." It was Jack's turn to look sceptical. "If that's really what she did, and you're looking for an alternative to suicide, forget it - unless you can find a way to administer that many tablets without the victim noticing."

"I know, I'd already thought that, that's why I'd like to see the official report. We met Eleanor's doctor this afternoon, and although he told us what the coroner had to say, I'd still like to see it for myself."

"Why, didn't you believe him?"

"I don't know. It's the first time I've met him and although I liked him and have no doubt that he's a good doctor, it's the fact that he was a personal friend of Eleanor's that's got me thinking. I'd have been happier if she'd simply been another patient."

Jack looked resigned. "OK, I can't promise you the report, but I can certainly have a look at it. I take it you'll believe me."

Mark grinned. "Of course, and thanks. Do you want another drink?"

"No, I'd better get going." He noticed Bob sifting through the contents of the file. "What are you looking for?"

"Anything that mentions a shotgun."

"Whose shotgun?"

"Any shotgun. It came up in conversation yesterday. Richard Mayling took his shotgun with him when he went missing, but I can't find anything about it here."

"That's because there's no record of it in there. Are you sure about this?"

"Of course I'm sure, I wouldn't be looking for it otherwise."

"It's a bit odd that it should come up now. You'd think someone would have mentioned it at the time, wouldn't you?"

"Aye - and I wonder what else they forgot to mention?"

CHAPTER THIRTY THREE

"Well, that completes the grand tour." Alex led Caroline into the sitting room. "What do you think of it?"

"It's a beautiful house. Thank you for showing me round, Alex. It's so strange, you know. The first time I saw this house I wanted to paint it, never guessing that I would one day be inside it - or that this was the very place I'd been searching for."

"And to think you nearly passed us by."

"Alex, would Hannah have known the names Ellwood or Grey?"

"Probably not. She came to work here when my mother married and there was nobody here of that name then. My mother might have told her of course, but I can't think why she would want to. Why do you ask?"

"No special reason, I was just thinking, that's all."

"Well, you're here now, and that's all that matters. You know, you do look very much like mother, especially when she was young. I'll show you some photographs later, if you like."

"Do you mind talking about her, Alex? There are so many things I want to know, but I realise it might be difficult for you so soon after her death."

"I don't mind, really. Talking about her seems to help in way. Perhaps later you'd like to visit her grave?"

Caroline nodded. "Yes I would. Is she in the graveyard through the woods or the one at the other end of the village?"

"No, she's here in the family grave."

"In that case I've probably already seen it, without knowing it of course. I wouldn't have recognised the name Mayling."

Alex smiled. "It's not even as simple as that. She's in the family plot originally bought by my... by our grandparents. Their name was Wakely. Mother's name hasn't been added yet so I don't think you'd ever have found us."

"Thank heavens for Emma Tucker and Reverend Cross, then."

"What made you start the search now Caroline, why not sooner?"

"Purely selfish reasons, I suppose. I'd thought about it on and off for years but while I still had my adoptive parents there didn't seem the need... and I think it may have upset them a bit." She suddenly looked sad. "They were wonderful people, Alex. I've been so lucky. But they died, first dad then mum within two months, and suddenly I was alone. The need to find my roots started as a vague idea, but as time went on it grew stronger until I became almost obsessive about it. I know I drove my friends up the wall. I talked of nothing else."

"Well it all paid off, didn't it? You're here, and I'm delighted about it. Apart from anything else you've saved me an awful lot of work."

"How do you mean?"

"I only learned of your existence a day or so ago, but immediately I knew, I was determined to find you. The trouble was I had nothing to go on. All I knew was a roughly calculated date of birth, the hospital you were born in and your Christian name."

"How did you know that?"

"Mother found out somehow and told a friend. He, in turn, told me."

Caroline looked thoughtful. "I wonder how she did it. That sort of information isn't easy to get."

"If you'd known her, you wouldn't ask. She was a very determined woman and, I suspect, so are you."

"Hmm. I suppose I am. It really is an amazing chain of events, isn't it?"

"Yes, amazing." They turned as Hannah's voice preceded her into the room. "Just think, if you'd gone to the pub, as I suggested, instead of the churchyard, you might never have found us." Her tone implied she rather wished that were the case. They both watched in silence as she poured tea. Without taking her eyes from her task, she asked. "What do you do?"

"I'm a painter. Illustrations mostly."

"That's interesting," Alex said. "Grandfather was keen on painting. He wasn't bad at it either; most of those pictures on the landing and in the hall are his work. Maybe you've inherited his talent."

Before Caroline could respond, Hannah muttered. "I don't think talent is something you inherit Alex. You've either got it or you haven't."

"How would you know?" Alex snapped.

"I don't know." Hannah's face reddened. "It was merely an observation. There's no need to bite my head off."

"Sorry," he mumbled quietly, then opened his mouth to say more, but changed his mind. How could he tell Hannah that her behaviour was becoming an embarrassment? He'd never known her be so rude. In an effort to lighten the atmosphere he smiled at Caroline. "I take it you're on an extended vacation?"

"Sort of. I'm free-lance, so I can take a break whenever I like. I really ought to go back soon."

Alex looked dismayed. "Surely you can take a little more time off, especially now?"

"I suppose I could, but I've only just got myself known on the publishing scene and I don't want to lose too much work."

"Of course you don't," Hannah agreed. "Time's money, and it's not easy for a woman on her own, having to support herself."

"That's true, but fortunately my adoptive parents left me well provided-for. Apart from my work I have the flat and some investments." She looked at Hannah with something like defiance in her eyes. "I don't really have to work at all, but I'm not very good at sitting around doing nothing. I like to be busy."

Having made sure they both had tea Hannah sat on the sofa directly opposite Caroline. "So money isn't a problem then?"

Alex began to feel extremely irritated. Did Hannah think she was after some sort of inheritance? Before Caroline could answer, he said. "I think we'd better get off to the graveyard as soon as we've drunk this. It looks as if it might rain." He swallowed his tea quickly. "Come on, we'll take an umbrella just in case."

As Caroline followed him out, Alex whispered. "I'm sorry about that, I don't know what's got into her."

"It's all right, she probably thinks I'm after the family silver." She laughed, then added quickly. "I'm not you know."

"I know, come on." He started walking down the drive.

"Hang on," Caroline tugged at his arm. "Isn't there a short cut through the woods?" She eyed the row of hedging.

"I never go that way, mother never let me..." he stopped abruptly. "What am I saying?" He laughed nervously. "Years of habit, I'm afraid. For some reason mother would never allow me to use the short cut, in fact, I've never been in there." He stared at the woods thoughtfully. "Why not? Let's see what sort of ghosts she was frightened of. How did you know about the short cut, anyway?"

Caroline explained her meeting with Hannah. "She just seemed to appear from nowhere, then disappeared as quickly."

"Yes, Hannah uses it all the time. Look, here's the path."

They followed a beaten track through trees and overgrown bushes until they reached a small clearing. A circular area, only about twenty feet in diameter, where nothing grew. Walking on a spongy bed of rotting leaves, they searched for the path through to the graveyard.

"We could be stuck in here for days." Alex joked as he

scanned the dense shrubbery.

"Look, there." Caroline pointed as she walked to a narrow gap in the bushes then stopped to stare at the base of a large oak tree near the edge.

Alex caught her up. "What have you found... oh, how odd?"

They stared in silence at a cluster of primroses. The plants, crowded tightly together, were bare of flowers but, in spite of their wilted leaves, showed promise for the following year.

"I wonder what it means?" Caroline murmured. "Someone has done this on purpose, they would never have grown like this naturally."

Alex didn't want to admit it, but he was beginning to feel exceptionally uneasy. The plants had been arranged with great accuracy to form a Christian cross.

Puzzled by the expression in his eyes, Caroline touched his arm. "It's a bit creepy, isn't it?"

He turned away quickly. "Come on, before the rain starts."

In the graveyard he breathed a sigh of relief. Now he could understand his mother's dislike of the Folly. It wasn't just the primroses; there was something evil about the place. He'd felt it as soon as they went in. Smiling to hide his anxiety, he said. "Mother's buried just over there." He guided her towards a large monument. "But I expect you already know that if you saw Hannah here the other day."

"No, this isn't where I saw her." She pointed towards the main gate. "She was down there."

"Really?" Alex shrugged. "I suppose she could have been visiting her mother's grave. I'll show you it later." He took her arm. "Our family plot is by the monument - here we are."

Caroline found herself before a stone sarcophagus enclosed by iron railings. "Heavens, it's enormous!"

"I think our grandfather envisaged a large family, and catered for all. He'd probably be quite disappointed if he knew there's only us left."

Impulsively Caroline stood on tiptoe to kiss his cheek. "Thank you," she said quietly.

"For what?"

"For saying 'us'. It makes me feel I belong."

Alex put his arm around her shoulders and turned her to face the grave. "You do belong. She was your mother too." He watched her as she silently read the inscription.

Reverend John Richard Wakely
Vicar of this Parish

1890-1959

Together they walked around to other side where she read aloud.

Lucy Eleanor Wakely
Beloved Wife and Mother

1895-1931

Caroline was close to tears. "It's hard to imagine the three people buried here are my family. I should have brought some flowers."

Alex squeezed her shoulder. "It's enough that you're here."

She rested against him. "I so wish I'd found you sooner, before she... Oh, I wish she knew I was here."

"I'd like to think she does." Alex turned her away.

"Come on, I think that's enough ancestry for one day." Walking slowly, she looked around. "It's kept well - the graveyard I mean. Who looks after it?"

"A chap from the village, old Jacob. He's been around for as long as I can remember."

"Well he does a good job - oh look, there are the flowers Hannah left the other day."

"Are you sure?"

"Certain, she put them in that stone vase, why?"

Alex walked towards it. "This is Jacob's family plot. Why would Hannah put flowers here? Her mother's grave is over... " He strode off looking puzzled.

Caroline followed. "What's the matter?"

"Well just look at the state of this." He gestured to an untidy heap of weeds. The headstone, leaning precariously backwards, was hardly visible beneath a tangle of ivy. Alex parted the stringy stems. "There - Martha Craddock, Hannah's mother. I can't understand why it's in such a mess. I thought Hannah looked after it - she comes here often enough."

"Why doesn't this Jacob fellow do something about it? All the other graves are neatly clipped, even the ones without headstones."

Alex shrugged. "Goodness only knows." He headed towards the main gate.

"Where are you going now?"

"There's just one more to see. I never come here without visiting it." He led her to the tiny grave with the plain stone cross. "Now this is really strange." He stared at a small bunch of wild flowers lying in the centre of the mound. "That's the first time I've ever seen flowers on this grave, except the ones I used to bring myself."

"Who's buried here?"

"I've absolutely no idea. I've always thought it must be a child, or maybe even an animal - whichever, for some reason it's always fascinated me."

"It's rather a sad little grave isn't it? No name or inscription, it's almost as if we're not meant to know who it is."

"Well, clearly someone knows, if they've brought flowers. I still think it's odd." He started making his way to the front gate. "We'll take the long route back, I think. We don't want to get caught in those woods in the rain - we'll get drenched."

Knowing this was just an excuse, Caroline followed in silence. She'd seen the expression on his face in Folly Wood. He'd been spooked - and if she was honest, so had she.

CHAPTER THIRTY FOUR

"Let's have another look at that map, Bob." Mark cleared a space on his littered desk.

The two men had spent the entire afternoon going through the Richard Mayling file. "You've already looked at it a dozen times. What exactly are you after?"

"I wish I knew. There's something here that we're missing, I'm sure of it." Mark ran his hands over the grubby parchment-like paper. "Jack said all the areas coloured red were searched and dug over, but look, the whole of Folly Wood is coloured in. They couldn't have dug it all, surely?"

Bob nodded wearily. "As I said before, the wood was the first place we looked. Every inch of it was examined but they didn't dig everywhere. Initially they went over it with spikes – prodding all the ground that didn't have something growing in it. If they found a spot where the soil was loose, they dug it up. Obviously, if the ground was hard and resistant there was no point."

"What about the clearing - was there a clearing in those days?"

"As far as I know it's always been there." He tried to sound patient. "You've asked me all this before. What is it, lad - what are you thinking?"

"God knows." Mark sat down heavily. "I'm sorry to keep banging on about it, but I'm sure this cross Alex mentioned is significant in some way. The trouble is, we need to know if the wretched thing was there before all the trouble started, but I can't tell from this map whether the clearing was ever dug up."

"I don't think it was, at least I don't remember it. I know they dug in some of the bushy areas, and they certainly had a go at the garden, but the clearing was solid ground – too solid..." he stopped when he saw Mark's expression. "I've got a nasty feeling I'm not going to like what's coming next."

Mark grinned wickedly. "I'm only thinking."

"I know, that's what worries me. Next you're going to ask me if I've got a spade."

"Well, have you?"

"I knew it! I just knew this was going to get tricky. Now look here, Mark, we can't go digging up the countryside on a whim."

"But it's not just a whim, is it?"

"A vague suspicion then, which amounts to the same thing. Anyway, there's bound to be a law against it."

"We don't have to tell anyone else about it, do we?" Mark was warming to the idea. "We'd have to go at night of course."

"Oh Lord, I can see there'll be no talking you out of it. When are we going?" His voice was flat with resignation.

"Tonight."

"That soon? We need to plan - get organised."

"What's to organise? A couple of spades and a torch, that's all we'll need."

"What we need is our heads examining - that's what we need."

Mark wasn't listening. "If we get there at dusk we can sit in the car until it's dark. Then, when we've made sure there's no one about, we can go in through the graveyard gates." He grinned. "What do you think?"

"I think you're stark raving mad." Bob said dryly. "What exactly are we looking for anyway? You're not hoping to dig up the missing vicar, are you?"

Mark shrugged. "I doubt we'd be that lucky, but there's still the question of this missing shotgun."

"You do realise what you're suggesting, I suppose? That we were all deaf dumb and blind all those years ago. Don't you think one of us would have found it?"

"Yes of course you would, but I've been thinking. Supposing someone shot the vicar and disposed of the body

242

somehow but didn't have time to deal with the shotgun? It could have been hidden almost anywhere until after the investigation was over, then buried with no chance of it ever being found."

Bob tried to smother a grin. "Aye, then they gave it a suitable burial of course, even planted primroses to mark the spot."

Mark snorted "I suppose it is a bit silly, but there's something there for sure, don't you think?"

"Well there's only one way to find out. What time shall we leave?"

There's nothing quite like a graveyard for stirring the imagination, especially at night. Moonlight, filtering through the trees, cast lengthy shadows across the burial mounds, throwing the marble, loaf-shaped headstones into stark relief.

From a distance the monument resembled the head of some grotesque creature, reminding Mark, briefly, of a holiday he'd taken in Egypt as a young man. All it needed, he thought, was a few carefully placed spotlights, and it could look as dramatic as the Sphinx with its famous Son et Lumiere.

"This must be the daftest thing I've ever done." Bob chuckled. "If anyone sees us creeping about in there with a spade each, they'll think we're a couple of body-snatchers."

"Who's going to see us? No one in their right mind would be traipsing around a graveyard in the dark."

"Exactly!" Bob opened the car door. "Oh well, we might as well get on with it."

Looking furtively from side to side, they crept through the gates and made their way stealthily between the graves to the path leading into the wood.

The moon disappeared behind a cloud as Mark led the way. "Give me the torch, Bob, I can't see a thing."

Bob did as he asked and followed silently, keeping as

close to Mark as he could. "I hate these places." He muttered.

"What?" Mark stopped abruptly causing the older man to cannon into him.

"Don't do that," Bob grumbled.

"Shh... someone will hear us."

"Who?" Bob glanced around. "They're all dead in here, at least I hope they are. Come on, get on with it."

They reached the clearing where Mark shone the torch around. "It's by an oak tree apparently - here it is."

"Good grief!" Bob stared at the floral memorial. "I can see what you mean, it's definitely man-made." The pale green leaves gleamed a ghostly white in the torchlight. "It's like a grave, isn't it?"

Mark handed the torch to Bob and placed his spade near the top of the cross. "Let's see if it is, shall we?"

"Hang on a minute lad, we ought to dig these up carefully so we can replant them... just in case."

"In case of what?"

"In case there's nothing there. After all, it might just be something the local kids have done."

Mark stared at the cross thoughtfully. "If it were any other shape I might agree." He placed his spade a few inches from the plants. "But just to keep you happy, I'll be careful."

The first few inches of topsoil offered no resistance, but as they got deeper it became rock-hard.

"I think we should have brought a pickaxe." Bob straightened and mopped his brow. "I'm amazed anything could grow in this."

Eventually Mark threw his spade down. "I'm beginning to think this is a waste of time."

"We'll just try a little further." Bob thrust his spade into the hole. It barely penetrated an inch when it hit something hard. "There's something here." He fell on his knees and started scraping the ground with his hands. "Give me the torch a minute."

"What is it - is it the gun?"

Without speaking Bob got to his feet. "There's nothing there, lad. We've just reached a tangle of roots from this tree. No one could have dug any farther down without cutting the roots out."

"Well that's that then." Mark was immensely disappointed. "Sorry Bob, I felt sure there must be something there."

"Never mind, come on let's fill this in and put it back to rights, then we'll go and have a pint."

The last plant was almost in place when Mark grabbed Bob's arm. "Listen."

"What?"

"There's someone coming along the path, can you hear it?"

Bob stood very still. "Who would be walking through here at night?"

"You mean, apart from us? Come on, we'd better get out of sight." Mark grabbed the spades and his jacket. "You get back to the car with these, I'm going to wait and see who it is."

"I'm not leaving you here on your own, we'll both wait."

Bob took the spades and threw them under a bush, then grabbed Mark and pulled him behind the great oak.

Together they waited, hearing nothing but the slow, steady crunch of heavy footsteps on the debris carpeting the ground.

"Can you see anything?" Bob tried to look over Mark's shoulder.

"Not a thing. I can't even tell which direction it's coming from - hang on, there's someone in the clearing."

"Can you see who it is?"

Mark put a finger to his lips and shook his head.

The footsteps had stopped, nothing moved. The two men froze, expecting at any moment to be discovered. The footsteps started up again, this time moving away.

"Who was it?" Bob finally asked.

"I don't know, there was just the ghost of a shadow. It was impossible to see without shining the torch on him. Here, that's a point, whoever it was didn't have a torch and must know this area very well."

Bob picked up the spades. "I've had enough of this, come on let's get out of here." This time he avoided the graveyard and led the way through the woods to the road.

They'd just closed the boot when a figure emerged from the gates.

"Oi! What are you doin' there?" The deep country burr echoed in the darkness.

"I might ask you the same thing." Bob's voice took on a note of authority.

"Why, if it isn't Sergeant Witchell. What brings you around 'ere?"

Mark heard Bob's sigh of relief. "Jacob! Well I'll be blessed! You're still looking after the old place then?"

"Aye, course I am. Who else would do it?" The man's weathered face broke into a toothy grin. "And all for next to nowt." Suddenly the smile vanished. "What's 'appened then? Why are you creepin' about round 'ere in the dark?"

Hopelessly lost for words, Mark was happy to let Bob do the explaining. "We were taking a short cut from the vicarage." He glanced up at the sky. "Thought it was going to rain."

"Nay. It won't rain t'night." The old chap twitched his nose in the air. "Can't smell it," he grinned. "Fancy a drink at the Lamb, then?"

"That's the best idea I've heard all evening." Mark spoke at last.

Jacob eyed him suspiciously. "Who's this, then?"

"This is Mark Jordan, he lives in Carlton, near me."

"Well, I s'pose if you're with Bob you must be OK."

Mark felt rough calloused skin as the man took his hand in a bone-cracking grip. "Was it you we heard in the woods just now?" he asked.

"In the Folly? Nay lad, nobody goes in there at night. You must be 'earin' things." He chuckled. "Spooked you, did it?"

"It did a bit," Mark grimaced. "Can we give you a lift to the pub?"

"Nay, I got me bike wi' me. You go on, I'll follow." The old chap's face creased into a mass of lines as he laughed. "Give ya chance to get 'em in."

"Aye, there's rum goin's on up there I can tell ya." Jacob swallowed the last of his second pint. "Dunno what, but summat." He banged his glass down with unnecessary firmness, indicating that another pint wouldn't be unwelcome.

Smiling sardonically, Bob took the empty glass. "All right, Jacob. I've got the message. What about you Mark?"

"Not for me, I'm driving." Mark tried to contain his impatience. The old chap had alluded to what he persistently referred to as 'rum goin's on' since he'd joined them in the pub. He tried again. "What sort of goings on, Jacob?"

"Nowt I can put me finger on, but some fool keeps shiftin' the flowers about. It only needs someone to complain to the authorities - well you know who'll be for the high jump, don't ya?"

"Shifting flowers, really?"

"Aye, every time there's a funeral, summat gets shifted."

"Where to?"

"To t'other graves - always the same two, mind." Jacob's brows drew together in deep furrows. "One of 'em I know, but t'other ain't got no markin's on it."

Bob returned with the drinks in time to hear this last piece of information. "There's only one un-marked grave, the one Alex mentioned... with the stone cross."

"Aye, that's the one." Jacob concentrated on his beer.

"Jacob, it's your job to keep the graveyard up to scratch, isn't it?"

"Aye, that's right." He eyed Mark suspiciously. "Why d'ya ask?"

Choosing his words carefully so as not to offend, he said. "I just wondered why the Craddock grave has been left to nature?"

"Them's Hannah's 'structions." Jacob defended. "She said I weren't to waste me time on it. She never cared much fer 'er folks, y'see."

"Hmm, I see."

"Funny lot them Craddocks. They never cared much 'bout 'er, so I s'pose she be gettin' 'er own back."

"Have you seen the primrose cross in the woods, Jacob?"

"Aye, seen summat like it afore - pet's grave I s'pect."

"Where have you seen it before?"

"The church in Kerridge. The gardener there fancies 'imself as summat of an artist, always doin' summat different like that. Last Spring 'e cut turfs out in the shape of letters, arranged 'em to say 'God Is Love'. Silly bugger didn't reckon on the grass growin' did 'e? 'Ad to keep goin' and snippin' round the edges wi' a pair of scissors."

The two men looked at each other. Bob asked. "Has it been there long - the one in Folly Wood?"

"Years." Jacob sipped his drink. "Weren't always primroses though, at first it were fresh flowers laid out - prob'ly nicked from the graveyard."

"And you think it's a pet under there?"

"Aye, couldn't be owt else, too small. Aye, it'll be a dog or a cat or summat."

"Have you ever seen anyone tend it?"

"Nay, never seen anythin'. Just let me catch the so-and-so that keeps pinchin' them flowers though. Someone's tryin' to get me in trouble, that's for sure."

"I'm sure nobody would blame you, Jacob."

"Oh yes they would, it's my plot they keep puttin' the flowers on. My old Dad bought that plot donkey's years ago, when ma died. Tended the graves 'imself in those days... kept 'is plot the best o' the lot. He were a grand ol' boy my Dad. When 'e went, God rest 'is soul, I took over the job. Funny though, after 'e were buried, that's when it all started, the flowers I mean - just kep' turnin' up – aye. Aye, it's a rum do."

Bob glanced at Mark's thoughtful expression. "Well lad, I think it's time we made a move. That wife of yours will think we've got lost."

Mark dragged himself back to reality. "You're right, it's getting late." He stood up. "It's been nice talking to you Jacob."

The old chap nodded. "Aye, likewise."

Mark started to walk away, then stopped. "There's just one thing, Jacob, when did your father die?"

Jacob rubbed his chin. "Let me see - it were 1962, I think. Why d'ya ask?"

Mark shrugged. "No special reason, just curiosity. Goodnight, Jacob."

CHAPTER THIRTY FIVE

Mark tried to pinpoint exactly when things had begun to change. When had research for a book become the serious investigation of a murder? And how long would it be before mild curiosity became obsession? He stared blindly ahead oblivious to the brilliance of the changing sky. It was all starting to feel horribly familiar. How had Jack put it – déjà vu? Well, he was right, and it would have to stop.

A small movement close by brought him back to reality. He was surprised to find Susan sitting quietly beside him, contemplating the evening sky. "Hello, how long have you been there?"

"About ten minutes. Where have you been?"

"Been?"

"I've spoken to you twice to no avail. In the end I decided the view was more entertaining. Just look at that sunset."

Her skin glowed, translucent in the fading light. Only a slight furrowing of her brow marred the smoothness of her complexion. Mark took her hand and held it to his lips. He wanted to tell her so many things. How he felt about her; his thoughts and anxieties, but as usual the words wouldn't come. Instead he said. "Sorry darling, I was miles away."

She knew what he was feeling. She also knew how hard it was for him to put it into words. He could write reams without embarrassment, but speaking his thoughts aloud didn't come easy. "I know you were," she said at last. "I've been expecting this - I've seen it before, remember. It's the book, isn't it? Can I help?"

"I wish you could. It's a bit premature to call it a book, though. All I have so far is a jumble of notes, all seemingly unconnected. This one's got me beat."

"Maybe you're trying too hard. Leave it alone for a while - it'll come. It did the last time, didn't it?"

He looked at her curiously. "The last time?"

"The last time you broke away from your usual style of writing. I know you want me to think this is a biography - but it's really another mystery, isn't it - a murder mystery?"

Mark shifted in his seat. He'd been careful not to tell her too much about his suspicions. "What's this, another premonition?"

She smiled knowingly "I don't need to be clairvoyant to see history repeating itself. Or to see that you're worried." She watched his chin set stubbornly. "Look, we've been here six years and in that time you must have written half a dozen books. None of them, except the Christie thing, had you staring into space and chewing the end of your pencil for hours on end. And, when you and Bob go sloping off after dark with a couple of shovels and a torch, I'd be hard pressed to convince myself that in a sudden burst of horticultural enthusiasm, you'd decided to tidy up the garden."

"There's no fooling you, is there? OK, so you're right, as usual, but I don't want you getting involved – I mean it, Susan."

"Oh don't worry," she assured him. "I'm having absolutely nothing to do with this one. Just promise me you'll be careful."

"I promise."

The distant sound of the phone ringing saved him from further explanations. While she went to answer it he tried to fathom what it was about the Maylings that bothered him so much. After all, what had he got? A suicide, which in the end, would probably turn out to be exactly that. Eleanor Mayling had terminal cancer, which was a plausible enough reason for taking her own life. The missing vicar had probably run off with some rich widow, and their investigation into the primrose cross had given him nothing but a backache. So far, the only interesting part of the whole affair was his talk with Jacob – and that, he realised, was the moment when everything changed.

"That was Alex," Susan called from the kitchen. "We're invited to tea tomorrow."

"Oh, that's nice."

"I said we'd be there about three o'clock."

"For goodness sake Tim, sit still!"

Mark glanced to the passenger seat where Tim wriggled impatiently on Susan's lap. He could feel her tension as well as hear it in her voice. "Why don't you put him in the back if he's being a nuisance?"

Susan remained silent. She'd been looking forward to tea at the vicarage until Hannah telephoned to insist they brought Tim with them. Now she would be on tenterhooks all afternoon. In her mind's eye she could see it all. There would be valuable china smashed on the floor, sticky finger marks on polished antiques, and heaven knew what else. "I just hope he behaves himself, that's all."

"Come on, he's not that bad."

She smiled reluctantly. "I know, it's me. I'm probably fretting unnecessarily, but it's hard to relax when you've got an inquisitive four-year-old to keep an eye on."

"Stop worrying. Once we get there I doubt you'll see him for the rest of the afternoon. Hannah will be only too happy to take charge. She loves having children around."

"Let's hope she feels the same way when we've left."

Any anxieties Susan had disappeared as soon as they arrived. Before Mark had switched off the engine, Hannah was running down the steps, her entire attention centred on Tim "Well, hello young man. It's about time you came to see us."

Tim eyed her curiously. "Who are you?" He demanded. "Is this your house?"

Susan's eyes rolled heavenward. "Here we go. I'm sorry,

252

Hannah, you're about to be given the third degree."

Hannah laughed and immediately looked ten years younger. Sweeping the little boy into her arms, she said. "Well he wants to know things, don't you sweetheart?" Bouncing him playfully up and down she carried him into the hall. "Would you both like to go into the sitting room," she called over her shoulder. "This young man can come with me." Squeezing Tim gently, she whispered. "I've got a special job for you."

"What?"

"You can help me cut the chocolate cake - do you like chocolate?" They disappeared into the kitchen leaving Mark and Susan to find their own way.

"Feel better now?" Mark whispered the question.

"I can't believe it. I wish I hadn't farmed Tim out to Eve when they came to lunch the other day, things might have gone a lot smoother with him around."

"That'll teach you." Mark opened the sitting room door. "Can we come in?"

Alex came to them immediately. "Of course - where's Hannah? No, don't tell me, she's with Tim. Well, that's her taken care of for the afternoon. I shouldn't be surprised if we have to get our own tea. Susan, come and sit down and make the most of it, you won't see Tim again this afternoon."

Susan crossed the room, smiling at the young woman who was standing by the fireplace. "Hello, it's Caroline, isn't it?"

Before Caroline could answer, Alex said. "As usual, I'm a bit late with the introductions. Why don't we all sit down and see how long it takes Hannah to tear herself away from the kitchen?"

It was fifteen minutes precisely when Hannah entered with the tea trolley. Clearly anxious to get back to her young visitor she said. "You can do the honours, can't you Alex? Tim and I are going into the garden."

Susan looked anxious. "I hope he's not being a nuisance, Hannah?"

"Bless you no, he's as good as gold. Don't you worry my dear, he'll be just fine with me."

Susan didn't doubt it for a moment. The transformation in Hannah was spectacular. "Well, if you're sure?"

"You just relax and enjoy your tea. Alex, if you want anything we'll be down in the orchard."

"All right, Hannah, I think we can manage. After this we're going over to the graveyard, so you can play in the garden to your heart's content."

"The graveyard? Surely you can think of something more entertaining to show your guests?" Hannah's attitude verged on scathing. "I can't see what the fascination is, you've virtually haunted the place lately. Anyway, you know where we are if you want anything."

Susan couldn't help noticing how Hannah effectively managed to exclude Caroline from the conversation. Whether the housekeeper disliked the girl, or whether she was just suspicious of her motives, wasn't immediately apparent but, either way, Caroline was going to have a tough time gaining Hannah's approval.

"Come on you lot, dig in." Alex interrupted her thoughts. "Then we'll go and deposit your flowers, Caroline."

Once inside The Folly, Susan regretted having expressed a desire to see the primrose cross. Everything was there to remind her - the woods, the pungent odour of rotting leaves, the eerie silence - suddenly she could see it, just as she had seen it six years ago. Helen's pale blue dress; her matted black hair and decomposed features - she shivered violently.

"Are you cold, Sue? Would you like my jacket?"

"What?" She felt Mark's arm around her shoulders. "Oh, no I'm fine." She smiled, briefly, and walked briskly ahead.

A few minutes later, staring in fascination at the primrose cross, the feeling of unease intensified. "Strange isn't it?" She managed to mutter before strolling away. "Shall we go on through, Caroline?" Anxious to be away from there, she linked arms with girl and urged her towards the path.

Following at a distance the two men spoke quietly. "I was surprised you found nothing there," Alex remarked.

"So were we. Both Bob and I felt sure there would be something." He looked around as they reached the graveyard. "Where are the girls?"

"There they are." Alex pointed to where they stood by a grave near the path.

Mark started towards them. He saw his wife's body stiffen and sway heavily against Caroline. Within seconds he was there to catch Susan before she collapsed to the ground. He looked from her stricken face to Caroline; the girl's clear, grey eyes were wide with fright, and rapidly darkening to the colour of wet slate.

Mark felt the muscles in his jaw tighten as he followed her frozen gaze. He could tell immediately, by the grubby tweed jacket and mud-covered boots, that the body was Jacob, and he didn't need to examine the lifeless form to know he was dead. The awkward angle of his head was evidence enough; the bloody mass where the back of his head had been merely confirmed it.

The pressure of Susan's weight against him lightened, as she began to regain her strength. He called to Alex, "Take the girls back to the house, will you," but Alex didn't move. "Alex!" Mark barked, "Pull yourself together, man!"

"What?" Alex tried to focus on Mark's face.

"I said take the girls back to the house, and then phone Harold police station - ask for Jack Witchell. I'll stay here."

Left alone, he studied Jacob's body carefully. It would have taken considerable force and more than one blow to smash his skull in that way. There was a dreadful finality to death, he thought, and with it came acceptance. It shocked him to realise that he wasn't surprised, that somehow, he knew this had to happen. Thoroughly sickened at the sight, and with himself, he turned away. Dear God was it happening again - was he to be responsible for another tragedy?

Unable to bear it he wandered aimlessly among the graves until he came to the Mayling sarcophagus. The grass inside the railings needed cutting and someone would have to dispose of the dying wreaths. Who would look after the graveyard now? His eyes fell on a single blood-red rose, the bloom still fresh and fragrant. A plain white card attached to the stem fluttered and turned. The words, written neatly and precisely in stark black ink, read:

Until we meet again,
Rupert

A flurry of activity near the road caught his attention. When he saw Jack striding up the path, he tore the card from its fixing and slid it into his pocket. He didn't try to fathom his reason for doing so, and having secreted the card he put it from his mind.

"It's over there, Jack." He pointed across the graveyard.

Jack Witchell nodded calmly, and walked along with him. "Where are the others?"

"At the house. Alex took Susan and Caroline back."

"Is my uncle here?"

"No, but I wish he was."

Jack studied Mark's face. "Why?"

"Well, he would have known what to do. I think I've mucked things up a bit."

"What on earth are you talking about?"

"Well, I sent everyone off, didn't I? I suppose I should have made everyone stay where they were. – the scene of the crime, and all that."

In spite of the situation Jack tried to suppress a smile.

"If I may say so, my friend, you've been reading too many books. I imagine you were all together when you found him?"

"Yes but..."

"And did they all go back the way they came?"

Mark nodded. "Yes, through the Folly."

"Well in that case, any damage caused would have occurred on the way in, not on the way out. And, at the risk of sounding facetious, it would be very hard to accept that three of you stood by while the fourth did the old boy in." As they reached the body Jack's attempt at humour vanished. "Bloody hell! Whoever it was made sure he was dead, didn't they? All right lads," he called to his men. "Cordon it off. Bowman's on his way. Tell him I'll be up at the house." Taking Mark's arm and leading him away, he said. "Bowman's the pathologist - bit of an old woman, but he knows his job. Come on, let's see how the others are doing."

They entered the hall to a chorus of angry voices, of which Hannah's was the loudest. "There's been nothing but trouble since you got here. Why don't you go back to London?"

"Hannah, for goodness sake, what's got into you?" Alex tried to make himself heard.

"Me? What's got into me? You're asking the wrong one, Alex. Don't you find it rather strange that she turns up, out of the blue, just as soon as Eleanor was gone? And now this - this..." Hannah spluttered to a halt as the door opened.

"It rather looks as though you've started the inquest without us." Jack Witchell said dryly, then looking around, asked, "Where's Susan?"

"In the kitchen with Tim." Hannah's tone had softened considerably.

Jack turned back to the hall. "Go and collect your family, Mark. Take them home, I'll be in touch later. Now, if the rest of you will sit down, maybe we can get this over with quietly and simply."

Crossing the hall to the kitchen Mark smiled to himself. It was the first time he'd actually seen Jack in his official capacity - very impressive.

Susan looked up as he opened the door. "Oh, thank goodness you're here. There's the most awful row going on in the sitting room."

"Not any more, there isn't. Jack's stunned them all into silence. What was it all about anyway?"

"I'm blowed if I know. Alex rang Jack, then called Hannah into the sitting room. When he told her what we'd found in the graveyard she went potty. Started saying all these things were happening because of Caroline. I must say, she wasn't making much sense - she just flew off the handle, blaming Caroline for everything and anything she could think of. I didn't want to get involved so I crept out and came to find Tim."

"Right, well we're going home. You look exhausted, love. Come on young fellow." He scooped the toddler up into his arms.

"I don't want to go home." Tim wailed. "I want to stay and play with Hannah."

"She's busy now, and what about Max and Lexer, they're waiting at home for you." Mark knew mention of the dogs would do the trick. Determined to get Susan home as soon as possible, he strode out to the car.

Susan settled back for what was to be a silent journey home. She knew Mark would be deep in thought and she was grateful for it. Suddenly she felt very weary and needed to sleep, but even with her eyes closed the sight of Jacob's body was still there, imprinted on her memory – along with Helen's.

CHAPTER THIRTY SIX

This time she was awake before the scream. Grateful for that at least, Susan sank back against the pillows and waited for the immediate panic to subside. She was tempted to switch on the bedside lamp but didn't dare. Mark slept like the dead, but the light might disturb him. She tried to see her watch in a shaft of pale moonlight from the casement window. It was either five past eleven or five to one, either way she hadn't slept for long.

Gradually the horror of her dream began to fade as reality reasserted itself in familiar sounds - Mark's sonorous breathing and Lexer stirring by the side of the bed. She stared up at the ceiling, knowing that it would be hours before sleep came - it always was. It was a familiar ghost that haunted her, recurring erratically and never in quite the same way. The location this time was the graveyard but, as always, the doll's severed head was there, following her, blood dripping from its roughly slashed throat, the hideous grin, leering, taunting until she awoke screaming. But this time it hadn't worked - at least she hadn't screamed.

With exaggerated care she slid the covers away and sat on the edge of the bed. Immediately conscious of her swollen waistline, she smiled. Maybe pregnancy was the reason - the nightmare had been monotonously frequent when she was expecting Tim. She stroked Lexer's silky coat. "Come on," she whispered, and together they padded downstairs.

She grabbed the saucepan just as the milk bubbled to the top.

"What's up Sue?" Mark's anxious voice made her jump causing droplets of scalding milk to splatter onto the floor.

259

"Here, be careful." He took the saucepan from her. "Sit down, I'll do it. In fact, I think I'll join you."

She watched him pour more milk into the pan. "I'm sorry I woke you."

"It's all right." He put the saucepan on the hob. "Was it the dream again?"

"Yes." She raked her fingers through her hair. "I'm beginning to think pregnancy makes it worse - more frequent. After all, my hormones are leaping about all over the place at the moment. What do you think?"

Mark yawned. "Possibly - I suppose it was the doll again?"

"As ever, only this time I was in a graveyard."

"That's hardly surprising, is it?" He poured the heated milk into two mugs and joined her at the table. Studying her carefully and trying not to sound worried, he asked. "When's Kathleen coming again?"

She looked startled. "Whatever made you think of her?"

"It's just that you've been a bit touchy since you've been seeing her."

"I was touchy, as you call it, before Kath arrived. If anything she's been quite a help, and to answer your question, I think she's coming the day after tomorrow."

"Still ghost hunting, is she?"

Susan shook her head. "I think she's given up trying to find Mary."

"How did she get on at the cottage hospital?"

"Not very well. The doctor who treated Mary remembered her, but after sending her on to a psychiatrist for further counselling, he lost track of her. Kathleen contacted the psychiatrist. He vaguely recollected Mary mentioning London. It seems she wanted to try and find Helen's boyfriend, Steven. After that, he assumed she was going back to her cottage in the lane." She took a sip of her milk. "Her old cottage is still empty isn't it?"

"Most of the time. It's rented out to tourists, but they're few and far between."

"But what about all Mary's things?"

"Eve's got them. Nobody knew quite what to about her belongings, so Eve offered to store her clothes, and Amos has got her furniture in his garage."

"I didn't know all this."

"Ah, well, you don't ask as many questions as me, do you?"

"Well, who told you?"

"Bob. He's been doing a bit of digging. It seems Kath roped him in for some support."

"Really? She didn't mention it."

Mark shrugged. "Probably forgot. Anyway, apparently Mary rented the cottage from the people who own Gibson's farm, and according to them the rent is still being paid regularly each month by banker's order."

"But surely they can't let it out to tourists, it's not legal, is it?"

"I wouldn't know. Bob says old Gibson's no crook, and that if Mary ever comes back, he'll make sure she gets her dues. Personally, I can't see her ever coming back – but when did I ever get anything right?" He finished his milk. "Mind you, if she does come back - I just hope it's not imminent."

"Why?"

"We've got quite enough strange goings on as it is, without Mary Tyler adding to the confusion."

Susan digested that and decided he was right. "Mark, talking of strange goings on - when I was expecting Tim, apart from the nightmares, do you remember me being particularly forgetful?"

"Not especially, why?"

She fished in her dressing gown pocket and produced a key. "This."

"Is that the back-door key that's been missing all week?" She nodded. "Where did you find it?"

"Behind the plant on the window ledge, but it wasn't there yesterday, or the day before. In any case, I've cleaned the ledge since the weekend, I would have seen it, wouldn't I?"

"Maybe Tim found it and put it there, or Maude?"

"Tim can't reach the ledge and Maude would have told me, she was here helping me turn the place upside down looking for it."

He could see she was getting upset. "Well, don't get into a state about it, love. You're tired out, you've had a rotten day, and now that wretched nightmare - it's only a key, after all."

"That's not all. I found it because I had to move the plant to close the window." She bit her lip and looked at him steadily. "I closed it before we went to bed, I know I did."

"Which window?"

"The little one by the door."

He got up to examine it. "I can see what's happened, come and look." She went to stand beside him. "Look, if you don't pull the handle hard enough the catch doesn't close properly. See, one gust of wind and its open."

"I suppose you're right." Shrugging, she turned away. "Sometimes I think I'm going mad."

Mark smiled. "I seem to remember you having doubts about your sanity when you were expecting Tim. I think you were right the first time, put it all down to hormones." He curled an arm around her waist. "Come back to bed, you'll laugh about this in the morning."

Knowing she wouldn't sleep, she smiled weakly but did as he asked. The morning was a long way off, and besides, she didn't want to laugh about it, she wanted to make sense of it.

CHAPTER THIRTY SEVEN

Jack Witchell was beginning to feel like a one-man band. If it wasn't enough that they were already as thin on the ground as police protocol would allow, last evening his detective sergeant had broken his ankle. What was the man thinking about climbing trees at his age? He should have left the bloody cat to fend for itself. Impatiently, he pushed his foot down on the accelerator and wondered, not for the first time, if some inexplicable lunar activity was having an effect on the crime rate. Between the hours of midnight and nine, two cars and a bicycle had been stolen, someone had broken into the off-licence, a pensioner had been mugged in Castleton, and now, on top of everything else, there was this godawful business in Ashbridge.

Jack had spent most of the morning delegating and making it known to all that he needed some help. Eventually it arrived – in the ungainly shape of Detective Sergeant McManus. At this point, Jack was starting to suspect a conspiracy. The fact that he and McManus disliked each other was well known throughout the station, and most of the time Jack managed to avoid working with him. This time, he had no choice - he'd have to bury his prejudices and trust the man to get on with the job in hand.

It was ten forty-five by the time he reached the Harold Road. He was an hour late but, all things considered, he'd cleared the confusion of the morning pretty well. The uniformed branch was dealing with the break-in and car thefts, and McManus had been entrusted with the Castleton mugging. Jack knew he could relax. McManus might be a foul-mouthed, cigar-smoking, whisky-drinking excuse for a detective, but he knew that, with all the subtlety of a charging bull elephant, he would eventually come up with the truth of it.

"Sorry I'm late, it's been one of those mornings." Jack

steamed into the Royal Oak and slammed his briefcase onto the bar. "Right, let's get on with it because I haven't got all day. Mark, I want to you to tell me everything you've dug up on the missing vicar - and no leaving bits out because you think I'm going to read the riot act. I want to know everything."

"About the vicar? I thought this was going to be about Jacob?"

"It is."

"Do you think there's a connection then?"

"Well don't you?" he barked.

"Hang on a minute," Bob interrupted. "Just calm down, Jack. So you're late, and someone's ruffled your feathers, but that's hardly our fault. And if this is going to get heated, I think it might be a good idea to go somewhere a bit more private. Someone's bound to come in for a drink sooner or later, and you don't want this broadcast around the village, do you?"

Jack wondered how his uncle always managed to take charge of a situation – and why such a natural leader had never progressed beyond the rank of sergeant. Suddenly he smiled. "You're right and I'm sorry. As I said, it's been a bad day." He looked from one to the other. He'd started this badly and now they were both on their guard. "Look, why don't you grab that table in the corner, I'll see if Joan can rustle up some coffee."

Bob, who knew his nephew better than anyone, had recognised the signs at the outset. He waited until they were all seated before saying, "All right lad, let's have it, what's on your mind?"

Jack looked steadily at is uncle. "There's no point in beating about the bush, so I won't." He turned is attention to Mark. "How many people know about this book you're writing?"

"Apart from Bob, Susan and Maude, the first person I spoke to was Alex."

"What was his reaction?"

"He seemed very enthusiastic."

"And Hannah - what about her?"

"To be honest I don't think she had any feelings about it one way or the other. In fact, she more or less implied it would be a waste of time."

"Anyone else?"

"I think David Latham knows, I'm sure Alex must have told him. And then there's Caroline."

"Yes, I spoke to her yesterday." So far Jack hadn't heard anything worth writing down. "All these people, are they aware that you've transferred your interest?"

"Transferred – I'm not sure what you mean."

"I mean, when you started your research you made it clear you were looking into the life of Eleanor Mayling, didn't you?" Mark nodded. "Well, somewhere along the line the missing vicar took centre stage – how many people know that?"

Mark suddenly found himself without a straightforward answer. "I imagine they all do. Come to think of it, the vicar has always been the biggest curiosity – Eleanor was simply the catalyst." He studied Jack's troubled face. "You think it's happening again, don't you? Just like the last time, when I tried digging into people's lives. I ask questions, and things start happening. Well, if it makes you feel any better I've decided to abandon this one."

"I'm not casting blame, Mark."

"I know, but after the last time..."

Jack interrupted. "I'm also not asking you to stop. This time, though, I want to be informed every step of the way. I don't want you to do anything without telling me first, and I want to know exactly what you've got so far." He looked from Mark to his uncle. "That goes for both of you – I mean it."

Bob could see his nephew had the bit between his teeth, and he knew why. Jack had suffered tremendous feelings of guilt over the Abbot case and was determined to control events this time. He looked at Mark. "Sounds fair enough, doesn't it?"

Mark nodded. "I'm only too pleased to hand it all over to you Jack, believe me."

The Chief Inspector nodded. "Did you tell Jacob about your book?"

Mark frowned at Bob. "Did I? I can't remember, I don't think so."

Bob shook his head. "Couldn't get a word in edgeways. He kept banging on about mysterious happenings in the graveyard; something about the flowers being moved around. He was worried about someone putting flowers on his family plot – thought it might get him the sack."

"Now that's interesting." Jack rubbed his chin thoughtfully. "Did you notice, Mark, that was where you found him - sprawled across his family grave?"

"Really? To be honest I didn't take much notice of the grave, the sight of him was enough."

"Wasn't very pretty, I agree."

Bob shifted forward in his seat. "I don't suppose there's any point in me asking you about it, is there?"

Jack grinned at his uncle. "I'm surprised it's taken you this long."

"I didn't dare, the mood you were in when you arrived."

"There's not much to tell anyway. Even a complete novice could see he died from head injuries. Several blows to the back of the head caused the damage. The first would have knocked him out, the following blows, of which there were many, finished him off.

"What about the weapon?"

"A spade - it was found several feet from the body, covered in blood. All very straightforward."

"What about prints on the handle?"

"Not a chance. It's one of those old wooden jobs, thick with the mud of ages. I'd say it was his own spade."

"Doesn't sound premeditated, does it?"

"No, I don't think it was." He looked at his watch and started to pack up his things. "I'm going to have to fly or I'll be late again. Now look you two, I meant what I said, I want to know everything. OK?"

The two men nodded and watched him leave. Bob smiled at Mark's expression. "Don't take too much notice of Jack's mood earlier on. Most of that bossiness was because he was late. He's been like that since he was a young lad, can't abide tardiness, it's almost phobic."

"I felt as if I'd had my knuckles rapped."

Bob laughed. "And you may well have before the day's out. Have you seen the time? You should have been home for lunch half an hour ago."

Mark stood in the doorway at Crane cottage. "If I wore a hat I'd throw it in first," he called.

Susan emerged from the kitchen. "Luckily for you, it's only salad." She smiled patiently. "Once I knew you were meeting Jack I abandoned all thoughts of cooking. Did you find anything out?"

"Only what we already know." He quickly changed the subject. "Joan George send their love."

He followed her into the kitchen. "Where's Tim?"

"In the garden, you can call him if you like, it's time for his antibiotic."

He watched her take a capsule and deftly pull the two ends apart, spilling the contents into a small glass of water. The tiny grains dissolved almost immediately. "Those have certainly cleared up his sinus problem, haven't they?"

"Yes, it always amazes me how little there is inside these things, and how a few grains can have such a powerful

267

effect." She looked up at him smiling, until she saw his expression. He was staring at the wall as if he were seeing a ghost. "Mark, what on earth's the matter?"

"What? Oh, nothing, I was just thinking. Did you go and see Maude this morning?"

Susan nodded. "I told her about Jacob and the nightmare. As usual she put everything into perspective. We've decided pregnancy does nothing for my reason."

"But works wonders on your looks, you're positively blooming."

"Flatterer - go on, fetch Tim. Thank goodness this is the last pill, he hates it, although it's not so bad since Hannah told me to dissolve them like this." She walked to the door to call Tim. "Anyway, since you've skirted around it, what did happen this morning, what did Jack have to say?"

"If you must know I got told off - at least I think I did. Jack seems to think this whole situation is a repeat performance of the last time I tried to write a true story."

Susan said nothing. Secretly she was relieved she wasn't the only one feeling uneasy. This whole business with the Maylings, and now Jacob, had stirred up memories she would sooner forget. For a long time she'd managed to put it to the back of her mind, except on odd occasions when her shoulder ached, then she would be reminded of the day she'd come close to being murdered.

"Is your shoulder aching love?" Mark's voice seemed to come from a great distance.

She realised she'd been subconsciously rubbing it. "No, not really, I just get a twinge now and then, it's nothing." She tutted impatiently. "Where is that child? Tim!"

"I'll fetch him. He's probably down the bottom of the garden."

Left alone, Susan's hand involuntarily went back to her shoulder. Although the hospital had made a good job of patching her up, a thin line about an inch long and slightly raised remained as a constant reminder of that day on the hill. She snatched her hand away - this was ridiculous! Why now, after all this time? She could see it all so vividly, hear the rain beating on the roof of her car as she waited outside the church, feel the ground squelch under her feet as she trudged through the long grass to the back of the building, the door creaking, the hooded figure, the glint of steel... "Oh God!" She covered her face with her hands.

"Sue, what's the matter?"

She felt Mark's hands on her shoulders, then Tim clutching at her skirt. "Mummy, mummy..." The fear in his voice brought her to her senses.

Forcing herself to smile she bent down and kissed him. "I'm all right sweetheart, I just had something in my eye, that's all."

"Has it gone now?"

"Yes, it's gone, come on it's time for your pill." She handed him the glass."

"Ughh." The toddler wrinkled his nose, but obediently drank the contents.

"Can I have a sweetie now?"

"Just one, then you can go and play again."

Mark watched in silence until he'd run off happily with the dogs. Leaning against the sink with his arms folded, he said. "Well you might have fooled him easily enough, but you'll have to do better with me."

With difficulty at first, she told him how recently she'd become more and more obsessed with memories of the past. "It's like a series of flashbacks, each one more vivid than the last. I can't understand it, I didn't have this sort of reaction when it happened."

"Maybe that's why. We all thought you were a bit too calm about it."

"But why now?"

"A combination of several things. You're already feeling a bit fragile, then finding Jacob yesterday, after all, it's happened before, hasn't it?"

She laughed mirthlessly. "I seem to be developing a talent for finding dead bodies, don't I?"

"You know, Sue, we've never really talked about it, not properly."

"There didn't seem any need. With Jim Abbott's death the mystery ended. What was there to talk about?"

"I don't know." Mark was lost. He didn't know what to say to make her feel better.

"There is something – we never talked about why Jim Abbott did what he did. I know we all read Helen's diary, but did we give enough thought to its accuracy? She wrote about what she saw through a child's eyes. How much credence can you give to an imaginative seven year old?"

"What exactly is the point of this, Sue?"

"Well, what we don't know - and what I can't understand - is why Jim killed Christie in the first place."

"Because he was insane." Mark said simply.

"But he wasn't – not before her death."

"Maybe it was because he found out she wasn't his child."

"It's a bit extreme, don't you think? Why blame the child? Why not get mad at his wife or, better still, Len Tyler?"

The furrows on his brow deepened. "Sue - what are you saying?"

"I'm saying, maybe he didn't kill Christie - maybe he just... oh, I don't know what I'm saying. I just know that, for me, there's always been a question mark over it."He looked at her in astonishment. "I can't think why you're doing this – why are you putting yourself through it all over again? It's over, Sue. Jack said at the time, with one fell swoop you closed the case - the old one and the new."

270

She smiled at him tolerantly. "What you'd call a suitable ending, eh?"

"Hardly suitable, but it was an ending. I thought you'd accepted that."

She released a long sigh. "I have really, let's forget it. Come on, your salad's getting warm."

CHAPTER THIRTY EIGHT

There was something magical about the hour before dawn, Mark thought. It had a mystical quality and a familiarity that he felt comfortable with. It was his hour – a time when his fog-bound brain would clear, when depression would lift and – when many a book had been finished.

He glared at his keyboard, screened by its neat plastic cover. There would be no frantic clatter of keys that morning, there was no book to finish, or, for that matter, to start.

At the window he stared through the darkness to the meadow beyond. A faint orange glow warmed the horizon. Very soon now sunlight would be flooding the land and blinding his eyes - and still he had no answer.

He became aware of a faint stirring from above. The dogs would waken first, then Susan. He smiled. Whatever Maude had said to her yesterday had worked, for she hadn't stirred in spite of his bumping around in the dark. He wondered, wryly, if he should seek a consultation with the old lady himself, maybe she could untangle his muddled thoughts. He returned his attention to the horizon; the thin orange line was rapidly widening. In a few minutes dawn would give place to sunrise, and the magic would be gone with the night.

Knowing the answer must be somewhere among the jumbled pages on his desk he proceeded to sift through his notes, methodically going over everything that had happened since Eleanor's funeral. He analysed every word - his thoughts, things people had said. Snatches of conversation came and went - unfinished sentences - who knew about his research? Eventually his eyes fastened on the plain white card he'd torn from Eleanor's grave, and the name seemed to leap up at him - Rupert!

Exhausted, he finally fell asleep at his desk, but not before he had a fair idea of what had happened to the missing vicar and subsequently poor, unsuspecting Jacob. After that, everything else fell into place and he knew, beyond doubt, who had killed Eleanor Mayling – and how. Dawn had finally broken.

By nine o'clock he was in Bob's kitchen pouring out the whole story. He looked at the ex-policeman anxiously. "Well say something for goodness sake, even if it's only to tell me you think I'm mad."

"I think you're right, lad. The trouble is, what do we do now?"

"I was hoping you'd have some ideas about that."

Bob wandered to the window. "We'd have a hell of a job proving it - unless we can get a confession."

"I did think about ringing Jack, but what could he do without concrete evidence?"

"Nothing, nothing at all."

"We could always have a go ourselves?"

"What, try to get a confession? And how do you suppose we do that then - thumbscrews?"

"Well, we can't just sit here and do nothing. "Mark started pacing. "Look, I've got an idea, but I really think we'd better phone Jack first. You know what he said about telling him everything."

Fifteen minutes later, speeding along the Harold Road, Bob was starting to worry. "I wish I'd been able to get hold of Jack. He isn't going to like this one little bit."

"Did you leave a message?"

"Of course I did, but goodness knows when he'll get it." As they neared the junction at Cherry Lane, he asked, "Are you going to call in and see Susan first?"

"No, it's best if she doesn't know what's going on and besides, she's going to be tied up all day herself. Kathleen's going back to Derby tomorrow so the pair of them are spending today doing the rounds. First they're taking Tim to playschool, then, after seeing Eve and Blanche they're having lunch with Maude. This afternoon, believe it or not, Kath wants to go up to the old church. Apparently it's Jamie's idea. It's the last of the spectres that have haunted her for the last six years and he thinks this trip will effectively complete the exorcism."

"How does Susan feel about this?"

"Sue's all right. We went through the same ritual just after we were married. She was getting to the stage where she avoided looking up the hill altogether, so I took her up there one afternoon. She was a bit uneasy at first, especially when we went into the woods, but eventually she got to grips with it. I think she's hoping to do the same for Kath."

Bob was unusually quiet. He didn't altogether approve of the exercise but couldn't explain why. "What time are they going?"

"I told you, after lunch. Why?"

"We'll be back by then, won't we?"

"I should think so - again, why?"

"I'd just feel a bit happier about it if we went with them. I don't like the idea of those two traipsing about up there alone."

Mark slowed the car down. "You're starting to worry me, what's on your mind?"

"I wish I knew."

Mark glanced at his expression and immediately pulled into a lay-by. "OK, let's have it."

Bob shifted in his seat. "It's this Mary Tyler business. I know you're glad Kath couldn't find her, but I rather wish she had. At least we'd know where she was."

Mark's face set grimly. "You think she's back in Carlton, don't you?"

"I don't know anything, it's just a feeling. The fact that the cottage is still rented in her name worries me, add to that these odd things that keeping happening..." He looked directly at Mark. "Susan told me about the key and the open window – and one or two other things that have happened."

"Like what?"

"Same things as before. Gates open when they shouldn't be - noises behind the garden wall, and the dog. I know Lexer's getting old but he hasn't completely lost his marbles - or his hearing. Susan says he growls at the slightest sound."

"Why didn't she tell me all this?"

"She did."

Mark bit his lip. "Yes, she did, and I told her she was imagining it." He switched on the ignition. "Right, as soon as we get to the vicarage I'm going phone and tell them to wait until we get back."

Bob released a long sigh. "Good lad."

Hannah greeted them with a smile. "Hello, this is a nice surprise. I'm afraid Alex has just gone out to get some milk. He shouldn't be long, though, would you like to come in and wait?"

"Thanks, Hannah." Mark answered. "May I use your phone?"

"Of course. Use the one in the sitting room. I'll be in the kitchen if you want anything. I'm afraid I can't offer you any tea until Alex gets back with the milk, unless of course you'd like coffee. I know there's some cream in the fridge."

"Coffee will be fine, Hannah." Bob followed her across the hall. "I'll come with you and let Mark make his call in peace."

Bob looked anxiously at Mark when he finally joined them in the kitchen. He mouthed the words. "Did you speak to her?"

Mark nodded and pulled a chair up to the table. "She's not very happy about it, but says she'll wait."

"Good."

Alex strode in, swinging a carrier bag and grinning broadly. "Hello, you two. It looks as though I'm just in time with the supplies. I've bought some fresh rolls." He looked from one to the other. "Have you two gentlemen had breakfast?"

"Yes thanks, but don't let us stop you." Mark's facial muscles seemed to have frozen but eventually he managed a weak smile. "Hannah's already offered us coffee."

The three sat together while Hannah set out cups and saucers. Bob, feeling someone should break the silence, asked. "Where's young Caroline this morning?"

"She went back to London yesterday." Alex pulled a face. "I tried to persuade to stay a bit longer, but evidently there's an interesting job coming up and it's important that she gets it."

"Is she coming back?"

"I hope so. We talked about it and she agrees there's no reason why she can't work here, but..." he inclined his head towards Hannah. "Anyway, we'll see. If she does come back she can use my grandfather's studio. He had it built into the attic years ago. There's masses of windows providing plenty of light - ideal for her."

"It'll need a good clear-out, Alex." Hannah poured coffee for each of them. "And a lick of paint."

Mark sat quietly making no contribution to the conversation at all. It was all getting a bit tricky. He knew he'd have to throw a wet blanket over the proceedings eventually, but how?

Without warning, Hannah gave him the opportunity he needed. "How's young Tim now?" she asked.

"Much better thank you, Hannah. That was a marvellous idea of yours with the capsules. I wish we'd known about it before. How did you come to hear about it?"

"I must have read it somewhere."

"Actually, your advice has had quite a profound effect on things." Mark watched her closely. "They're going to do fresh tests on Eleanor's blood."

His words couldn't have had a greater effect if he'd announced war had been declared.

Hannah froze, the coffee pot slipped from her hands and smashed loudly on the stone flags.

"How can they?" Alex demanded. "She's buried, for God's sake - surely they're not thinking of..."

"Exhuming?" Bob interrupted. "No, of course not. In certain cases they keep samples of body fluids, especially after a death in suspicious circumstances."

"But what are they looking for?" Alex spluttered.

Mark hadn't taken his eyes off Hannah. "Gelatine." He said simply.

Hannah stared back at him, eyes narrowed, her expression a mixture of defiance and fear. A thin vapour of steam rose and fell around her ankles, as she stood amid the shattered crocks. Dark splashes of scalding coffee mottled her thick stockings, but she appeared not to notice.

"Gelatine?" Alex repeated.

Still returning Hannah's stare, Mark nodded. "That's right. Capsules are made of a gelatine substance which, once ingested, dissolves and releases the drug into the bloodstream. If Eleanor did swallow all those capsules of Nitrazepam, a certain amount of gelatine would remain in her system, and would show up in tests."

"So if they don't find any gelatine...?"

"It proves she was murdered." Mark finished for him, "It would be such a simple thing to empty the grains from the capsules and keep them until there was enough. Dissolved in a drink, hot sweet chocolate for instance, Eleanor would be completely unaware she was swallowing a lethal dose." Sitting squarely back in his chair, his next words surprised even Bob. "Is that how you did it, Hannah?"

"Are you mad?" Alex was on his feet and standing beside her.

Still holding her gaze, Mark ignored the young man's indignation. "It will show up in tests, Hannah - one way or the other."

"I don't believe this." Alex put an arm around her ample shoulders. "It's all right, Hannah, don't listen to him... I'm here, I'll..."

At last she moved. With sudden speed she pushed Alex away and turned on him, her face contorted with hatred. "You're here? Is that supposed to be a comfort?"

Bob and Mark were on their feet, prepared to grab her. "Stay where you are." She spat the words out as she turned to face them. "Yes, I killed her." Hannah's normally expressionless face hardened as she glared at Mark through flinty blue eyes. "So you've figured it out at last - and now you think you know it all."

"Not all of it, Hannah." Mark spoke gently.

Suddenly the fight seemed to go out of her. She turned away, shoulders drooping, and slumped into a chair. "I knew this day would come eventually. Twenty-eight years is too long to keep a secret, but that's what we did, Eleanor and I. I think we might have gone on with it until the end of our days if Eleanor hadn't made a mistake." An ugly flush stained her cheeks. "She told one lie too many you see, and to the wrong person - me." She looked at them without expression. "You'd better sit down all of you, it's a very long story."

"I knew Eleanor long before I came here to work. She didn't know me, of course. I was just a village kid. I used to watch her whenever I could, in the village, at church – I suppose it was envy. I wanted to be like her, you see. I wanted what she had. Hardly surprising really, seeing as she had everything. Her father made sure she wanted for nothing, clothes, jewellery - you name it, he made sure she got it.

Then, when Richard Mayling came to Ashbridge, he made sure she got him as well."

"It was an unhappy marriage right from the start, and made for all the wrong reasons. Richard married her because he thought he'd inherit all Reverend Wakely's money. He didn't know the old boy had spent every penny of it on this house. As for Eleanor, God knows why she went through with it. Maybe she loved him at first, who knows? If she did, it didn't last. At the end she hated him. He told me that himself - Richard told me everything."

"Were you and he...?"

"Lovers?" She silenced him with a glare. "Oh yes, and if things hadn't gone so dreadfully wrong we'd be together now. He talked of leaving her, and I think he would have, but Eleanor won again - just as she always did. If only I'd known then that Eleanor, the highly respected vicar's daughter, was no better than I. If I'd known she had a lover of her own, how different things might have been." Suddenly her eyes filled with tears. "But I didn't know, if I had I would have waited." Hannah's head fell forward, her shoulders shaking as she sobbed.

At last she raised her head and prepared to continue. Mark watched, with a certain amount of sympathy, as tears slid silently over the puffy flesh and ran into the deep crevices either side of her mouth. "Tell us what happened, Hannah."

With both hands she roughly rubbed her face dry. "It was the night of September fifteenth, 1962. That's when it all happened. Eleanor had gone out that night so, as usual, I went into Folly Wood to meet Richard. We always met there whenever we had the chance. He'd drunk far too much at dinner so I suppose I should have waited before telling him my news, but I was so excited, you see. I thought once he knew I was expecting his baby he would leave her, and we'd go away together as he'd always promised." She ran the back of her hand across her nose and sniffed loudly. "I don't think

I'd ever seen him so angry. He called me filthy names, told me to get rid of it, said I was crazy if I thought he could be trapped like that. We had the most dreadful row, both screaming and saying dreadful things – until he became violent. He was like that because of the drink, you see. I knew the best thing I could do was leave and wait until he was sober – he was a different person when he wasn't drinking. But I persisted, saying more terrible things until he hit me with such force I fell and banged my head against something hard – maybe a large stone – I don't know. For a moment I was senseless. I wasn't sure what was happening - then I saw Eleanor. She was on the other side of the clearing. There was someone with her, a man, but I couldn't see his face because it was so dark. I was still on the ground when I saw her pick up the shotgun Richard had left by the oak tree. She aimed the barrel directly at him and shouted, 'Leave her alone, Richard!'

"Richard turned away from me, but I got to my knees and tried to pull him back. He was so angry, screaming abuse, then he put his hands around my throat and started to shake me. 'I'll kill you, you whore!' he shouted.

"Eleanor's voice carried above everything. 'Let her go Richard or I'll shoot you - I mean it!'

"At almost the same time a man's voice cried out. 'No, Eleanor - no!'

"Suddenly there was loud bang; it seemed to echo all through the woods. Richard let go of me instantly. At first I thought he was shot, but when I could focus I saw the other man, he was on the ground clutching his ankle and rolling around in pain. Eleanor told me afterwards that he'd grabbed the barrel of the gun and pulled it down. She hadn't meant to pull the trigger, it just went off - the man was shot in the foot.

"Richard suddenly let out a cry and ran towards her. I think he knew the man was Eleanor's lover because he said. 'Give me the gun, I'll finish him off.' She tried to run but he caught her. They struggled for what seemed like ages. I heard the material of Eleanor's dress rip, and then blood appeared on her shoulder. Finally he punched her in the face. The shotgun seemed to just leave her hands, flying through the air until it landed a few yards in front of me. By now, the other man was trying to get to his feet. Richard lunged at him then, and they both fell on the ground. They rolled this way and that, then suddenly the man was on top, straddled across Richard's chest. He had his forearm under Richard's chin, pressing on his throat. I could see Richard couldn't breathe - I thought he would die.

"Suddenly everything seemed to be happening in slow motion. I could no longer hear Eleanor's sobs, or the crackle of twigs breaking as the men fought, I was conscious only of Richard. I had to stop this man from choking him. I knew there was another shot in the barrel, so I picked up the gun and aimed." Hannah's tears fell uncontrollably. "I hadn't reckoned on Richard's strength, though. He forced the man's arm away and rolled him onto his back just as I pulled the trigger. The bullet went into the back of Richard's head. He died instantly, right there at the foot of the oak tree where the primroses are. After that everything was quiet. I don't know how long we all stood there, or when the other man left, but suddenly there was just Eleanor, and me. She started shaking me, and said. 'Leave this to me Hannah, you go back to the house and stay there, I'll come soon.'

"I remember thinking, she doesn't know that we were lovers, she thinks Richard was forcing himself on me, that I meant to kill him. And that's the lie I've lived with all these years."

"Who was the other man, Hannah?"

"I don't know, she never told me."

Bob passed her a handkerchief. "What happened after that?"

She dried her eyes. "Eleanor came back to the house alone, but she was very nervous and kept looking out of the window. She said. 'There's someone out there, Hannah, but I don't think he knows what happened.' She went on to tell me about Tom Field, a lorry driver who'd stopped to let his dog out for a run. Eleanor said she threw her shoe at the creature to distract it, then moved away from Richard's body.

"When this man found her, he thought she'd been attacked - which was partly true, I suppose. Anyway he didn't see the body, which was all that mattered."

Hannah looked up at Bob. "Do you think I could have a glass of water?"

Without a word he went to the sink while she continued. "Later that night Eleanor and I buried Richard. 'We'll just say he's disappeared.' she said. 'No one will be surprised, they'll just think he's gone off on one of his binges. By the time they all realise he's not coming back it will be too late, there will be nothing to find.'"

Knowing what the answer would be, Mark asked. "Where did you bury him?"

She laughed then, a harsh ugly sound. "Where nobody would ever find him." She looked from one to the other. "And nobody ever did." Her eyes settled on Bob. "Led you a merry old dance didn't we - fooled the lot of you. Your lot searched everywhere they could think of, everywhere except the one place you would expect to find a body - the graveyard." She laughed again, insanely. "Ever tried letting a dog loose in a graveyard expecting him to find a corpse?" She stared at Mark defiantly. "There was going to be a funeral, you see, the very next day. The plot was already dug, so we just dug a little deeper, wrapped Richard in a blanket, laid him in the bottom of the hole then covered him with soil and flattened it down - easy." She looked almost proud of herself. "The next day the funeral took place, as planned. The coffin was lowered on top of him, and that was that."

"Who took the service, though?"

"Yes, now that was a bit tricky. Because Richard couldn't be found we had to call in the vicar from Harold. Nobody was surprised, everyone knew of Richard's reputation."

"It was old Jacob's family grave that you put him in, wasn't it?"

She stared at Mark with narrowed eyes. "So you figured that out too, did you?"

He nodded. "It was the date. The only funeral to take place that week in September was Jacob's father. That, together with the flowers that kept turning up there - and then there's Caroline, she saw you."

Hannah snorted. "Caroline!" She spat the name out. "Somehow I knew she'd be trouble - still, what could I expect from another of Eleanor's bastard children?"

"Another?" The question tore itself from Alex's lips.

Ignoring it, Mark asked. "Why Jacob, why did you kill him?" He tried not to look at the astonishment on Alex's face and stared steadily at Hannah.

"You seem to have all the answers, Mr Jordan, you tell me." Her lips curled into a sneer.

"He saw you, didn't he?"

She nodded. "Up until now I'd managed to pick times when I knew he wouldn't be there, but I got careless. Lately, it didn't seem to matter so much. I suppose I didn't really care any more. Anyway, I was late and he caught me putting the flowers on his father's grave. If he hadn't started shouting, things might have been all right – but then he threatened to report me. I got angry then - too angry."

There was a long silence, then Mark said, "How have you managed all these years, you and Eleanor? Everyone thought you were so close."

"Don't you see? Eleanor never knew the truth of it. She firmly believed it was all Richard's fault, that he'd taken advantage of me. She didn't even know I was pregnant. I suppose I would have told her, eventually, but I only carried him for four months." Once again, tears filled her eyes. "I buried him in the graveyard, too."

Alex suddenly spoke. "The plain stone cross near the gate." He was beginning to understand. "But why did you stay, Hannah? You could have gone away, started a new life."

She stared at him, wide-eyed. "Because of you of course. You were Richard's child, all that remained to remind me of him. I used to pretend you were mine, until..."

"Until you discovered Richard wasn't Alex's father." Mark spoke now. "How did you find out?"

No longer surprised at the extent of his knowledge, Hannah simply continued. "One morning Eleanor gave me some letters to post. Among them was a large envelope addressed to her solicitor. I was suspicious, she may have changed her will, I needed to know, you see. Anyway, I opened it and found I was right, it was a new will but I needn't have worried. The only alteration was a small bequest to this man, Tom Field." She looked at Alex. "There was another envelope inside addressed to you, she wanted you to have it after her death." She sneered. "That's when I knew she'd fooled us all."

"Do you still have the letter?" Alex asked.

She nodded. "It's upstairs, I'll fetch it for you." She rose wearily and crossed the room. At the door she turned. "You'll be none the wiser though. It tells you everything you need to know - except who your father is." The door closed quietly behind her.

In the following silence the three men listened to her footsteps as she climbed the stairs, then walked along the landing to her room. Suddenly she was descending, her pace quickening as she reached the hall. All eyes were on the door, waiting. But Hannah didn't stop; she was running now, past the kitchen to the front door.

Alex looked sharply at Mark. "She's running away."

Bob was on his feet. "I was afraid of this." He reached the door as the blast reverberated through the house. Seeing Alex and Mark move to follow him, he spoke firmly. "No - leave this to me." He stepped into the hall knowing what he would find.

The doors to the gun cabinet were wide open. Hannah was propped against the wall, the rifle butt resting on the carpet between her knees, the barrel still in her mouth. A dark mass of blood and tissue splattered on the wall behind her head had begun to trickle down onto her shoulders. Bob stooped to pick up a long white envelope lying on the floor beside her. He turned to see Mark and Alex transfixed in the doorway. Walking steadily towards them he tried to obscure the sight of Hannah's body from Alex. Standing squarely in front of him he put the envelope into his hands. "This will probably answer all your questions, lad." He nodded to Mark. "Take him into the sitting room and stay with him. I'll phone Jack."

CHAPTER THIRTY NINE

Mark was beginning to find the silence oppressive. He badly wanted Alex to say something – anything - even if it was only to tell him, in the plainest terms, to push off.

In the immediate aftermath, Mark had left Bob to deal with the formalities, while he concentrated his attention on Alex. Once he'd got him into the sitting room and placed a glass of scotch in his hands, he seated himself in a chair close by and waited. He looked at his watch. Forty-five minutes had passed since Jack had arrived. Since then, all he'd heard was muffled voices, doors slamming and the sound of gravel flying as a constant flow of vehicles came and went. At some point Jack had put his head around the door. His grave brown eyes had swept the room and finally settled on Alex. He seemed about to say something - then changed his mind. Instead, with a brief nod to Mark, he closed the door.

Mark refilled Alex's glass then watched from the window as Jack's car pulled away. He was off the hook for the moment, at least. Eventually, he knew he would be called upon to explain his part in all this, and he knew that wasn't going to be pleasant, but right now his immediate concern was for Alex. Apart from occasionally raising his glass to his lips he had barely moved. At some point the unopened envelope had slid from the armrest to the floor, but Alex had made no attempt to retrieve it.

"Aren't you going to open it, Alex?" Mark waited for a response, but none came. He picked up the envelope and laid it on Alex's knees. "Maybe you'd prefer to be alone while you read it?"

"Huh?" Alex looked up vacantly. "Oh, Mark. I'd forgotten you were there. Has everyone gone?"

"All except me and Bob."

"What about Hannah?"

"They've taken her away. I think it's all clear out there

now."

Bob put his head round the door. "Have you got a minute?"

Mark nodded and stood up. "I'll be outside if you want me, Alex."

In the hall, Marks eyes went straight to the gun cupboard. Apart from a strong smell of chlorine, nothing remained except a dark damp patch on the carpet. Bob pulled him away from the door and led him to the kitchen. "Jack reckoned he didn't like the look of Alex so I've called the doctor. He should be here any minute."

"Good thinking."

Bob nodded. "He's not exactly delighted with all this, you know." He lit the gas under the kettle.

"I don't suppose he is - what are you doing?"

"Making some tea. That lad can't go on drinking scotch all day - and I don't think he should stay here alone, do you?

"No I don't - but he may not have to."

"What do you mean?"

"Don't ask me to explain it, it's just an idea - was that the doorbell? I'll get it, it's probably David."

David Latham strode into the hall. "Damned awful business, this. And Hannah, of all people! What the devil's happening in this house?"

Closing the door and leaning against it, Mark said. "Hannah shot herself because she was found out. She murdered Eleanor." He watched the doctor's clear grey eyes darken with emotion.

"But why - how?"

"Hannah only tolerated Eleanor because of Alex. When she found out that he wasn't Richard Mayling's son and that it had all been a lie, anger drove her to murder. As to how, well, we know now why the sleeping pills you prescribed didn't seem to work. I believe Hannah collected the pills from the chemist but before giving them to Eleanor, emptied them. She may have left them empty or filled them with a harmless substance such as baking soda. Anyway, she went on like this until she thought she had enough, then one night - gave her the lot."

"Good grief! How did you find all this out?"

"It's a long story David, and it can wait until another time. Right now, Alex needs some support."

"Where is he?" The doctor walked towards the sitting room.

"Just a minute, David. Before you go in, there's something I'd like to ask. You are Rupert, aren't you?" The doctor opened his mouth to answer, but before he could speak, Mark drew the card from his pocket and placed it on the table.

A look of resignation settled on the doctor's face. "How did you guess?"

"My son. He named you Paddington after his favourite bear. Rupert was Eleanor's name for you, wasn't it?"

"She and everyone else in the village. It's a nick-name from our childhood." He smiled crookedly. "There's something else on your mind, isn't there?"

"It's none of my business really, but for the first time in his life Alex is alone..."

"You're going to say, 'and needs a father,' aren't you?" The doctor came towards him and put a hand on his shoulder. "You're a clever man, Mark, you should have been a policeman."

"I've been told that before."

"Tell me, how did you know?"

"Several things. Your friendship with Eleanor, this card, but it's your eyes that put the lid on it. Just like Alex, the way they darken when something upsets you." He gave the doctor a penetrating look. "Caroline's are just the same."

"So you've guessed that as well." He smiled and picked up his bag. "One day, Mark, we'll talk, you and I... I'll tell you the story of my life, as long as you promise not to put it in a book. Right now, I'm more concerned for Alex, so if you'll forgive me..."

"Will you tell him, David?"

"Oh yes. Maybe not today, but I will certainly tell him. There's been too much secrecy in this house, too much by far." He walked to the living room door.

For the first time Mark noticed a slight limp. "So it was you in the woods that night."

The doctor turned to see Mark staring at his feet. "Yes, it was me. Eleanor wounded me twice that night. The first was when she refused to come away with me, the second was a bullet in the foot. It was hard to tell which was the more painful." He smiled sadly. "Now you know it all. I'll be in touch, Mark." He nodded briefly and went into the sitting room.

Mark found Bob in the kitchen drinking tea. "Come on, we'd better be on our way."

"What about Alex?"

"David's with him. I don't think he'll be needing us again today."

Bob stood up. "There's just one thing I want to know. What you said, is it true? Would there really be traces of gelatine in Eleanor's blood?"

"Search me, I haven't the foggiest, and I was banking on Hannah not knowing either."

Bob's face was a study. "Well you had me fooled, lad. I thought you knew what you were talking about."

"So did Hannah." He walked to the door. "Are you coming? I wouldn't put it past Susan to get fed up with waiting and go on up to the church without us. Come on, I'll tell you the rest of the story on the way back."

Bob hurried after him. "You mean there's more?"

CHAPTER FORTY

"Mark's going to be furious, Susan, we really should have waited a bit longer."

"You don't know him as I do, Kath. We could still be waiting at midnight. Once he gets involved with something, time has no meaning. I can't think why he wanted to come anyway."

Kathleen chuckled. "Maybe he's still searching for an ending to that book. After all, this is where it all started, isn't it?"

"And ended." Susan stopped to catch her breath. "I often wish he'd never started the wretched thing, and I doubt that he'd find that last chapter up here, anyway."

Kathleen turned to study her. Susan's eyes seemed over-bright and her face was flushed with exertion. "Are you sure this isn't too much for you?"

Susan linked her arm through Kathleen's. "Of course not. The fresh air and exercise will do me good."

"Look, if you find it becomes too tiring, just say so and we'll go back down." Susan squeezed her arm. "I'll be fine."

Kathleen looked up at the sky. "I'm glad it's warm and sunny. Whenever I've thought about this hill, I've seen it in the rain. It's always a bleak and desolate spot. Maybe after this I'll see it in a different light."

"To be honest, I'm surprised you want to see it at all." Susan smiled and quickly added, "That's not a criticism – just an observation."

"Your observation, or Mark's?"

"Mine. Mark thinks pretty much as you do. He's a great one for facing up to things and..."

"And laying ghosts?" Kathleen finished.

Susan nodded. "Yes, that too. Come on, let's get on with on with it."

They continued in silence until they reached a point mid-way between the village and the old church. "Let's have a breather, shall we?" Kathleen turned to face the village. "Now this is the view I want to remember." Her eyes scanned the rooftops of Carlton. "Do you know who lives in my old cottage now?"

"A couple from London bought it, but they only use it for holidays. It's empty most of the time."

A wistful note crept into Kathleen's voice as she turned away. "I hope they'll be happier there than I was."

"It wasn't all miserable, was it?"

"Not in the beginning." She looked up the hill. "Come on, we're nearly there now."

They completed the last few yards in silence. Susan would be glad when this particular trip down memory lane was over. The week's exercise might have laid a few ghosts for Kathleen, but it had resurrected one or two of hers.

"It's in an even worse state than I remembered." They stood where the gate had once been. Kathleen studied the crumbling walls and empty, faceless windows. "I suppose someone will pull it down in the end."

Together they negotiated the weed-covered path to the front of the building. The absence of both doors created more light, so it was possible to see the length of the hall without entering.

"You don't want to go in do you, Kath?"

"Why not? We're here now, might as well."

Susan's heart sank. She really didn't want to go any further. Since reaching the top of the hill she'd tried to shake off a rising anxiety. "Do you want me to come with you?" She tried to keep the tension out of her voice.

Kathleen turned to look at her. "Would you rather I went alone?"

Feeling foolish, Susan smiled nervously. "No, of course not. I'm just being silly. I'll come with you"

Inside, very little had changed. There was a litter of crisp packets and sweet wrappers that hadn't been there before, and part of the roof had fallen away, which created even more light. Cautiously picking her way over rotting wood and shards of broken slate, Susan followed Kathleen to the far end where the stage was still intact. She felt very strange, as if someone was walking over her grave.

Kathleen climbed the rotting wooden steps and turned to face her. "I once read the lesson from here, you know."

"Did you?" Standing centrally at the foot of the stage, Susan looked up at her wondering how she could be so calm. The place apparently held no terrors for her.

Moving to the edge, Kathleen smiled down at her. "Do you feel anything?"

Susan shook her head. "Nothing." She said simply.

"That's odd... you're standing on the exact spot."

Susan looked down at the floorboards. What did she mean, what spot? She couldn't mean the spot where Christie died - how would she know - she wasn't there? "Oh dear God!" She could feel her heart thumping against her ribs, as she looked up into Kathleen's eyes, grown large and bright with insanity.

Returning her horrified gaze with a smile twisted with hatred, Kathleen whispered, "Why did you come back, Christie?"

"It was you." Susan's mind was racing. "You killed her!"

Kathleen chuckled. "Of course it was me, but you know that, that's why you've come back isn't it - for revenge?"

"And Helen - did you...?"

Suddenly Kathleen threw back her head and laughed, a deep, hollow, malevolent sound. "Why are you playing these games, Christie? You know I had to. Helen found out, didn't she? It took her a long time, though. Poor little Helen never was very bright, but she got there in the end."

"But everyone thought it was Jim." Susan wanted to keep her talking while she tried to figure out what to do.

"Yes, poor sweet Jim, he always was a fool. He'd do anything I wanted - anything." She laughed again. "He couldn't have killed you or Helen, too soft. Well you know that too, don't you? He tried the last time and made a botch of it, ended up getting killed himself." Kathleen shook her head. "Typical, such a fool."

Susan could suddenly see it all so clearly. Jim's devotion to Kathleen had been total, even to the point of covering her crime. That's what had driven him mad, years of coming to terms with the knowledge that his beloved Christie wasn't his child, and the horror of knowing that his adored wife was responsible for her death. "What about Len Tyler, did you...?"

Kathleen's attractive features contorted into an ugly mask. "Len Tyler killed himself – the only thing he ever got right, the weak, useless creature - but we're wasting time, Christie. This isn't why we're here." She lifted her bag and opened it. "You know what we have to do, don't you?"

Susan stared in horror as Kathleen slowly drew a knife from the bag. The blade glinted in a shaft of light from the damaged roof. "Kath, it's me, Susan," she tried to reason. "Christie's dead - already dead." Taking a step back she watched as Kathleen moved to the side of the stage. Oh God, not again! Surely not again! Memory flooded back, the rain, the muddy path, running, slipping. It was the same – but different. Last time she'd had help. Maude was waiting outside - but not this time - this time she was alone.

She took another step back and rocked unsteadily as her heel caught on a broken rafter. She looked to the stage. Kathleen was coming down, her gaze fixed, the knife gripped tightly in her hand... Susan looked around frantically for something to defend herself with - there was nothing.

With menacing slowness Kathleen moved forward, ever nearer, never taking her eyes from Susan's retreating figure. "It's no good, Christie, you can't escape this time."

"I'm not Christie!" she screamed. "For God's sake, Kathleen, I'm Susan!" Still moving backwards, she knew she was near the doorway. If she could just get outside - then she would run. This time it wasn't raining, the path was dry and she stood a better chance of keeping her footing - of getting to the village. Her mind was racing, maybe George would be out in the yard, he would hear her if she shouted. Another step and she would be outside. Bracing herself to turn and run, she suddenly found she couldn't move, her shoulders were held in a vice-like grip. At the same time someone shouted – it was a voice she didn't recognise.

"Mother!"

Susan watched Kathleen's expression change from maniacal hatred to abject terror. An agonising scream tore itself from her lips, as the woman charged forward, the knife held high, the blade pointing directly at her. Again she heard the voice. "No, mother - No!" Someone pushed past her - a man. Jamie's fist caught Kathleen squarely on the jaw as she ran, full tilt, into it. But who was holding her shoulders? She wrenched herself free and turned sharply to stare into Mark's anxious eyes.

"Oh, thank God!" She fell against him, releasing a sob as he wrapped his arms around her.

"It's all right, love. It's all over now." He drew her out into the sunlight.

She pulled away and raised a tear stained face. "How did you know?"

"When Bob and I got back from the vicarage we found Jamie waiting outside the cottage." He grimaced. "Kathleen hasn't been in Derby all this time, she's been in hospital - a mental hospital." He looked behind him. "Bob, you can put that down now."

Looking past him, she saw Bob clutching a rotting piece of wood. Suddenly she started to laugh and cry at the same time. "And I thought I was alone." She wiped her eyes and took a step back into the church. "Jamie?"

Cradling his mother's head in his arms, Jamie looked up with tears in his eyes. "I'm so sorry. We thought she was better." He stroked the hair from his mother's forehead. "I've always suspected she killed Christie, but could never be sure." "But why, Jamie - why did she do it?"

"She blamed Christie for everything - everything that happened after she was born. I suppose it was because of how my father behaved. Once he found out Christie was Len's child, he changed. He still loved mother, but was never the same with her. The marriage inevitably went from bad to worse. She couldn't handle it, you see. Everyone thought she was the strong one, but she wasn't. She relied completely on Dad and I suppose she thought she'd lost him. Everything went wrong after that."

Mark moved forward. "Come on Jamie, let's get her into your car." He looked round for Bob. "I suppose you'd better phone Jack."

"Aye, and somebody had better contact the poor sod who owns that field, we've ploughed it up good and proper - again!"

CHAPTER FORTY ONE

"I got here as soon as I could, dear." Maude came through the back door at Crane cottage in a flurry of anxiety. "Now, what can I do?" She threw her things on the table and reached for the kettle. "I really think you should be lying down, you know. Why don't you go up now, dear? I'll bring you a cup of tea as soon as it's made." She stopped to study her young friend. "Maybe I should call the doctor, you look very pale."

"Maude, please!" Susan held up her hands. "I'm perfectly all right. Sit down for heaven's sake, you look far worse than I feel."

Maude collapsed into a chair beside her. "You're right, and I'm fussing again, aren't I? I'm sorry, but since Mark phoned my mind's been in a whirl." She pressed a hand to her forehead. "I can't believe it. Kathleen, of all people."

"I know. She fooled us all."

"What do you think will happen to her?"

Susan shrugged. "Jamie's taken her back to the hospital, I expect they'll sort it all out."

Maude studied her curiously. "I must say you're incredibly calm about it all."

"I suppose I am, but you know, in spite of what's happened I feel better now than I have for ages. All the nagging doubts, the questions - it's finally over. Perhaps we can all stop thinking about it now."

"I had stopped thinking about it. It's only you, my dear, that couldn't let go."

Susan grimaced. "I know, but I can now. With a bit of luck and some positive thinking I might even stop having those nightmares, and Mark, at last, can finish that wretched book."

"Before or after he's written the one about Eleanor?" Maude asked dryly.

"Ah, now there's another shock for you. You know Maude, between the Abbotts and the Maylings it's been a murderous six years, but I mustn't steal Mark's thunder. He can tell you all about it when he gets back."

"Where is he, anyway?"

"He'll be here soon. He's gone to fetch Tim from playschool - and he's collecting Jamie's daughter at the same time."

As she spoke the back door flew open and Tim ran across the kitchen into his mother's arms. Giggling with excitement, he announced, "Daddy says my friend can stay to tea."

Susan hugged him to her and peered over his head at the little girl standing cautiously in the doorway. She experienced a fleeting moment of unease before smiling into the child's strangely familiar, blue eyes. "Hello," she murmured at last. "What's your name?"

The pretty face, framed by a mop of unruly blonde curls, gazed up at her smiling sweetly. "Christie," she whispered shyly. "Christie Abbott."

THE END

About the Author

Sally-Ann Wilding was born and grew up in the South of England. From early schooldays writing was first a hobby, at times a solace but most importantly a compulsion. However, encouraged by her family to seek 'a proper job', she trained and has worked in all aspects of the beauty trade – she is now the owner of a successful and thriving salon.

Her interests range from gardening and jigsaw puzzles to psychology, crime and detection – the latter resulting in this first novel.